THE BOY WITH THE HIDDEN NAME

THE BOY WITH THE HIDDEN NAME

skylar dorset

sourcebooks
fire

Published by Sourcebooks Fire, an imprint of Sourcebooks, Inc.
P.O. Box 4410, Naperville, Illinois 60567-4410
(630) 961-3900
Fax: (630) 961-2168
www.sourcebooks.com

Library of Congress Cataloging-in-Publication data is on file with the publisher.

Printed and bound in the United States of America.
VP 10 9 8 7 6 5 4 3 2 1

For Megan and Caitlin, who bring
joy and laughter into my life.

CHAPTER 1

Y ou don't understand, miss," says a little man in an
old-fashioned bowler hat who is crawling out from
underneath the bench I'm sitting on. "We just really need
the book."

To say that I am annoyed is to put it mildly. All I want to
do is sit and eat my ice cream cone, and instead I'm getting
stalked by supernatural creatures who keep *literally* crawling
out of the woodwork. I mean that: the other day, a carving
on a balustrade at Trinity Church started talking to me. We
were there on a field trip, and it was difficult to hide.

This is what happens when you find out you are half-faerie
princess and half-ogre and then try to pretend it never happened and go back to leading a normal life.

"She doesn't have the book," Kelsey tells the little man,
who is now sprawled on his back on Boston Common, legs
still hidden under the bench. "How many times do we have
to keep telling you? She *doesn't have the book*."

The man scowls. "She *stole* the book."

"No, I didn't," I snap. "I didn't steal the book. Will Blaxton
and Benedict Le Fay stole the book. I just happened to *be*

there." And then I wince at my slip. I have to stop giving up the names of people I care about. There's power in a name.

The man points at me. "Will Blaxton is always trying to steal books. This is nothing new. He only succeeded because he has *you* now."

I bristle. "He doesn't 'have' me. And it was Ben. Ben made the difference."

"Well, where's Ben then?" asks the man politely.

The question of the hour, day, week. And if I knew the answer to it, I'd…well, I don't know what I'd do, because I'm angry at Ben for abandoning me on Boston Common after promising never to leave me, all so he could go in search of the missing mother who might or might not be someone we can trust. I know a lot about missing mothers who might be incredibly untrustworthy, since mine is the same way. Not that Ben listened to me about that.

"I have no idea where he is," I snap. "He's a magical faerie who can jump effortlessly between worlds and into enchantments. How am I supposed to have any idea where he went? And I don't know where Will is, although you ought to try Salem. That's where I was always able to find him. And I don't know where the book is. I'm just trying to eat my ice cream and complain about unreliable faerie quasi-boyfriends like a *normal teenager*."

The man frowns at me, his eyes narrow in displeasure. "You're not a normal teenager. You're the fay of the autumnal equinox. You're *trouble*."

Don't I know it, I think.

The man burrows his way into the ground beneath our feet.

Kelsey, because she's a good best friend who doesn't let herself be fazed when supernatural creatures appear and disappear all around us, licks her ice cream cone and says, "They're persistent, aren't they?"

"Here's what I think," Kelsey says the next day at school.

"That Emerson makes no sense?"

"That we should celebrate your birthday." Kelsey looks like she is bouncing with excitement over this.

I stare at her. "Celebrate my birthday? Now? But it's not really my birthday anymore."

"Correct me if I'm wrong, but have you ever celebrated your birthday before?"

"No," I admit.

"So then I think we should celebrate it."

"My birthday triggered the dissolution of the enchantment that had kept me hidden from evil faeries," I point out. "Doesn't really seem like something to celebrate."

"I think we should do something totally normal," Kelsey says as if she didn't hear me at all.

"Like what?" I sigh, resigned, because I don't even know what normal people do. I fail at being normal, and it's so frustrating.

"I don't know. How about a movie?"

A movie. I am astonished by how normal a movie seems. And so simple. Like being normal can really be *that* simple. "A movie could be fun," I say, because it sounds almost seductively indulgent to do this really normal, simple thing.

"Great." Kelsey beams at me, pleased with herself. "What do you want to see?"

I have no idea what's out. "Flip a coin?" I suggest.

"Great idea if we had a coin," Kelsey says with a grin.

"Oh, I've got a coin." I dig my hand into my pocket, pulling out a dime. "Picked it up this morning on the way to—" I cut myself off, looking at the coin in my hand and thinking of how I picked it up this morning, for no reason, so that it could come in handy at this point. All of the normality comes tumbling down around my ears. How can I pretend to be normal when I do things like this?

Kelsey takes the dime out of my hand, leans forward, and puts it on the empty desk off to the side. And then she says, "No coin toss. We'll do eenie-meenie-miney-moe when we get to the theater."

I am walking through Boston Common at dusk, on my way to meet Kelsey at the theater, when another little man in a bowler hat falls into step beside me. Why are there suddenly so many little men in bowler hats in Boston?

"About the book," the man says.

"For the last time," I grit out, frustrated, "I *do not have* the book."

"But you do have a black button, do you not?"

I do. And I hate that I do. I grabbed it the other day on my way through the Common, where it had fallen under a bench.

I don't say anything, but he looks at me meaningfully because clearly he knows that I have a button.

"Exactly," he says, as if it proves I am so special that I must have the book. And then he holds up his sleeve cuff, which is quite obviously missing a little black button.

Again with my stupid pack-rat tendencies. I walk on, absolutely refusing to give the little man the satisfaction of getting his button back.

Kelsey is waiting for me at the movie theater, and she notices immediately that I'm irritated.

"What's wrong?" she asks me.

"The usual," I tell her, and try to shake it off. "Let's not talk about it. Let's just be normal and go to a movie."

We do eenie-meenie-miney-moe as planned and end up with a random romantic comedy. Kelsey orders popcorn and soda. I don't feel like popcorn, so I stand a short distance away, playing with a napkin that was left on the counter. When Kelsey's ready, I go to crumple it into my pocket and then pause, realizing what I'm doing, and deliberately leave it on the counter exactly where I found it.

Which means, of course, that when we get settled in our seats, Kelsey promptly spills soda on herself.

"Damn it. I wish I had a napkin," she complains.

I say nothing.

CHAPTER 2

When the past few days of your life involve escaping from a faerie prison, stealing a magical book of power from the Boston Public Library, and being abandoned by the slippery faerie you've been inconveniently in love with for most of your life, getting ready for school actually starts to seem adventurous. Doing what would be normal for other people becomes a change of pace for you that is weirdly exciting. I'm being stalked by supernatural creatures. I can't even take the subway anymore, I feel like I'm so closely and viciously watched. Pretending that I'm just a normal teenager who goes to school is a fun bit of playacting for me.

I choose an outfit with care and do my makeup to accentuate my light blue eyes and brush my long white-blond hair until it gleams almost silver in the sunlight slanting through our lavender windowpanes. And then I look at the result. *Yes*, I think. I look absolutely put together and on top of things and not at all like I'm falling apart and heartbroken and refusing to acknowledge my destiny of leading some faerie *coup d'état*.

I take a deep breath and walk out of my bedroom—stepping

over the enchanted sweatshirt Ben gave me that I've left crumpled on my bedroom floor—and down the stairs. The grandfather clock on the landing chimes 2:15. Which is not at all the actual human time, but the grandfather clock doesn't keep that sort of time.

My aunts, True and Virtue, are knitting, working on the same enormous pair of socks they have been steadily working on my whole life. They barely look up at me as I pass through the room into the kitchen, looking for something that could serve as breakfast.

"Are you off to school?" Aunt True calls.

"Have a nice day!" Aunt Virtue adds.

I open the refrigerator door and stare at the contents, trying not to think about how my aunts are actually ogres who have raised me since birth because my homicidal faerie mother abandoned me on my father's doorstep. Oh, and then, for good measure, drove my father insane. We're ignoring all of that now. Because back before I knew any of that, my life was so simple and straightforward, and that's what I want back.

Unfortunately, as soon as I straighten and close the refrigerator, giving up on the idea of food, the sun goes out.

That is what it feels like at least. The room plunges into a darkness as severe as night. My aunts look up, confused. I tip my head and walk over to the window and look out. Where the sun had just been shining on us, there are now dense, black clouds roiling overhead.

I stare at them because those clouds are not of this world.

I look at my aunts, hesitate, and then say, "What—"

My aunts have gone back to knitting, even more furiously than before.

"You're going to be late for school," Aunt True says, and that is the end of that attempt at conversation.

My aunts hate it when I ask questions. It tends to destroy the world.

Kelsey is waiting for me when I open the front door. Going to school together is part of our routine. What is not part of our routine is the redheaded faerie standing next to her.

"Safford," I say in surprise, because I haven't seen him since Ben disappeared last week and Will disbanded our little band of revolutionaries, saying there was no point anymore.

"That's not good," Safford says, not taking his eyes off the clouds overhead. All of the regular humans going about their days on Beacon Street seem to think this is just a sudden weather phenomenon, but Safford is from the Otherworld and knows better.

"Where did you come from?" I ask.

Kelsey looks at me and blushes a little bit. "He just showed up." Kelsey and Safford have some sort of thing going on. If you can call it a "thing" when one half is a faerie. I know from personal experience that trying to have a relationship with a faerie is tricky at the best of times.

"I think you're going to need help," Safford says into the dark sky. "Lots and lots of help."

Annoyed, I look up and down Beacon Street for a break in the traffic so we can cross. "I'm not doing the prophecy anymore. I can't do the prophecy. We don't have the other three fays and we don't have Ben and you heard what Will said." Finally we cross the street together.

Safford says, "I think Will's wrong. I don't think this is out of your control."

"Safford," I say in exasperation as we walk down Boston Common toward Park Street, "I hate to break it to you, but this was never *in* my control."

"Of course it was. *Is*," Safford replies. "You're the fay of the autumnal equinox. It's *your* prophecy."

"It doesn't feel like my prophecy," I say. "It feels like all that happens is that I get violently pushed around by everyone and everything when I just want to live my li—"

The bell from the Park Street church tower suddenly flies out of its confines, wood splintering all around it, and lands with a heavy, dull impact only a few feet away, with one last clang of protest that rings deep vibrations through my bones.

After a moment of stunned silence, panicked commuters start behaving as if bells are suddenly going to fall from the sky all over the place.

"Exhibit A," Safford says. "They're getting rid of the church bells before they attack."

"Who?" I say, even though I already know.

"The Seelies. They can't get into Boston. It's protected. By an enchantment created by a faerie who's left," Safford points out frankly.

Ben. I glare at Safford, who is Ben's cousin and therefore probably on his side, but still. "Thanks for that reminder."

"I'm just saying I think we need to do something."

Commuters spill around us, desperate to get away from the bell sinking incrementally into the Common's concrete pathway. On our left, Park Street Church sits silent, its ruined bell tower splintering still. Off in front of us, the church bell at the Cathedral Church of St. Paul smashes its way through the rooftop, provoking more panic as it arcs over the Common and lands in the middle of a group of fleeing commuters. None of them seem hurt, but that's just a bit of luck. These bells could have easily killed people. And there are churches positioned like that all over Boston, clustered close together, all within throwing distance of each other. Church bells are going to be flying into crowds on every block of this city.

And I can't deny it anymore. Apparently trying to be normal means turning Boston into some kind of dangerous war zone. "We need to find Will," I say.

The T station is chaos. The subways are clogged in all directions, and compounding the problem, it seems like everyone on Boston Common has decided to take shelter in the station.

We give up before we even reach the turnstiles, turning back and struggling against the crowd, up onto the Common.

"What now?" asks Kelsey. "The ferry?"

"We don't have a choice," I agree.

"Why can't he have a cell phone?" Kelsey complains. "Supernatural creatures could really be a lot easier to get in touch with."

I start to respond but then hear someone calling my name, not really with intent but firmly enough that it slices through the chaos all around us. We all stop walking and look around, and it's Will, an absentminded professor type with graying brown hair, parting the crowd around us.

When he gets closer, I realize that he looks furious. "What are you doing out in this?" he snaps.

"We were going to look for *you*," I snap back. I gesture to the nearest church bell on the Common. "Look—"

"Yes, yes," he cuts me off, "and the sun has gone out. Both not-good things, but we can't stand out here talking about them, since who knows what's coming next. We're going to get inside, and you're going to get your sweatshirt."

I hate being ordered around like this. "No, I'm not. What does my sweatshirt have to do with any of this?"

"You and I are going to get this prophecy back on track," Will announces grimly.

CHAPTER 3

My aunts are annoyed to see Will. When we get there, they have every light in the house blazing in an attempt to fend off the unnatural darkness of the day.

"Oh no," Aunt Virtue complains. "What now?"

"We need to get the prophecy back on track," Will says.

This is an abrupt turnaround from the despairing and depressed Will who said that Ben had destroyed the prophecy when he left.

"I thought you said we couldn't after Ben left," I point out. Honestly, I just thought Ben was fulfilling a different prophecy, one my mother had taunted me with. *Benedict Le Fay will betray you. And then he will die.* But Will keeps insisting it's not actually part of the prophecy. I don't know what to believe anymore. Prophecies are so tricky, so hard to pin down, that as far as I'm concerned, we might as well not have them.

"I'm still not entirely sure we can," Will admits. "But take a look outside, would you? The *sun* has gone out. And the church bells are falling out of the towers as far away as Lexington and Concord. We have to do *something.*"

"I don't get it," I say. "The Seelies love light. Why would they put out the sun?"

"The Seelies love *their* light," notes Will grimly. "Can't have the Thisworld sun competing with their Otherworld light. Got to get rid of the Thisworld sun first."

"The Seelies can't get into Boston though," Aunt True says, wringing her hands. "Aren't you protecting Boston? Don't you have it locked from them?"

"The Seelies have been picking at the lock for a while now," Will says. "They're going to get in, sooner or later. Especially without a Le Fay enchantment to add to the protections. Our only chance is to get out now, while we can, and find the other three fays."

He says it like it's so easy. "How are we supposed to do that? I wouldn't know where to even *start* looking," I point out.

Will goes to answer, but Aunt Virtue cuts him off. "You mean to tell us that, after all this time, that foolish boy Benedict suddenly leaves and all of Boston is going to fall?"

"Boston was always living on borrowed time," Will says harshly. "We built it to be ready for battle, because we knew that sooner or later, the battle would come. You've just forgotten that. Well, the battle is here." Will gestures toward me. "She triggered it. It's coming. There's nothing we can do to stop it now. We have to take a stand, and we have to fight."

There's a beat. Kelsey says, "Let's get out of Boston then."

"No, you don't understand because you're *human*," Will informs her scathingly. "Boston is the *safest* place we can be.

Good luck with the rest of it."

"Kelsey's human," I say. "Won't she be fine? The Seelies, they want me, they want us, they want—"

"They want everything. You've met them. You've spent time with them. The Seelies have always been in the Otherworld because we kept them there. If you start to blur the lines between the worlds, they'll be everywhere. Fresh blood for them to feed off. They need fresh blood, you know. It used to be you could throw them a few changelings here and there. Younger blood, faerie or human, it didn't matter. They need the youth, the vibrancy. They feed off of it. And the most alive creatures in either world are humans—they live everything so *intensely*. So no. The humans won't be safe. Not if we don't hold the line in Boston."

"And we can't hold the line in Boston without Ben," I conclude.

"Or the other three fays," says Will. "Look, I can't read the prophecy anymore. It's a mess; it's too in flux. You can't predict the events that you're already *living*. All I can do is guess. We needed the other three fays. Benedict was supposed to help us find them. This is why you can never trust a faerie."

"We don't have Ben anymore," I say practically. "So what can we do without him? What does the book say?"

"Nothing useful," grumbles Will.

"Well, the Witch and Ward Society have been stalking me to get it back, so it must say *something*."

"Yes. It says that the key to all of this is Benedict's mother.

So now we know."

"Then give the book back," Kelsey tells him. "It's getting kind of annoying having little men popping up everywhere."

"I'm not giving the book back," says Will. "It was mine to begin with. Lord Dexter left it to me. I was only letting them *borrow* it."

"I don't want to get into whatever happened centuries ago with this book," I cut in. "I want to know how we get the sun to come back out. And how we can find the other three fays without Ben."

"We can't," Aunt Virtue says. "We should just forget about the prophecy and—"

"We can't forget about the prophecy. There is no status quo anymore, Virtue. Don't you see? We can't just wait for the next opportunity to come around to save the Otherworld. We need to do it *now*," says Will.

There's a moment of silence. I don't say anything because part of me feels guilty that I was willing to ever drop the ball on the prophecy. It was like I'd forgotten how terrible the Seelies are, forgotten my responsibility to a world I just learned existed but is depending on me to save it. I have no idea how to do it, and I doubt that I'll be successful, but I surely have to *try*.

"If Ben's mother is the key to finding the fays," Kelsey says slowly, "then shouldn't we be looking for Ben's mother?"

"Ben's mother, who up until a few days ago, everyone thought was *dead*?" Will retorts scathingly. "I've no idea how we would even begin to find her. Only Benedict would know, and he's *gone*."

"Thank you for repeating that as much as possible," I say, because it's not like I don't already remember every single *minute* that Ben is gone. "What about the guy who was guarding the book? He wasn't in that society, was he? He didn't try to stop us from taking the book, not really. So maybe he'd help? Maybe…he would have picked up some information about the book while he was guarding it, or something?" I feel like I'm flailing. "I mean, I don't know, but Ben seemed to think he was important, so…" I trail off, feeling like an idiot, but Will is looking at me as if I've just said the most interesting thing in the world.

"The Erlking," he says. "Of course."

"The what now?" says Kelsey.

"The Erlking. King of the goblins."

"The goblins," I echo.

I suddenly have a vague memory from long ago in my past, a past I'm no longer even sure I lived. Goblins have come up before in my life, have been referenced by my aunts even, but there's one time in particular… "Wait, that's what Brody was."

"Who?" asks Will.

I look at Kelsey. "Brody. We went to Salem Willows with him. Remember? Did we still live that?" The summer I met Kelsey, when we had a summer job together and went on a double date with some boys from school. Hot boys, both of them. Except one of them, Brody, the one interested in me, turned out to be…I can't seem to remember it clearly now. I seem to think he'd turned into a monster while I was kissing him, and then I pushed him into the water, and then… But the official story was…

"Of course I remember," Kelsey says. "He died in a shark attack, Selkie. It was awful."

That was the official story. He died in a shark attack. But he *didn't*. "No, he didn't, Kelsey." I turn back to Will. "Ben mentioned something about him being a goblin. Something." I am trying so hard to remember. How did I not remember all this before, when Ben was around? "It's all fuzzy now."

"Wait," says Kelsey, and her face is also screwed up in concentration. "You might be right. I think…I mean, he wasn't a goblin. Wasn't he a…monster? Was he a monster? But it was a shark attack." Kelsey gives up. "I'm confused."

"Yes," Will says. "Too many overlapping enchantments. But it wouldn't surprise me if you'd had a brush with a goblin before. They've been keeping a close eye on you. You're just as valuable to them as you are to the rest of us. They're really all around, most of the time masquerading as attractive humans. It's an ego thing."

"Brody tried to *kill* me." At least, I think he did. I wish I could remember the encounter better.

"You probably misinterpreted. You said he looked like a monster?"

I nod. I'm fairly sure he did. He was hideous and terrifying.

"Then he was in some distress, as goblins usually have no problem maintaining their disguises. He was probably asking you for help." Will shrugs, as if this is no big deal.

"And then I *killed* him?" I gasp in horror.

"You probably didn't. Goblins are very difficult to kill, and it wasn't like you had any special powers. I'm sure he's fine." Will continues to look very unconcerned about all of this. "You can ask the Erlking when we see him. I'm sure he'll know."

We decide to all go see the Erlking together, because Boston isn't safe anymore. I don't want my aunts to stay behind, and they don't want me to leave without them, and so we are agreed.

It is Will who says, "What do you wish to do with Etherington?"

And up until that moment, selfishly, like a terrible daughter, I had not really thought about my father. It's not because I don't love my dad—because I do—but because I'm not used to him being involved in stuff. And I'm used to thinking of him as being *safe* where he is.

But that was before I learned that Boston is about to turn into a battleground.

I look at my aunts, who look back at me.

Aunt Virtue says, "We will have to go get him."

Aunt True pulls out a white handkerchief, heavily

embroidered because she's probably been adding embellishments to it for centuries now, and blows her nose, her eyes weepy.

"How will we get him out?" I ask. I've never really thought about it, but surely we're not just allowed to walk in and retrieve our institutionalized family member?

Aunt True looks at me blankly with red-rimmed eyes.

Aunt Virtue draws herself up proudly and intones grandly, "We are the Stewarts of Beacon Hill. Who would dare to stop us?"

I decide that maybe they know better than I do about this, and anyway, it's nice to have something that someone else is in charge of.

"Selkie," Will says to me, "get your sweatshirt."

I hesitate. I took the sweatshirt off in a fit of anger right after Ben left me on the Common, because if he was going to walk away and abandon me, then I wasn't going to cling to his gift, even if it *was* supposedly keeping me safe. I don't know that it will work anymore, that Ben cares enough to be maintaining the enchantment over it, over *me*, because he *doesn't* care. He left.

Will walks over and stands next to me, stalled at the bottom of the stairs, looking up toward my bedroom.

"It wasn't about you, Benedict leaving," he tells me in a low voice. "I've never seen him so fond of anyone before, and I've known him a very long time, longer than either of us would care to remember."

I look at Will. "I don't care. I don't care why he left. I don't care what he was thinking. I'm not worrying about him anymore."

Will looks dubious.

I frown. "I *don't*. I'll get the sweatshirt if you want me to, but I don't care." I shrug to show how much I don't care, then say, "The only thing I'm worrying about is that my mother said Ben was going to die. That he was going to betray me and he was going to die."

Will shook his head. "She was saying it to get to you, Selkie."

"He did betray me," I point out. "I don't *care*, but I don't want him to *die*." I remember how my mother named Ben when we were trapped in Tir na nOg. Saying his name over and over with dangerous intent. Causing him pain.

"He's got a hidden name, Selkie. He's going to be fine. And if it really is a prophecy, then all we can do is find a way out of it."

"Fulfill part of the prophecy without fulfilling all of it?" I say hollowly.

"Get the sweatshirt," says Will. "It's the first step. We need to keep you as safe as you can possibly be."

"And you think the sweatshirt is still enchanted to protect me?" I am not nearly as sure about that.

"Benedict liked you more than I've ever seen him like any-body," Will repeats.

Which shouldn't mean anything to me, considering he also *left* me. But I can't help it; it does. So I jog up the stairs.

My sweatshirt is just where I left it, crumpled on the floor. I take a deep breath and pull it over my head, and then I take another deep breath and look around me at my room. I step onto the landing and peek out of the Palladian window, choosing one of the lavender panes, letting it tint Boston Common below into wavy purple. This is my home, and now it's a battleground, and somehow I'm the one who is leading everyone into battle.

Or something.

"Selkie?" Kelsey says behind me hesitantly.

I don't turn to face her.

"I guess this means we won't have to take the quiz on Emerson," I say, because that was what had been on our schedule for today, before all this.

"Yeah, that's at least one good thing to come out of all of this. We've been saved from having to pretend we understood any of 'Nature.'"

"You should go home," I say. "You should go home to your mom and—"

"You heard Will. It's not safe. What good would it do?" Kelsey comes up to the window and looks out of it with me.

"I called my mom," she says eventually. "She didn't pick up. I left her a message and I told her I loved her. I…didn't know what else to do. How can I say to her, 'Mom, I'm scared the world's ending, but don't worry, Selkie and I are trying to stop it'?"

"I don't know how I got us into this," I say, because I don't understand how it all spiraled so quickly to this moment here.

"You were you," Kelsey replies. "And I always knew you

were going to be a little bit crazy to be friends with, from the very beginning."

"You didn't think it would be this crazy."

"Maybe I had a suspicion," says Kelsey.

"Remember when all you had to worry about was cheerleading?"

"No," Kelsey answers frankly. "I don't. That seems like a lifetime ago. Look, the world might end, right? I want to be able to brag to my grandkids that I stopped it. So let's go."

I lean forward and hug her fiercely and say, "It's so good to have you here."

And Kelsey says, "Right back at you."

And then we head down the stairs together. Only I get distracted on the landing, looking at the clock.

Because it's stopped.

"Selkie?" Will says from the foyer. "Ready?"

"The clock stopped," I call down to him.

"What does that mean?" he asks.

I look down at him in surprise. "I thought you would know."

"Why would I know what that means? It isn't my clock. But I'm going to assume, based on recent events, that it is probably another portent of ill to come and we should get moving and not spend time winding it."

I am already on my way down the stairs. "Fine," I say to him. "I didn't need a *speech*."

My aunts are already outside, standing on the front stoop with Safford. They both look typically anxious, wringing their hands, and I don't blame them. I think of how they had to go through my entire existence worrying that all of this was going to happen someday and they were going to lose me, and it makes total sense to me now, all of the stuff that I dismissed as craziness on their behalf.

Aunt Virtue closes the door and carefully locks it.

Aunt True lays a hand against it, reverently and adoringly, sniffling.

"True," Will says to her, his voice very gentle. "Everything we've been through together, all of us, here, it does not end like this. Do you hear me?"

Aunt True looks up at him, eyes wide and welling with tears. "How can you be so sure?"

"Because I am not going to stand by and just give them Boston," says Will. "I lived on this hill when it was an actual *hill*, before its height was stolen to create new land. I was hanged out on that Common for being a witch. I will not surrender it to the Seelies. Not until one of them names me, and not a second before."

"That isn't going to be necessary," I say, trying to sound soothing. "We're going to take down the Seelie Court."

My aunts stand side by side, almost identical with their dark features and dark hair and matching long-sleeved black blouses and knee-length black skirts and black boots, all neat and gleaming. And they look at me, their eyes sad, like they're worried I'm so delusional that they don't even know what to do with me anymore.

Aunt True takes Will's arm. "Will," she begs. "Could you cast a protective charm? Please?"

He looks down at her. "I can't promise it would do any good, True, not now."

"Please?"

He sighs and glances back at the house. I don't see anything happen but something must, because, after a second, my aunt relaxes slightly and breathes, "Thank you."

Will nods once, brusquely, and then we set off down the Common together.

"So," says Will as we walk, "the plan is that we retrieve Etherington and then we go to the goblins."

He seems to be much calmer now that we have a plan, a direction. I think he was feeling rudderless without the prophecy, and it was making him panicked. I think of how panic-inducing it must be for someone like Will, who lives in a world where he's used to thinking he knows what's going to happen and suddenly he's lost that. It must be, in a way, like suddenly losing a sense, suddenly going blind or deaf.

"How are we getting to the goblins?" Kelsey asks.

"We're going to take the subway, of course," Will says matter-of-factly.

"The subway is a mess," Kelsey says.

"It's true," I agree. "The lines were all backed up. We were going to take it to go find you."

"It'll work for us," Will assures us confidently.

Park Street is crowded during rush hour on the best of

days, but it's worse today, balanced on the edge of a full-fledged riot. You can taste panic in the air.

"Everyone's trying to get out of the city before it falls," Will remarks, walking through the gates on the heels of a commuter. "As if that's going to do any good."

"Wait," I say, confused. "Aren't these…humans?" I hope no one is eavesdropping.

"Well, yes. But an odd, sudden storm just rolled in and church bells are falling out of towers," Will points out. "It doesn't matter what you are—you're getting away from here."

"The Red Line trains will be running, right?" Aunt True asks. "The human ones?"

"They should be. The human trains will run longer than our trains will," Will responds. "The goblins will fall back, but the trains will run as well as they can for as long as they can."

We go down to the Red Line platforms, reaching the platform in the middle, which is so packed you can barely move. Will walks without apology, pushing through the crowd. I try to keep him in my sight and make sure everyone else is still with us too.

We come out, finally, on the far side, near the fire exit stairway.

A train sounds its horn, rolling up to the station toward us on my left. At the same time, another train comes roaring in from the tunnel on my right, going in the opposite direction.

The bells chime then. An awful jingle-jangling sound that makes me feel queasy. My hands clench into fists automatically, and I back away from the fire exit stairway, where the sound seems to be coming from.

The trains to our left and our right have their doors open.

"Selkie," Will says slowly. He stands still, his eyes on the fire exit stairway, watching, waiting, tense. "The goblins live in the subway tunnels. Get into a tunnel, ask for the Erlking, and use my name."

"Wait, what?" I say, looking at him, confused. "Why are you telling me this?"

"Get on the train," he tells me.

I glance behind me. My aunts have already gotten on the train, although Aunt Virtue is standing with her hand on the door to keep it open. I look back at Will.

"Selkie," Kelsey says to me, and I look at her.

She is staring up at the fire exit stairway. Where a faerie has appeared, glowing palely in the dim T station.

The faerie is a Seelie. For a moment, looking up, I think it might be my mother. It isn't, but it could be; that's how strongly the Seelies resemble each other. Although I didn't think that when I was in Tir na nOg. Did they all look alike then? Or is it just that they all look alike now?

In my moment of confusion, all hell breaks loose. It feels like an earthquake shakes the station, the cement trembling under our feet, fine vibrations that increase to tremors. The regular commuters all look around in confusion that quickly tips over into fear then rises to a crescendo of panic.

And then the floor literally begins rolling underneath us.

"Go!" Will shouts, and I dart toward the waiting T, except that the pavement cracks right in front of me, rising in an impossibly high jagged cliff.

I try to scramble up over it, and I'm almost to the top when I hear someone say my name. It must be the Seelie, saying it with intent, because I cry out with the pain of it, and someone yanks hard on the hood of my sweatshirt, pulling me back through the crowd of people, and I scream in panic and wheel around to claw at whoever's holding me.

I collide with the being that grabbed me. Who turns out to be Will. He tumbles backward and into the open T door across the platform from where my aunts are. He manages to get hold of me and pull me in after him, and then the doors slide closed. The lights of the T flicker off and then back on.

And then Kelsey says, "Where the hell are we?"

CHAPTER 4

The train looks like the living room of some kind of fancy hunting lodge, with comfy chairs positioned in cozy little reading nooks around an enormous central fireplace. I am with Will and Kelsey and Safford. My aunts, who were the first people on the other T, the T we were all supposed to get on, were stuck there when the platform cracked between us.

"My aunts," I say, and reach for the closed doors, although I don't know what I'm going to do. How do you open subway car doors once they've closed?

And then the subway swings into motion, taking us away from the station. Away from the Seelie and the weird earthquake, but away from my aunts too.

I whirl back to Will. "No. Will. Take me back. I have to go back. I have to get them."

Will is massaging his face where I collided with him. "We can't go back."

"*We have to go back, Will!*" I scream at him. "We can't just leave them! There was a Seelie!"

"They're on their own subway train. They'll be on their way

now. And anyway, *you're* what the Seelies want, and you're here. That makes your aunts safer than they would be with you."

"Will—" I start, and then truly register the surroundings of the train around us. "Wait a second. Where are we? What happened? We're not even in *Boston* anymore."

"We are. We're just on an Otherworld train."

"The Otherworld trains go to the Seelie Court! They're evil!"

Will shakes his head. "Only the Green Line is evil. The Red Line should take us to the Erlking."

"It can't," I tell him. "It can't take us anywhere without my aunts and my father. We have to go back. This train has to stop, right now."

And then it does.

It screeches to a violent halt. The chairs skid forward, crashing against the wall. We all lose our balance, tumbling to the floor. The awful squealing of the wheels against the track ends, and the silence that descends is deafening.

After a moment, I say hesitantly, "Did I do that with the power of my mind?"

"No," Will bites out as he gets back to his feet. "You didn't. I told you the Seelies were after you, didn't I? We have to get off this train." Will is studying the doors.

"In the middle of a tunnel?" Kelsey asks.

"And go back for my aunts?" I say.

"No," Will snaps. "We can't go back for your aunts. Don't you get it? We're being *hunted*. The Seelies stopped this train. So we have to get out into the tunnels."

"And what are we going to do once we're there?" I demand hotly. "We have to go somewhere, we might as well go—"

"We'll go to the goblins." Will cuts me off brusquely and tries ineffectively to pry the doors open. "This is all *so* much easier to do when you've got a traveler with you," he comments, and then, "Don't tell Benedict I said that."

"Aren't you a wizard?" I ask. "Just magic it open."

"Sorry, I was busy learning important spells like disguising silver boughs to smuggle into prison for you and casting a protective enchantment over an entire city. I didn't bother to memorize the spell for *opening subway train doors*."

"You don't know the spell to *open things*?" I say in disbelief. And then the doors slide open.

I look at Will, who looks back at me, and then we both turn our heads.

Safford is replacing the emergency door release handle. "What?" he says at our looks. "Didn't you want to open the door?"

"Magic trains have emergency door release handles," says Kelsey.

"Safety first," says Will, and then, "Thanks, Safford." He leaps out the open doorway into the dark tunnel beyond then turns back to the rest of us. "Come on."

There is a moment when I stand at the edge, hesitating. I look at Kelsey and Safford, who are depending on me to keep them safe. I think of my aunts and my father. I don't know how I'm supposed to be keeping all of these people safe. And

I haven't even started to think about Ben, who is somewhere dangerous, undoubtedly getting himself into yet another situation where he will need my rescue.

I don't know what to do, but I believe that we are sitting ducks on this train. Better to keep moving.

I jump down after him.

Kelsey and Safford follow.

Will starts walking, and we trail behind him, for lack of anything better to do, I guess.

"Tell me how being in the subway tunnel is going to help us get to the goblins."

"Well, the goblins live in the subway tunnels. We were going to get there the civilized way, on the train, but this will work just as well."

"The goblins," Kelsey repeats in a processing tone of voice, as if she is taking careful notes for when she writes up her memoir of this experience, "live in the subway tunnels."

"Yes," Will answers crisply, as if Kelsey should have figured out much earlier in her life that goblins lived in the Boston subway. "Did you never wonder why your subway system is so excruciatingly incapable of functioning correctly?"

"I wondered that all the time," retorts Kelsey. "I never thought it was because of goblins."

"They sabotage the tracks," Will explains.

"Do they hate us?" I ask.

"No, they're just mischievous and frequently bored," Will replies.

"Can't they get hobbies?" grumbles Kelsey, and I don't blame her, because the malfunctioning subway *is* annoying.

"Brody didn't live in the subway tunnels," I say.

"How do you know where Brody lives?" counters Will, and he has a point.

"So the goblins will help us get to Ben," I begin.

"And we can use them to check up on your aunts and your father. The goblins have the run of Boston," Will says.

"The goblins," says Kelsey, in that same thoughtful tone of voice, "have the *run* of *Boston*."

Will rolls his eyes as if Kelsey has just revealed she doesn't know the alphabet.

The tunnel is very quiet. I expect there to be the rumble of subway trains from other places, but there is nothing but silence all around us. I listen harder, for the chiming of bells, for Seelies to rush up on us. I imagine, as I listen harder, that what I can hear is scuffling.

"Are there rats in the tunnels?" I ask suddenly.

"Of course there are," Will answers. "What kind of ridiculous question is that?"

I draw to a stop. "Ben told me there weren't any rats in the tunnels."

"Then he lied," Will answers, sounding unconcerned. "He's a faerie, Selkie, it's what he *does*. Anyway, what do you have against rats?"

I start moving again, but going very slowly, disgruntled over the revelation of Ben's lie. "That's right, you love rats," I recall.

"You love *rats?*" says Kelsey.

"I love all creatures," Will announces primly.

"All of a sudden you're Doctor Dolittle?" remarks Kelsey.

"This is the most inane conversation," Will complains. And then, suddenly, "Shh." He stops walking, holding his hand up. He stands there for a second, listening.

"Do you hear anything?" Kelsey breathes behind me.

"No," I whisper back.

But it is clear that Will hears something. He turns in a circle, looking all around us through the dimly lit gloom of the tunnel.

And then I hear it too: bells. The chiming jingle bells of the Seelie Court.

"*Run!*" Will commands, and I don't need to be told twice, but I can't tell where they're coming from.

"Which way?" I ask, vaguely panicked, turning around, trying to figure it out. It sounds like they're coming from all directions, like they are all around me, the chimes bouncing off the walls and echoing through my brain.

"Away from the train," Kelsey says, and it makes sense. They would be heading toward the train, right?

We tear down the tunnel, but I think this is fruitless. Seelies can move fast, faster than we can run. A small trickle of dirt hits me square on the nose. I brush it away, but then another trickle of dirt hits me, and then a pebble.

"Oh my God," Kelsey says, at the same moment I'm realizing it. "They're going to make the tunnel cave in."

"*Run!*" Will urges us again, and we keep running, although I don't know what the point of it is, and then, suddenly, in the space we just vacated, comes a great crashing sound, and the tunnel vibrates with the reverberation and dust kicks up all around us. Will has drawn to a halt, and I draw up beside him, coughing, and look back where we've come from.

The entire ceiling of the tunnel appears to have caved in. We are facing a huge wall of debris.

"We barely made that." I wheeze.

A voice off to our left says, "You're much safer on this side. Which was the point. We would never have actually *buried* you."

A man steps forward as he speaks. He is dressed all in black: black pants, black button-down shirt, black shoes. He looks a little bit like a funeral director, to be quite honest. An unexpectedly cute one, with gleaming dark hair and a quick smile that he sends in our direction. I guess he thinks that his comment about not burying us was reassuring. He sticks his hands in his pockets and rocks from his heels to his toes and back again.

"We need to see the Erlking," Will tells him.

The man's amusement seems to grow. "Yes, he thought you might be paying us a visit." He takes a few more steps forward, standing nose to nose with Will now. He smiles. It is not a very friendly smile, even if it must be admitted that it's an attractive one. "He looks forward to hearing your explanation."

He makes it sound like, actually, this is not a good thing at all.

Will smiles back. Also not a very friendly smile. "I look forward to providing it."

The man, smile cemented on his face, turns on his heel and walks away, looking over his shoulder at us. "This way," he says sweetly and winks for good measure.

"You heard him," Will says to us and starts following him.

"Who is he?" I ask, keeping my eyes on him, because he could easily fade into the darkness of the tunnel, dressed all in black as he is.

"What do you mean, who is he?" Will looks at me in surprise. "He's a goblin."

"*He's* a goblin?"

"What did you think he was?"

"I thought goblins were…" I trail off.

"I told you: most of the time they look just like us. All these preconceived notions. Really, humans understand very little about the Otherworld. We're natural tricksters; we're sending false information out into your world all the time."

"Let me get this straight," interjects Kelsey. "Goblins are really…hot guys?"

Will rolls his eyes. "So simplistic." He pauses. "Some of them are female."

The tunnel has opened up abruptly, and we are standing on an overlook that looks out over a vast and glimmering city. It isn't a modern city—there are no skyscrapers or anything like that—but it's clearly a sizeable settlement, with sleek and gleaming structures. Even the roads below us seem to catch the light. The ceiling drips with what look like stars but can't possibly be, because we are still underground. The light is dim and artificial, coming from countless numbers of torches scattered everywhere we can see, hovering over our heads and planted into the wall. And it is loud, loud with the sound of lives being lived. There are people calling to each other and laughing, as well as an insistent tapping noise.

I hear Kelsey gasp, and she and Safford and I stand there, staring out over this.

"What…" I begin, but I don't even know what question I want to ask.

"Come along," Will calls impatiently, and I tear my gaze away. There is a set of stairs leading down into the city proper, and Will is already halfway down them.

I run to catch up with him, because now I am overflowing with questions and I want him to answer them. The first thing I say isn't a question at all. "We're in a subway tunnel, Will."

"No, you're not. You're in Goblinopolis." He turns away from me and resumes walking down the staircase.

"Goblinopolis?" I repeat in disbelief.

"Their name, not mine," Will assures me.

"It's a city," Kelsey exclaims, and I hear her running to catch up to us. "It's an entire *city*."

"Yes, I know."

"Are we still under Boston? How can we still be under Boston? How can there be a city under Boston?"

Will sighs and turns and looks at both of us. "Don't you think, by this point, that it's time for the two of you to stop being so surprised by everything that happens? Now keep up. We don't want to lose our escort." He starts walking back down the stairs.

"There's a goblin city in the subway tunnels under Boston," remarks Kelsey, "and he thinks that's totally normal." She looks at Safford. "Do *you* think this is normal?"

"No," he admits. "Faeries don't normally associate with goblins."

"Why not?" she asks.

"I don't know. Tradition, I suppose. They live underground, and we live aboveground. Why should we associate? And there's the fact that travelers and goblins don't get along, so I think that we just fell into the habit of…not getting along." Safford frowns briefly. "Actually, now that I think about it, most Otherworld creatures have just fallen into the habit of not getting along, after the Seelies came to power. It was easier not to trust anybody at all than to trust someone and be named for your trouble."

It sounds awful, and Safford looks sad. Kelsey takes his hand and squeezes it a bit. Safford looks at her gratefully. I look away so as not to ruin their moment.

Will, predictably, ruins the moment. "Really," he calls up

to us, "if you get lost in Goblinopolis, I'm not stopping to look for you."

I know it is a hollow threat, but we pick up the pace anyway, half skipping down the staircase. At the bottom of it, our guide is waiting. His smile is still plastered in place, but he looks tense and annoyed nonetheless.

"This way, if you please," he says and leads us through the streets.

I cannot quite figure out what the roads are paved with, and I spend a lot of time trying to, scuffing my shoes over it. Could it be…tin? That is the best I can come up with. There are no cars, but goblins are walking all around us, going about their business. They spare a few curious glances for us, but mostly they are busy with what they are doing, darting in and out of shops and hailing friends. The buildings look as if they are made of silver. Some are highly polished and reflect everything, while others have grown tarnished. It is impossible to drink everything in.

"Please close your mouths," Will says to us. "You look like tourists."

The streets branch off of each other in a dizzying array. We could be in Boston, except we are *underground*. I am quickly lost, but I'm really unable to pay much attention, since this whole thing is so absurd. The goblins look just like regular people, only all of them are extremely *pretty*, to a ridiculous extent. It's like walking through a city populated with celebrities. They're all well dressed and well coiffed, and I wonder if it's some sort of rule, this attractiveness. Maybe they kill the ugly babies; that would seem like an appropriately goblin-y thing to do. It's true that Brody was pretty hot, at first, but then he turned into a monster, and I don't quite understand why none of them look like the monster Brody turned into.

We come to a square with a park in the middle. It looks just like a regular square, only prettier, like everything else down here. The grass is an expanse of smooth and inviting velvet, and members of the populace are sprawled on it, a few of them with rats that appear to be pets.

"But…how are they growing grass?" asks Kelsey.

Will sighs heavily. "It's *enchanted*."

We walk through the park and come at length to a river that seems to be trickling through the city. On the other side of the river, nestled in its own velvet lawns and surrounded by a golden fence, is a gleaming copper palace. It is not tall, not a fairy-tale castle with spires or anything like that. It sits low to the ground, hugging the gardens around it, and it is perfectly symmetrical, with rows of Palladian windows winking at us in the torchlight. And every once in a while, one of the windowpanes is lavender.

"Lavender panes," I say, because it is the only thing I can think to react to.

"Who do you think figured out how to make the glass fade to purple?" Will asks me, and the answer, I assume, is *goblins*.

There is a wide footbridge over the river, delicate and pretty, with the same golden fence as surrounds the palace lacing over it. We follow our escort across the bridge and up to the huge golden gates. There is a guard at attention, dressed in a black uniform with a bit of gold braid along the shoulders of the jacket. He looks at us warily as we approach and says to our escort, "What do we have here, Folletto?"

"Picked them up on patrol," our escort replies.

The guard looks at him. "And you brought them *here?*"

"Well, you know who they are, don't you?"

The guard whistles piercingly, and a little boy in the same black uniform comes running up from a little seat by the bridge that I hadn't noticed before.

"Go and tell His Majesty that Will Blaxton and the fay are here to see him," the guard tells him. "With…others." The little boy slips nimbly between the rungs of the fence and races up to the palace.

The guard looks at us with renewed interest. "*Really?*" he says, as if he had been expecting something totally different.

I look at Will.

Will looks bored. He yawns.

We stand there in silence. Safford fidgets a little bit. I twist the ties of my hood around my finger. And then the little boy comes running out. He slips through the fence again and looks at the group of us.

"Which of you is Mr. Blaxton?" he asks.

"Me," answers Will.

The little boy bows to him and, when he straightens, says, "His Majesty apologizes for keeping you waiting, sir."

Then the little boy snaps his fingers, and the golden gate swings open.

"Excellent," Will says. "I shall tell him not to mention it." He winks at the guard as we file through the gate.

CHAPTER 5

We are in the court of the Erlking. Whatever that means. The palace is gorgeous, but I would have expected nothing less. The gardens were beautiful, and the doors opened for us onto a lovely room full of marble and gilding, with a painted ceiling high above us and many sets of French doors opening onto a terrace along which fountains have been positioned, the water catching torchlight everywhere. There is a harp in the corner that seems to be playing itself, not so much a tune as a few notes plinking once in a while. Safford has gone to one of the doorways and is regarding the terrace, but I stand in the middle of the room with Kelsey, uncertain whether we should really be moving. You never know when you might cross a boundary in the Otherworld. It's exhausting, like trying to determine tipping customs in Europe, only worse, of course.

Will looks very at home. He is standing by one of the fireplaces, looking at the enormous portrait hanging over it, which is of an extremely attractive man in a black velvet suit and black riding boots, a cape jauntily flung back over his shoulder. He has one hand resting on the intricately jeweled hilt of a sword at his hip, and the other hand rests on a marble table beside him. On his head sits a large bejeweled crown, flattening black hair into cowlicks that peek out from the back of his head. The expression on his face in the portrait is self-satisfied, a smirk dancing around his lips, amusement in eyes a brilliant shade of blue.

The thing about this portrait is that once you look at it, nothing in the room seems nearly as interesting.

After a couple of minutes, footsteps sound over marble, far away from us but approaching swiftly. Safford turns from the window, looking wary, and Will takes a step away from the fireplace, looking with interest in the direction of the footsteps.

And then the man from the portrait sweeps into the room. He is dressed in the same black velvet as in the portrait, the same black riding boots, with the same black cloak billowing out behind him as he moves. It's what he wore that day outside the Boston Public Library, when we retrieved the book that told us about Ben's mother. I wonder if he ever wears anything else. I mean, it's working for him, but still.

There is no crown on his head, but the sword swings at his side. His hair is that shade of black that seems to almost gleam blue, much darker than Ben's hair, so dark that it seems impossible and makes me think of silly poetic things like raven's wings and ebony. It is carefully disheveled all over his head in a devil-may-care sort of way.

He walks immediately over to Will, arms outstretched, exclaiming, "William Blaxton."

Will smiles at him. "Your Majesty," he says and then hugs him.

"We have much to discuss," says the man and gives Will what can only be described as a hard look, belying the joviality of his tone.

Will pauses. "Yes," he agrees.

"First, though." He turns to me and smiles. "You are the fay," he proclaims.

"Hi," I say warily, a little thrown by his manner, which is halfway between welcoming and imperious.

"Lovely to meet you formally," he says, "as there wasn't time for such niceties when you stole the book from me."

"It wasn't your book," Will says.

"It wasn't *not* my book," the man retorts. "But now, now, this is a conversation that should not be had in such an uncivilized manner. There are other guests." He looks at Safford and Kelsey expectantly.

"Kelsey, Safford," Will introduces, "this is the Erlking."

He bows very gracefully, pulling the cape dramatically about him as he does so. "Normally I would say, 'Very much in your service,'" he says. "'Any friend of Will's' and all that. But recent occurrences being what they have been, I offer you a conditional welcome."

"Conditional?" Kelsey echoes faintly. Her cheeks are a bit pink, and I don't blame her, because the Erlking head-on is a little much to take.

"Will has explanations to make. If they're not acceptable,

I will, of course, have your heads." He says it so lightly that Kelsey actually laughs, assuming it's a joke, and the Erlking looks at her quizzically, as if she is an interesting curiosity, which makes her laughter dwindle to a stop.

The Erlking looks back at Will. "Shall we dine then?"

"Of course," Will responds.

The Erlking smiles, looking genuinely delighted. I cannot figure out how old he is—he is clearly a king and carries himself with the authority of one, but there is something boyish about him as well. "Excellent. I love a feast." He whistles, and the same little boy who delivered the message from the guard comes racing into the room. "There you are," the Erlking says to him. "Please tell the dining room we are having guests for dinner." The Erlking pauses and looks over at us. He looks suddenly uncomfortable. "I'm so sorry, forgive me, but…faerie or human food?" He looks to Will. "You are in mixed company." He turns back to us. "Which would you prefer, ladies?"

"Human food," I answer. "Definitely."

He inclines his head graciously. "So be it." He turns back to the little boy. "You heard Her Ladyship. A human feast, if you please."

The little boy nods. "Yes, Your Majesty," he says and races out of the room.

The Erlking turns his attention back to us. The harp in the corner of the room plinks a few notes, and he frowns in its general direction. "Heavens below, what *is* that thing doing?" He walks over to it and shakes it a bit. The harp jangles in response. The Erlking sighs and turns back to us. "It's depressed. It's been depressed ever since I had to send the piano in to be fixed. It can't even get itself to play proper music anymore, which is at least an improvement over the terrible dirges it was playing before. I keep trying to tell it that the piano will be back soon, but you know how musical instruments are. They never believe a word you say."

The little boy comes racing back into the room.

"Ah," the Erlking says to him, "is dinner served?"

The little boy nods. "Yes, Your Majesty."

"May I have the honor then?" the Erlking asks Kelsey and me politely, holding out an arm for each of us.

I had thought it possible that the portrait had exaggerated the blue of the Erlking's eyes, but if anything, they are more intense. He is undeniably compelling, and I hear myself saying, "Of course," and settle my hand in the crook of his elbow.

Kelsey does the same on the other side, and the Erlking leads us out of the room and into the next, which is a large dining room with a beautifully set table. There are two chandeliers hovering overhead, each crowded with hundreds of tapered candles, and the china and crystal and silverware all flash in the candlelight. The table is covered with food, and my stomach audibly growls. I hadn't realized until that moment how hungry I was.

"How did they have time to do all this?" Kelsey asks.

"Time?" echoes the Erlking blankly, as if he doesn't understand the question. He pulls her chair out for her and seats her, and then moves around to the other side of the table and pulls another chair out. "For you," he says to me when I stand there stupidly watching him.

"Oh," I say and scurry over to him. I've never had a guy pull out a chair for me before, and I'm not quite sure that I pull the whole thing off as elegantly as you're supposed to, but whatever. "Thank you."

He sits to my left, at the head of the table, and Will takes the seat to my right, with Safford opposite him.

A violin comes floating into the room and begins crooning a soft sonata from near the roaring fire in the fireplace.

"The violin," the Erlking remarks, "is not depressed. I think it quarreled with the piano and is hoping it never comes back." And then he holds out his hands expansively. "Please. Help yourselves."

I hesitate and look to Will for guidance, and he pulls over a bowl of mashed potatoes and puts a heaping amount on his plate. I follow his lead, and for a little while, there is silence as we help ourselves to food.

The Erlking is not eating. He is settled back in his seat, cradling a goblet of wine in his hand and watching…me.

I look at him, self-conscious under his gaze. I am sure I am blushing. "What?"

His eyes stay on me, and his lips curve into a smile. "You were the reason for Will's last visit. A fay of the seasons, he told me. And would we consent to have her sheltered in the city above us. And look. Here you are." He sits up abruptly and sets his goblet of wine down. "And now we discuss it." He fixes Will with a hard look. "I mean to exist in peace, and you know those are my intentions, but I cannot find myself with any other option than to acknowledge that my people are presently at war."

"Not with us," Will denies.

"Oh no? Who was it who took the book out of the room? That was the term of the treaty, Will Blaxton: that the book of power would be locked into the room by the Witch and Ward Society."

"There was always going to come a time when we would need that book, Kainen, and you know it."

"Do you really dare to use my name here?" the Erlking demands.

"Yes. Because you let us leave with the book. Which is something your people don't know, do they? And all this is to save face. You know that there are greater issues afoot, or you wouldn't have let Benedict get away from you. You could have stopped him with a fingertip."

The Erlking watches him for a moment, his eyes glittering sapphires in the candlelight. "I have heard rumors."

"The rumors are true. We can deny it no longer. The battle we have long suspected is nearly here. Might be here already."

"I thought that was what this meant." The Erlking holds up a pocket watch, face out. The time reads 11:09. I have no idea whether that's the right time or not. I suppose it's the right time somewhere in the Thisworld or the Otherworld.

"Why?" Will asks. "What happened to the time?"

"Well, it kept time perfectly, for centuries or hours, depending on the time you're keeping, and then suddenly, today, it stopped."

I look up, food forgotten, thinking of the grandfather clock on the landing at home. "It stopped?"

The Erlking nods. "And then when it began ticking again, it was eleven o'clock. You know what happens when clocks strike twelve."

"What happens?" I ask.

The Erlking gives me a disapproving look. "Don't you read your histories? The enchantments all end."

I think of the enchantment around Boston. "Which means the Seelies will get in."

"Exactly," says the Erlking, replacing the pocket watch and resuming eating as if this isn't terrifying.

"But…" I think of the grandfather clock. "We'll never know how long it will take to strike twelve. It doesn't move linearly."

"It will now," responds the Erlking, still calmly eating. "It will move through the eleven o'clock hour until it strikes twelve. Of course, we cannot know how quickly that will happen, you are correct, but we know that whatever time is being kept, we are fifty-one ticks away from the twelve o'clock hour. So we are in the middle of a fight for our lives, and *you* have given the book to the faeries." The Erlking looks hard at Will.

I realize at that moment that I have no idea where the book went. There was so much other stuff going on, I managed to lose track of it. I lost track of the book of power. I'm terrible at this.

Will says, "Do you really think that I would do that? We needed it, for the next step of our mutual defense, so we took it. But they don't have it."

"Who has it then? Because I've already spoken to the Witch and Ward, and they've a warrant out for its discovery. And in the meantime, they've abandoned the city."

This seems to catch Will's attention. "Have they? Already?"

The Erlking snorts. "Frederick and Henry were never ones for bravery, were they? You were the one who set the whole thing up, and they just accepted the privilege of lording over it. But they were never going to fight for it."

"That is hollow flattery," says Will after a moment.

"Which you have always been susceptible to," says the Erlking and sips from his goblet.

"Will you fight for it?" Will asks without acknowledging the Erlking's point.

The Erlking is silent for a moment. "I let you have the book, didn't I? I think I've made my choice." He puts his goblet down. "What is it that must be done?"

"We need your army."

"So I assume."

"The Stewarts must be protected. They are currently exposed in Boston."

The Erlking nods. "We can bring them to Goblinopolis."

"And they'll be safe here?" I ask anxiously. It doesn't seem like such a bad place. Maybe it's part of the spell the Erlking is weaving, but it seems much safer than Boston, cozy and protected instead of sharp and cold and exposed. And the Erlking did not stop Ben when he could have, has not yet stopped us. I can feel myself starting to trust him, even though it seems strange that I should trust a goblin more than I should trust faeries.

The Erlking looks at me. "They'll be safe as long as there are goblins left to fight. If Goblinopolis should fall, then of course I can guarantee no safety, as I shall be gone myself."

He says it so calmly, so simply. I swallow the nervous pit in my stomach and nod and realize that I have entirely lost my appetite. It actually seems a betrayal of my family that I'd had any appetite at all to begin with.

"There's something else," Will says.

The Erlking arches an eyebrow at him. "You ask for my army and my protection, and you still seek more?"

"Benedict's been tricked. Trapped."

"Benedict Le Fay has been *tricked*?" repeats the Erlking. "Pray tell, how does one trick a Le Fay?"

"Very cunningly," Will responds. "We need him for the prophecy, if we have any chance of winning this war, so we need to find him."

"You need a traveler? Really? That's what you need to win? In that case, I shall withdraw all of my armies as soon as you retrieve him."

"You know that's not how prophecies work, Kainen—"

"Why are you here?" The Erlking's voice is cold, and I shiver with it. "I have no interest in helping you find a traveler. I say good riddance to him."

"You want the prophecy to be fulfilled as much as the rest of us do. And we need Benedict to do it. And you can find him, can't you? The goblins have always been able to hunt travelers."

"Goblins hunt many things," the Erlking replies. "That doesn't mean we can find things that don't wish to be found. If your traveler is any good, he will never be found. And if he *isn't* any good, then the Seelies will have already gotten him, no?" The Erlking says this very casually.

I frown at him, because I am furious at Ben but I still don't like to hear people casually discussing his death.

The Erlking notices, turning his gaze onto me. "You disagree?"

"He's looking for his mother," I say as if in his defense.

"His mother?" the Erlking echoes. "His mother was named centuries ago. Or yesterday, depending on the time." The Erlking pats at his chest, where he replaced the pocket watch.

"Not according to the book. The book says she's the only one who knows where the other fays are, and we need to find her to get to them. This doesn't have to do with Ben; this has to do with everything else. I don't care if we ever find Ben."

The Erlking looks at me for a moment before arching one of his dark brows wryly up. He looks as if he doesn't believe me for a second, which is really irritating. Then he says, "Well, if the book told Benedict that his mother is still alive, it must be a trap. It's a book of power; the words in it could be traps just as much as they could be truths. Lord Dexter was on our side unless he wasn't. You know how the saying goes: never trust a faerie or a wizard or an ogre or a gnome. Never trust anything except a goblin."

"That's not how the saying goes," sighs Will.

"If Benedict's mother were still alive, where is she? Why would she have kept herself hidden for so long?"

"Because she had a price on her head," Will says. "Because she had to hide to survive."

I look at him. "Hang on, I thought *you* thought this was a trap too."

"It can be true and still be a trap," Will replies. "But you're right—we don't have any other option. If she's the one who hid the other fays, we need her. And if anyone could have stayed hidden all this time, it would have been her. She was the best enchantress in the Otherworld."

"Her son isn't so bad at it, from what I hear, and he couldn't get his hiding enchantment to hold up," the Erlking points out, tipping his head my way.

"Selkie's enchantment was supposed to break," Will says. "Otherwise the prophecy would never have been fulfilled."

"Then why not just wait until the rest of the enchantments break?"

"Because we don't have time, as you just pointed out.

Because the clock is ticking, and we didn't coordinate our battle strategy with Benedict Le Fay's hidden, named-or-maybe-not-named mother, and because you know there are other prophecies in motion that you do not want to be fulfilled."

There is a long, tense moment. I feel like I can hear the Erlking's pocket watch tick forward another minute, but that might just be my nervous imagination.

The Erlking finally says, "Where would she have been all this time?"

It's such an impossible question for me to contemplate. I know almost nothing about the Otherworld, so I don't even know where to look. At least if you lose someone on planet Earth, you have a general idea of where the continents are, of where that person might *be*. Yeah, he might be on the other side of the planet, but you could get in a plane and you could start searching systematically, street by street, if you really had to. I have to find a faerie who may or may not exist and I don't even know the *geography*. I might as well roam the Earth, asking every random person I encounter, "Do you think you might be a faerie?" in order to find the other three fays.

The Erlking goes on, "Who would ever want to have been caught harboring such a fugitive from the Seelies? The Seelies will destroy you for no reason, never mind *this*. She would never have been able to shelter herself for so very long—"

He cuts himself off, and I realize in that moment that he's had an idea, an idea he doesn't want to share with us.

"What?" I demand.

He swallows and looks at Will and then back to me and admits reluctantly, "Unless she went to the Unseelie Court."

"And who's that?" Kelsey asks.

"The Seelie Court's worse half," Will explains, and I remember Ben mentioning them before. "The only small pocket of the Otherworld that's not under Seelie control is under Unseelie control, and they are even worse than the Seelies, which is why the Seelies never conquered them. They let them be because they couldn't be bothered. If you were hiding from Seelies, you'd hide there. But only if it was your last resort. Because the Unseelies would betray you back to the Seelies in a heartbeat. You can't trust faeries as a general rule, but the Unseelies have never even heard the word 'trust.'"

"That's where Ben thought she was," I note.

"If she's anywhere," agrees the Erlking.

"Well, whether or not she's there, that's undoubtedly where Ben went to find her. We have to go to the Unseelie Court."

The Erlking starts to laugh. He flings back his head in hilarity, his laughter booming about us, echoing off the marble walls of the dining room.

"Why is that funny?" I demand.

"The Unseelie Court is closed to visitors," he says with a smile. "How do you propose to get in?"

"How did Ben get in?" I counter. "How did his mother get in?"

"They're travelers. They can get in anywhere. Like locked rooms with books of power that no one is supposed to have access to." The Erlking gives Will a dark look, as if to remind him that that is not forgiven; then he looks back at me. "*You* cannot just walk into the Unseelie Court."

"That's where I was hoping you might come in," Will inserts.

The Erlking's amusement fades. "Will," he says and sighs.

"You're the only one who can get us in," Will tells him.

"I don't disagree with *that*." He sighs again and looks briefly to the ceiling. "All these years…True, there are constant battles with the encroaching humans, but mostly they have been ages of peace and prosperity."

"I can see that," Will says. "I think of how you were when you came to me, this ragtag little band of miners, and I see what you've done with the place, and the truth is you've done marvelously, Kainen, no one can deny that. But it won't work. You can't keep them out of this one. The Seelies will destroy everything this time if we don't stop them. And your armies won't be enough. We need the other fays. And we need a Le Fay."

The Erlking regards him heavily for a moment and then looks back to me. "I have heard rumors," he begins, searching my face. "The most fantastical rumors. Church bells in Tir na nOg, I have been told. A silver bough, for the first time in memory. Is it true? Did you escape from Tir na nOg?"

"Yes," I answer firmly.

"And now you propose to march into the Unseelie Court?"

"If that's what we have to do to find the other fays," I answer again, stubbornly this time.

The Erlking's eyes narrow slightly, studying my features closely. "Aren't you just *extraordinary*," he murmurs.

"I'm just trying to fulfill my prophecy and save the world," I say. "All in a day's work."

The Erlking looks back to Will. "I thought there would be so much more time before this moment," he says sadly.

"We all did," responds Will.

"Well." The Erlking sighs and says solemnly, "You and I rose together. If we are to fall, may we fall together too." He lifts his wine goblet toward Will.

Will leans over me and clinks his goblet against it firmly. The sound is sharp and crystalline and chilling.

"What time is it?" I hear myself ask.

And the Erlking looks at his pocket watch and says, "11:11."

"Make a wish," says Kelsey softly.

I don't. Instead I slip a butter knife off the table and into my pocket. Seems more useful than most of the other things I take.

The Erlking has horses, and they look almost exactly like normal horses, except for the very important fact that they don't have any eyes. Where their eyes should be is just… smooth skin.

Kelsey and I stand there looking at them.

"Don't say anything about how they don't have eyes," Will warns us. "You'll offend the Erlking."

Kelsey and I look at him and then back to the horses. They paw blindly at the ground with their hooves.

"They're cave horses," Safford explains helpfully. "I've heard about these."

"Why don't they have eyes?" asks Kelsey.

"Because they don't," Safford answers.

"Ah, here he comes," remarks Will, and I turn to look over my shoulder.

We are standing outside the Erlking's stables, and the Erlking himself is walking toward us over the expanse of enchanted grass that separates the stables from the palace. His cape is billowing out behind him, and he is walking swiftly, pulling on a pair of black leather gloves, his sword swinging by his side. The little boy servant is skipping beside him to keep up with his pace, holding a small bundle.

The Erlking does not look happy. He had sent us out to the stables while he called his advisers together—*He's a king*, Will told us, *he can't just up and leave*—and I discern the chat with his advisers might not have gone as well as hoped.

"All set?" he asks, taking the reins of the horse that the nearest servant leads to him. He speaks in clipped, brusque tones, very different from the smooth, urbane charm he used before. He looks at us briefly before taking the bundle out of the little boy's hands. It is some sort of rucksack that he is fastening onto his saddle.

"Ready," Will confirms and swings onto his cave horse.

Kelsey and I exchange a glance.

"We don't ride horses," I state.

The Erlking, settling atop his own horse, stares at me. "You don't ride horses?"

"They don't ride horses much aboveground anymore," Will tells him apologetically.

"It is so uncivilized," the Erlking complains. "Nobody has any sense of propriety anymore."

"Kelsey can ride with me," Safford offers, his voice bright with hope.

"Fine." The Erlking waves one gloved hand dismissively. "The fay can ride with me." He turns to the servant next to his horse. "Help her up."

The servant, without warning, fastens his hands around my waist and lifts me as if I weigh nothing. I make a noise of surprise and, after a bit of inelegant scrambling, manage to get myself onto the horse behind the Erlking, which requires me basically to sit on his cape. I wonder if he's going to be upset about that and decide not to mention it.

"Let's go," he says. "The sooner we get going, the sooner we get this over with. The clock is ticking."

"What time is it now?" I ask.

"11:12."

"We've only lost another minute?" I say, surprised.

"The Seelies must be having trouble with the Boston enchantments. We did do a few things right all those years ago, eh, Will?"

"It was only a few minutes ago, Kainen, wasn't it?" replies Will.

The Erlking urges the horse forward, and I immediately wrap my arms around his waist to keep from falling backward. We move forward at a slow, ambling walk. I'm torn between wishing we were moving a little faster and being terrified of falling off.

Everyone is silent. The Erlking's mood doesn't seem to welcome small talk. For a little while, we wend through the streets of Goblinopolis, keeping next to the river, and the people all seem to recognize their king and gape at us as we pass before them, remembering to bow low and deep. The Erlking doesn't acknowledge any of this, and we just keep plodding forward.

The outer limit of the city is marked by a flat wooden bridge over a bend in the river, very unlike the light and elaborate bridge leading to the palace, and there is a gatehouse at the end of it. A goblin dressed a little like one of the Three Musketeers sweeps his hat off his head and bows graciously to us as we pass, and then, almost immediately, the world becomes dimmer and dimmer and dimmer, until we are moving through a darkness so black that it matches the Erlking's cloak, the lights of Goblinopolis well behind us. In fact, the only way I know the Erlking is there is because I have my arms around him. I cannot see him at all. Nor can I see anyone else in our party, although I can hear the hooves of their horses and the rhythm of their breaths. The darkness closes in all around, making me feel claustrophobic, and I realize now why cave horses don't have eyes: what would they look at?

"Can't we create some sort of light or something?" I ask finally, when I can bear it no longer. It seems to me that we have been walking through pitch blackness for hours, and I am beginning to hear sounds at the edge of my consciousness. The dark keeps pressing in on us from all sides.

"You're better off not seeing," the Erlking replies, which is not very comforting.

It *is* comforting to hear someone else's voice in this intense world of night, and to keep him talking and because I genuinely mean it, I say, "Thank you for this. For helping."

"I haven't much of a choice," he responds, sounding grim.

Maybe it's not the best time to try to talk to the Erlking, I decide.

"Close your eyes," he says to me after a long moment of silence, and he sounds a bit softer. "It won't bother you as much if you close your eyes."

I do as he suggests, and he's right—the darkness is much more bearable when I'm not trying to see through it.

I fall asleep. Probably not surprising, since it's been a while since I've slept and the world around me is so dark and the rocking of the horse and the warm velvet of the Erlking's cloak are comforting. I wake up when the rocking stops. The Erlking has drawn our horse to a halt, and he is sitting up straighter in the saddle. There is an alertness to him, almost a quivering, and I get the sense that he is listening to something I can't hear.

"We stop here," he decides at last.

"Stop?" I echo, alarmed. "We don't have time to stop."

"We have plenty of time," the Erlking replies. "It is barely a quarter after the hour."

"But…stop *here*?" I can't help but say. I don't want to stop here. I want to get out of this eternal darkness.

"It's nighttime," he tells me.

"It's been nighttime for hours."

"No, it hasn't. You overworld creatures are really appalling at telling time underground. Go on, hop off the horse."

"I can't see the ground," I tell him. "I'm not hopping off this horse until I can see the ground and I can verify that there are no rats on it."

"You're quite troublesome," the Erlking sighs.

"She's half ogre," Will explains, and then there is light. It's probably not very bright, but it's so dazzling after the darkness that I squint and the Erlking throws up one hand to shield his eyes from it. It is an orb of light, hovering over our heads.

"Some warning would have been nice, Will," the Erlking grumbles.

"Sorry," Will says, not sounding it.

"Did you do that?" I ask.

Will nods, looking almost offended at the question. "I am a wizard, you know."

"Yes, and you even know some useful spells," I agree and then survey our surroundings. It's a small, round dirt room, I supposed you could call it, almost like a clearing in the middle of tunnels. The ceiling is close over our heads, and the "room" has a number of narrow, dark openings.

"Did we come through one of those tunnels?" Kelsey asks, looking at the openings as Safford helps her off their horse.

I follow her gaze, noticing how tiny the tunnels are. The walls and ceiling must have been right on top of us as we'd traveled. Just thinking of it makes me claustrophobic.

The Erlking looks unconcerned. "That's why I said it was better that you not be able to see. Are you going to hop off the horse anytime soon?"

"Oh," I remember. "Yes." I slide gracelessly off the horse, feeling stiff and sore.

The Erlking dismounts gracefully, of course. "If Will starts us a fire," he remarks, fiddling with his saddle bag, "we can eat."

Will, scratching his head with one hand, waves at the ground with the other, and there is a fire, dancing merrily. Another good spell. Will's wizardry is coming in useful. Why don't *I* have any magic?

"Excellent," says the Erlking and pulls something out of

his saddle bag. He thrusts it into my hands without a word and then leads the horse a short distance away. Safford's and Will's horses seem to sense where he is and follow.

I look down at the bundle in my hands and realize it's food. Bread and cheese and what looks like dried meat. And some oranges. The Erlking has thought to feed all of us. I am relieved.

Will takes the food out of my hands and pins some bread onto a fork he's conjured, stretching it out toward the fire to toast it.

"Why can't you just conjure food?" asks Kelsey.

"Because that would be like conjuring oxygen," Will replies as if that's some kind of answer. "Can't be done."

Kelsey shrugs at me and sits close to the fire. I follow suit.

"Are you sore, Kelsey?" Safford asks her anxiously.

"I'm fine." She smiles at him.

The Erlking is apparently done with the horses. He comes over to the fire. "You should heat the meat. It'll take the spell away," he tells Will.

"Oh, I was wondering about that," Will says and conjures another fork that he hands across to me.

I put a piece of meat on it. It is thick and leathery. "What spell?" I ask.

"It's been glamoured to be dried," Will explains. "It isn't really; it's perfectly fresh, should be delicious."

The meat is delicious, pressed with a slice of cheese between pieces of toast.

The Erlking passes around the oranges, and everyone struggles with them, but I pull the butter knife I'd taken out of my pocket and slice into it cleanly, pulling out the wedges and sharing them with Kelsey.

"Where did you get that?" Will asks.

"I borrowed it," I say.

The Erlking lifts his eyebrows at me but says nothing.

When we are done eating, the Erlking announces, "We should all get some rest."

"*Rest?*" I say. "But…"

The Erlking holds out his pocket watch. "11:12," he says. "Holding steady. We can rest."

"But what if they suddenly pick up the pace?" I ask anxiously.

"My pocket watch will chime at the quarter hour; it will wake us up. We should get some rest."

"Big day tomorrow," remarks Will hollowly.

"Do you know if my family got to Goblinopolis safely?" I ask the Erlking.

He looks at me blankly. "How would I know that?"

"They have musical instruments with emotions, but they don't have *cell phones*," Kelsey mumbles.

Will waves his hand and conjures us blankets. "Would you rather have cell phones or newly conjured blankets?" he asks.

I think of all the people I want to talk with right now. "Cell phones," I say. "Why can't I conjure up a cell phone? Why can't I conjure up *anything*?"

Will looks surprised. "You're not a wizard."

"Right, but I'm a faerie and I'm an ogre and I can't do *anything*."

"You're good at naming." Will sounds bewildered.

"Which is horrible, by the way." Using someone's name to hurt them—kill them. My one and only superpower.

"The Seelies used good naming power to conquer the entire Otherworld. I wouldn't dismiss it so easily, if I were you," says the Erlking.

"Okay, *yes*, but still. I want to enchant meat so it looks dried but it's really fresh. I want to be able to light up an entire cave. I want to be able to do *something*."

"First of all, you might never be able to do those things. It's like saying to me that you want to be a concert pianist and a ballerina and an acclaimed painter. You can't be everything. Second of all, they all take practice. Nobody gets to be a pianist or a ballerina or a painter overnight. You're a faerie, and you're naturally good at naming, which is actually a very, *very* special thing to be. The rest of it will take time. Remember, it took you time to learn how to *walk*. You're not going to learn how to be a faerie in the space of a couple of hours."

I know what he's saying makes sense, but I'm resentful. I have a prophecy to fulfill, and I'm tired of feeling terrified for my life all the time. I wish I felt like I could do something to make myself feel better.

And then the Erlking says, "You're you. You're exactly what we've been waiting for. Half faerie and half ogre and you. What could be better than that?"

"And you've already done things that nobody has ever done before in the history of the Otherworld," adds Will. "How can you be complaining that you don't have special powers when you escaped from Tir na nOg?"

"That…" I can feel Safford and Kelsey both looking at me, and I wish that I hadn't started this topic of conversation. "That was Ben. And luck."

"It was you," Kelsey says. "Maybe it was a bit of all of us, but that's how the world works, even the Otherworld. Stronger together than apart."

"A bit trite," says Will, "but if it makes you feel better, sure."

"Everyone's a critic," huffs Kelsey.

The Erlking says, "It is time for everyone to go to *sleep*."

CHAPTER 6

Everyone else seems to fall asleep immediately, but I am not tired, since I took that long nap during the journey. I lie awake, watching the magical fire crackle and trying to keep my breaths deep and even. Because I am awake, I know when the Erlking leaves, creeping stealthily away from the circle of the fire. I sit bolt upright, straining to see past the firelight, to figure out where he went, but he is dressed in black, and he fades into the shadows all around us.

I sit by the firelight while everyone else sleeps, waiting for him to return.

When he does, I don't even hear his approach until he speaks. "You're awake," he says, his voice low, and then he settles onto the ground beside me.

"Where did you go?" I ask, keeping my voice low as well.

"Reconnaissance. Ear to the ground kind of thing. The Unseelie Court doesn't stay in one place, you know, but they seem to know we're coming. They're staying quite still right now."

The firelight flickers over his face, and I study his profile. It's a handsome profile, but it's creased with worry.

"How will you get us into the Unseelie Court?" I ask him.

He doesn't look at me when he answers a moment later. "A long time ago, the goblins were dying out. We were held prisoner by the Seelie Court, trapped in mines where humans had invaded, losing our battles for our homes. Will had started Parsymeon—now called Boston—and I wanted to come here, with as many goblins as I could. A new world, an undiscovered world, a world where we could build our defenses and become entrenched and *thrive*. But none of us could come to Parsymeon without the permission of the Seelie Court. We were enchanted into place, always mining to bring them jewels, to craft their coronets and forge their bells. No one can do it as well as a goblin, you know. Everyone else lacks the *delicacy*."

He pauses for a long time. I hold my breath, waiting for the rest of the story.

"In those days," he continues, "I was young, and I was daring. I would save my people, I thought. It is how youth is. You are foolish and headstrong and think you can do everything." He sighs heavily.

"You're a king," I point out to him, feeling he is in need of comforting. "You were just doing what you had to do to save your people."

"Oh," he replies. "I wasn't a king then. I was just a boy. I was a boy with a plan, to use my one great talent to save my people."

"And what was your talent?" I ask, transfixed now.

He looks at me for the first time, and he sends me a smile that is simply breathtaking in its suggestiveness. "*Seduction*," he answers silkily.

I swallow thickly. "Oh," I croak.

He looks back into the fire, breaking the spell. "All goblins are natural seducers, of course, but I was the best seducer in generations. Or I had that reputation in those days. The Seelie Court doesn't pay attention to the reputations of goblins. Why would they? So I got myself chosen to be the goblin that delivered the latest shipment of treasure, and then it was easy. They are surprisingly susceptible to seduction, Seelies." He falls silent.

"And then?" I prompt.

"And then I stole the talisman. Broke the enchantment."

"What's a talisman?"

"The physical embodiment of an enchantment. All truly strong enchantments have one."

I look down at my sweatshirt.

"Once you have stolen the talisman of an enchantment from the person or people to whom it is entrusted, the enchantment ceases to work properly. It begins to crumble. And that's what happened. I stole the talisman, and we goblins emerged from the mines where we'd been imprisoned, and we came here, to Parsymeon, which has been a dream of a place. We've been very happy here." He looks almost wistful now.

"And is that how you became king?" I ask him.

"Yes. The goblins hadn't had an Erlking for generations.

While the Seelies had ruled us, we'd fallen into disarray. Upon being made free and independent again, we reinstituted the Erlking, and I was voted into the position."

"That was after you came to Parsymeon?"

"Yes."

"So that's why Will calls you by your name?"

The Erlking shrugs. "It isn't quite my name, although it is close enough." He leans back on his elbows, looking into the fire. "He knew me before I had a title. There aren't many beings around anymore who remember me from that time."

"Do you like it? Being king?"

He looks at me. "I thought you wanted to know how I was going to get you into the Unseelie Court," he remarks wryly.

"Oh!" I remember. "I do."

"The Seelie I seduced, she was flung from the Seelie Court. Do you know what happens to faeries who are exiled from the Seelie Court?"

"They don't get named?"

"Not right away. Seelies like to play with their prey first. Haven't you noticed?"

I had noticed that actually. I shudder and look into the fire.

"So if you're an exiled Seelie trying to avoid the inevitable naming to come, you go to the Unseelie Court."

I stare at him. "You're going to get us into the Unseelie Court by using an ex-girlfriend?"

He looks grimly at the fire. "Not pleasant, I know. Will's lucky I like him. And that, well, I don't really have a choice if

I'm going to save my home. The clock is ticking." He takes out his pocket watch, glances at it, and then shows it to me. 11:13.

"But doesn't she hate you?"

"Hate me?" he echoes blankly, looking at me in bewilderment. "Why would she hate me?"

"Because you stole the talisman from her and got her exiled from the Seelie Court," I remind him.

He shrugs. "Oh, *that*. You fail to comprehend: I am very, *very* good at seduction."

We fall silent for a moment. I lean my chin against my knees and stare into the fire. And then I venture, "I...met one of your people. Once."

"Oh," the Erlking says. "Yes. Brody. Sorry about that. He was just supposed to provide us with a progress report. I was worried that we were running out of time, that we weren't *ready* for this. But I suppose we would never have been ready, no matter how long it took."

"I..." I take a deep breath and plunge forward. "Did I kill him?"

The Erlking looks at me, startled. "Kill him? What? No."

My relief is tempered by the Erlking starting to laugh. He tries to keep himself quiet, laughing into his cape, but he is clearly highly amused.

"What's so funny?"

"You. Thinking you could have killed a goblin just like *that*. No. We can be named like any other supernatural creature, but we are much harder to kill by conventional methods."

"I knew his name."

"Brody isn't his name. We wouldn't give you the correct name, the way Benedict didn't give you his."

I think of Ben, who has always been Ben, because he held back the power of his name from me. "Yeah, well, never trust a faerie, right?" I say, wishing I could hold back the bitterness.

"Never trust a Le Fay," the Erlking corrects me. "You know that he might be at the Unseelie Court. You know that he also might *not* be at the Unseelie Court."

"I don't care either way," I say with a bravado that I'm not sure I feel.

The Erlking rolls onto his side to face me. "It is a very dangerous thing, you know, to have lost your heart to Benedict Le Fay. He is an expert in *enchantments*. You can never know that anything about him is real."

"The way you are an expert in seduction?" I can't resist saying.

"Touché," the Erlking laughs, and then, "You are quite remarkably fearless."

I'm really not. I'm afraid all the time. I say instead, "I'm not in love with Ben. I'm not falling for his enchantment this time. I know way too much about him. And we've been through too much. I'm kind of sick of saving his life."

The Erlking smiles. "Oh, the delicious things I would do with an indebted Le Fay. Call in your favors carefully, fay of the autumnal equinox."

"I'm not calling them in at all. I don't want anything to do with him. I'm going to fulfill this prophecy, with or without him. This isn't *about him*." But even as I say it, I hear my mother's voice in my head. *Benedict Le Fay will betray you. And then he will die.* This *isn't* about him. But it's not entirely *not* about him either.

"When Will came to me, when he asked if I would consent to your being hidden at Parsymeon, if I would help him to protect you…I made my choice then. Not the most popular choice I've made as Erlking—prophecies are tricky things, and you can never be sure if you are bringing about your downfall or your victory—but it was the choice I made. Sometimes you have to gamble with the birds. Will saved us, offered us shelter, at a time when we needed it. How could I deny him the ability to do the same for you? And then it came complete with a traveler invasion. Travelers are hugely troublesome beings; always getting into trouble, you can't keep them out. They were constantly stealing jewels from our mines, and there was no way to stop them. Until we evolved, of course."

The Erlking rolls onto his back. "Anyway, sometimes I think I should have objected to Benedict's presence. But his enchantment was useful, necessary. None of the rest of us are as skilled at hiding things. We needed him. We might need him still. All the same…" The Erlking glances over at me. "I'd be careful of him, were I you."

CHAPTER 7

We are woken by the Erlking's pocket watch chiming at us.

The Erlking looks at it and confirms. "11:15."

"We should get going," says Will.

The Erlking doesn't reply but just walks over to the horses.

"Here," says Will, handing us some pieces of dried fruit.

"If you heat it up, does it become fresh fruit?" Kelsey asks him.

"Don't be absurd," Will replies, as if her question made no sense at all.

Kelsey sighs.

"Let's go," says the Erlking, swinging himself gracefully into his saddle.

"How long until we get to the Unseelie Court?" I ask, clambering gracelessly onto the horse behind him.

He winces as I tug accidentally on his cloak, tightening it around his throat, and reaches up to adjust it and give himself some air. He doesn't say anything, just urges the horse onward.

I cannot tell if I feel like I understand him more or less

after the conversation last night. I find the Erlking a strange mixture that I can't quite read. Will appears to trust him implicitly, but I'm not to that point yet.

The day is just like the previous day, darkness all around and unceasing forward movement, and finally I ask again, "How long until we get to the Unseelie Court?"

"We're there," he answers me curtly.

I blink at his back, which I can only locate in the darkness because I know it is right in front of me. "What? When did we get here?"

"A while ago."

"Why didn't you say anything?"

"What was there to say?"

"'We're entering the Unseelie Court.' That's what there was to say."

"I didn't think it was important."

"It looks the same as everything else."

"That's why I didn't think it was important. Shh."

I am offended. "Don't 'shh' me—"

"*Shh*," he says again more firmly and draws his horse to a halt. "Will," he calls. "What is that?"

"Nothing good," I hear Will's voice answer from the darkness behind us.

"What does that mean, 'nothing good'?" I ask. "What can you hear?" I am straining very hard to hear something, anything, but all it sounds like is silence to me. Maybe, very far away, the sound of water dripping.

"I think it's a dragon," comes Will's voice, hushed, as if the dragon might hear us talking about it.

We are all very silent. But no matter how quiet we are, I cannot hear anything.

I am about to say that when, very suddenly, a stream of fire licks its way toward us, accompanied by a loud roar, flames curling through the darkness. The horse rears under us, and I grab at fistfuls of the Erlking's cloak to keep from falling off. The flames subside, the darkness darker now and heat still lingering in the air. The creature is no longer roaring, but the echo of it is ringing in my ears. The Erlking is trying to soothe the horse, which is now prancing sideways.

"I thought you were going to be able to use your wiles with your ex-girlfriend," I remark sarcastically.

"I said I could use my wiles to get us in. I never said she wouldn't kill us once we were here," he retorts and then twists to call over his shoulder, "Everyone okay?"

"We're fine," Kelsey responds, sounding a bit shaken.

Will, by way of answer, sends a light orb shooting out in front of us, illuminating the landscape.

We're in the middle of a cavern, stalactites dripping from a ceiling high above our heads, through which Will's orb is bobbing and weaving. Directly in front of us, the ground disappears into a yawning ravine several hundred feet across. There is a bridge suspended across it, floating magically, and there, on the other side, is a squat, heavy, black castle.

"That's the Unseelie Court," says Will.

"I don't suppose we can just cross over the bridge," I note grimly.

"Not with a dragon underneath it," remarks Kelsey.

On cue, the dragon, from out of sight in its pit, belches fire that rolls over the bridge in hot billows.

"Get off," the Erlking says to me, and I manage to clamber off the horse. He swings off gracefully and strides purposefully over to the bridge, stopping just at its edge, looking down.

"Well?" Will asks him.

He shakes his head a bit. "You can't even see the bottom, it's so deep." He steps back, frowning at the bridge.

"Well, we have to get across somehow," I say. This was my only idea, the thing I said we had to do to fulfill the prophecy. We can't have spent all that time getting here just for it to turn out to be a waste. "Can we enchant the dragon somehow?"

"I can cast a protective spell that will block the fire from reaching the bridge," Will says. "The dragon isn't really the issue."

The dragon roars, flames momentarily engulfing the bridge in white heat.

"I can't wait to hear what's really the issue," comments Kelsey, staring at the embers left behind by the flames, "if it's not that."

"The bridge is enchanted," explains the Erlking impatiently. He is pacing up and down the cliff, looking irritated. The Erlking, I realize, doesn't like being *still*. When Kelsey and I just look at him, he continues, "It isn't really *there*."

We look back at the bridge.

"It's not?" I say.

"It's there as long as the Unseelie Court wants it to be there."

"Oh," I realize. "So we could get halfway across and…"

"Yes," he concludes grimly. He turns decisively from the bridge and looks at me. "We have to go to the Unseelie Court, you claim. We have to find Benedict's mother to find the other fays to keep the prophecy on track and defeat the Seelies."

"Yes," I respond.

"This isn't because you hope Benedict is there and you've gotten yourself all starry-eyed over the best enchanter in the Otherworld, is it? Because I'm not doing all of this just because you're under some sort of spell."

I draw myself up, offended. "He left me," I say. "It was his choice. I wouldn't be here if I was just *chasing* him. The precious book of power said that his mother hid the other fays, and we need the other fays for the prophecy, and you said this is where his mother is."

"We also need Benedict for the prophecy," Will says. "I think. If I'm reading it right."

"But that's *secondary*," I insist.

The Erlking continues to look at me for a long moment. Then he nods. "Then I'll go first," he says and turns to face the bridge.

"Wait," Will protests. "What?"

"I am the least valuable," the Erlking proclaims steadily,

regarding the bridge. "The most expendable. There is no prophecy about me the way there is about the rest of you. And I am the most likely to be trapped by the bridge, since I'm the one who upset a member of the Unseelie Court. The rest of you are innocent. Well, as innocent as you can be in the Otherworld. Which in your case, frankly, isn't very. But anyway. I'll go first. Alone."

There is a long moment of silence. I feel like one of us should protest—he's only involved in this because we asked him to be—but I'm worried that instead he'd suggest sending across Kelsey or Safford, who are also more expendable than me, and I don't want that to happen.

I look at Will, who sighs and rubs at his temples.

The Erlking turns away from the bridge and walks over to Will. "You can cast the enchantment to block the dragon, right? I don't need to be worrying about that too." He is unstrapping the sword from around his waist.

"Yes," Will tells him. "Of course. What is that?"

Because the Erlking is now holding the sword, sheathed in its scabbard, out to Will. "Here's something nobody else knows, Will. This sword is the Seelie talisman. I can't have it vanish with me, if I do vanish. Take it, and keep it safe, and bring it back to Goblinopolis for me. Do you promise?"

Will nods and accepts the sword. "My word of honor," he promises, and he tries to say it very brusquely but I can tell he is touched by the trust in the gesture.

"Excellent." The Erlking turns back to the bridge and walks

confidently over to it, standing on the very edge. "Ready?" he asks Will.

"The spell is already cast," Will answers him.

The Erlking steps onto the bridge without a moment of hesitation. I think we are all holding our breath there on the edge of the cliff—I know I am—but the Erlking strides confidently along the bridge. His cloak drifts in his wake, and the dim light from Will's orb picks up the blue sheen to his dark hair. The dragon breathes fire but it passes up and over the bridge in a fiery arc that would be beautiful if it wasn't so obviously very deadly. The Erlking's rhythm does not hitch. He gleams and billows his way across the bridge and then steps onto solid land on the other side, where he turns and executes a bow in our direction, gathering his cloak dramatically around him.

"Is it safe then?" I ask, even though I know the answer.

"Safe enough for him," Will responds.

"Should we all go over at once?"

"No," says Will. "If it disappears and kills all of us at once, then that is far worse than it disappearing and killing just one of us, at which point the rest of us can try to come up with an alternate plan."

"Then who should go next?" I ask. And suddenly I hear myself saying, all in a rush, to Will, "I think you should go last."

Will regards me with surprise. "Really? Why?"

"Because you can get everyone back to Boston easily. And

you'll know what to do to protect my aunts and father, as much as you can. If you go, I'll have no idea what to do to save them."

Will looks at me for a moment. "But you're the fay—"

"What will it matter if I'm left all alone? I won't know what to *do*."

"Selkie," Will says gently. "You'll be *you*. You've gotten us to this point, haven't you?"

"And I left my entire family back there and who knows what's happening to them. Please don't fight me on this. You can save them. I can't. I'm going next."

And then, before there can be any more discussion about it, I run over and onto the bridge.

"Selkie!" Will and Kelsey shout from behind me, but I am already on the bridge and there's nothing they can do now.

I keep running, focused on the Erlking on the other side of it, watching me expressionlessly. The bridge feels very solid under my feet; I find it difficult to believe it's not real, except for the fact that I can't see how it's moored to land in any way.

Then, just like that, it's not real. The bridge disappears underneath my feet, and I am falling through space. I can't even scream; I can't gather breath to do it. I tumble, head over feet, surrounded by blackness. I can't even see the dim light of Will's orb, and panic rises up and overtakes me just as someone's arms fold around me, catching me solidly against him. I am still falling but I am no longer alone.

I twist my hands into his shirt, and I know who it is before he even speaks.

"Close your eyes," Ben's voice says to me.

I don't have time to react before we land with a thump on solid ground, and it is bright all around us. We are clearly no longer in the dragon's cavern. We don't seem to be anywhere near there. We're in a green, grassy meadow, and the sun is bright in the sky above us. Ben is there, dressed in only one layer, a long-sleeved, bright blue T-shirt that makes his eyes seem like they could almost be blue. Except for how they are also green. And gray.

"Are you okay?" he asks me urgently.

"Ben," I pant, because the panic hasn't quite subsided and I can't quite catch my breath and where did he *come* from?

"Are you okay?" he snaps at me, his hands roaming over me not at all the way I would have fantasized about back when I was still in love with him (which I obviously no longer am), but as if he is making sure I have not broken any bones.

I realize that I am sprawled on the grass with the sky directly over my head.

"Are you okay?" he demands again, and his face swims back into my vision, his unclassifiable eyes and that beautiful mouth he has and all that artfully tousled hair.

I am *furious* with him. I lift my hand and give the side of his head a solid whack.

"*Selkie*," he exclaims, as if he is *surprised* that this is my reaction to him. *Surprised!*

I sit up as he rubs at the side of his head and looks hurt. "You look *fine*," I complain to him, because he ran off and left me and he looks as if he went on *vacation*.

"What?" He looks bewildered.

"You're *fine*. You idiotic…" I struggle for a word to call him. "You idiotic *faerie*."

"You're angry with me for being *fine*? I just saved your life."

"My life was only in danger because *you left me*," I retort. And that's not quite true, but whatever. Logic isn't the most important part of an argument, right?

Ben looks amazed. "Were you were coming to *rescue* me?"

"No." I fold my arms, belligerent. "I'm coming to find your mother, because it turns out we didn't have any choice. We had no other ideas how to find the other fays."

"You need to find my mother?" Ben echoes.

"How did you know where I was?" I ask him, because it's suspicious to me that he turned up at the perfect moment.

He looks at me for a moment. Then he smiles at me, the kind of smile that would have made me giddy in earlier times, before he abandoned me in the middle of Boston Common. "Selkie Stewart," he says, and he says it nicely, and it *feels* nice, and that's not fair. "I missed you."

I hate him, I think. "Funny that *you* missed *me*, since you're also the one who *left*," I point out scathingly. "*Benedict Le Fay*."

He winces, his smile faltering. "Are you really still angry about that?"

I blink at him, astonished. "Did you really think there would be any chance at all that I wouldn't be?"

He looks uncomfortable. "It was…a while ago. Wasn't it? I'm unclear on the time being kept, so I—"

"It wasn't a while ago, Ben," I snap at him, "and it wouldn't matter if it was. It wouldn't matter if it was *whole entire lifetimes ago*. I would still be angry with you for *leaving me* when I *asked you to stay*."

Ben looks uncertain. "Selkie—" he begins.

I cut him off, because I don't want to hear it. "Where are we?" I ask instead. "Where have you taken me? Where is everyone else?"

"Everyone else?" he echoes. "Like who?"

"Will and Kelsey and Safford. Did you think I came here alone?"

"You were alone last time you came to rescue me," he reasons.

"I'm not *rescuing* you," I remind him. "And I'm not alone. I have friends now. Friends who stick with me and help me. We need to go back and get them. They'll be worried, because it isn't like me to go away and *abandon* them."

Ben is silent for a moment, and when he speaks, it is brusque, not light and comfortable the way it had been before, almost as if we are strangers meeting for the first time. I wonder if he's decided that I'm a lost cause. I would be perfectly okay with that, I tell myself; in fact, it would be the best thing, and I ignore the part where I feel as bereft now, suddenly, as I did when Ben first disappeared on Boston Common. Like even though he is right in front of him, he is still somewhere I can't find him, and he always will be.

"Where are they?" he asks me.

"Well, they were right beside the dragon pit. They were going to cross the bridge next."

"The dragon pit," he repeats. "Wait, were you coming to the Unseelie Court?"

"How do you not know where I was? You were just there."

"You were in distress. So I went to *you*. I didn't know where we were. What were you doing at the Unseelie Court?"

"Coming after your mother. I've just told you that."

"How did you know my mother was at the Unseelie Court?"

"We didn't really know. We just guessed." I look around the bright meadow. "And clearly we're not at the Unseelie Court now. Wait…" I am being seized with recognition as I take everything in. I look back at Ben. "Is this your home? Where I met your father?"

"No." He looks around himself. "We are at the Unseelie Court. This part's just been enchanted to look this way."

"By you?" I guess.

He doesn't have a chance to answer, because someone calls his name, behind him, off in the distance. "Benedict!" the voice shouts, a woman's voice. Ben looks over his shoulder, and even as he does so, abruptly, the woman is right there in front of us. She is tall and willowy and lithe and pale, her spun-gold hair floating gently in the warm breeze wafting over the meadow. She is dressed in a flowing dress the hues of a sunset, made of some material that seems to keep subtly shifting colors. She smiles at me, the smile of a Seelie, a smile that makes me feel cold.

I stiffen and debate shifting away from her on the grass of the meadow.

"How did *you* get here?" she asks me, smile still on her face, and then looks at Ben. "Aren't you going to introduce me? She must be a friend of yours, for you to have granted her passage."

"She's the fay of the autumnal equinox," he answers her, his eyes steady on mine. "And this…." His chin tips ever so slightly in the direction of the woman standing next to him. "Is my mother."

CHAPTER 8

I thought Ben's mother would look like Ben. Instead, she looks, well, like *my* mother. I gape at her a little stupidly for a moment but I don't really know what else to do. I'd kept saying we needed to find Ben's mother so she could tell us where she hid the other fays, but Ben's mother is acting as if she has nothing to do with any of this craziness surrounding us.

"The fay of the autumnal equinox!" she exclaims in a voice like a purr. "Oh, why, Benedict, she's lovely. What a beautiful job you did with her, my dear. He's been so coy about you," she addresses me. "I thought for sure you must take after the ogre side of your family, but look at you—you're *lovely*."

I don't know what to make of this speech. I smile tightly and glance at Ben, who is giving nothing away, his eyes, gray-green now, shuttered as he regards me.

Ben's mother turns to him. "Where did she come from?"

"Linking enchantment," Ben answers lightly. "She was in distress, so she was brought to wherever I was."

"Clever enchantment," praises his mother, and I suppose it would be, except that it doesn't seem to me to be at all what happened. I've been in almost constant distress, for one thing. For another thing, Ben came to *me*.

Ben shrugs.

"Well," Ben's mother says to me, "you are a very lucky little fay that Benedict is so clever. And now you are here, we must have a feast."

I don't want to have a feast. "That's not necessary," I say with a smile. "I don't want you to go to any trouble. I just need to know—"

"No trouble at all," she assures me with that icy smile still lingering on her face. Then she vanishes.

So much for asking her about the fays and getting out of here quickly. I turn to Ben. "Look—" I begin.

"Don't—" he starts, but I talk over him.

"We need to go get everyone else and—"

His mother appears at his shoulder again, her eyes narrowed at me. "Everyone else?" she echoes. "Who's everyone else?" She looks to Ben for an answer.

"Friends," Ben replies with an easy smile. "Friends Selkie was traveling with."

"Oh?" She looks back to me. "Where are they?"

I don't know what I thought meeting Ben's mother would be like, but she's too much like my mother for my comfort. I wanted to just *ask* her about the fays, but now I don't know if I should. *Never trust a Le Fay*, says the Erlking in my mind.

"Not sure," I lie. Or maybe I'm not lying at all. Who knows if they are still by the dragon pit, since they probably think

I'm dead? But I do not want Ben's mother to know where they are.

She studies me closely and then says slowly, "Well, then. I will have the guards keep an eye out for your friends, won't I?" She vanishes again, less abruptly this time somehow, more like drifting away.

I look at Ben, but he moves forward before I can say anything, his lips directly on my ear as he breathes, "Are they by the dragon pit?"

I nod. And before I know it, we are there, Ben's hand curled into mine. We are on the side near the castle, and the Erlking is beside us, blinking at us in astonishment.

"Selkie!" exclaims Kelsey from across the pit, bouncing up and down in her excitement.

I wave at her.

Surprise evident in his voice, Will says, "Benedict."

Ben, having registered the Erlking next to us, takes three enormous steps away from him, dropping my hand to do so. He doesn't acknowledge Will's greeting from across the dragon pit. He looks at me accusingly. "You never said anything about an Erlking."

"Not *an* Erlking, *the* Erlking," the Erlking corrects impatiently.

"Stop it," I interrupt their squabbling. I look at Ben. "Go across to the other side and bring the rest back over here."

Ben hesitates, looking across to the other side. I can feel it in him, the uncertainty in the way he is standing.

It startles me. This should be the part where he excels, where he wants to show off. "Ben?" I ask.

Then he vanishes. I look across to the other side, where he reappears. Then he is back on my side with Kelsey, and then gone again.

"*Selkie!*" Kelsey flings herself on top of me, hugging me tightly. "We thought you were *dead*." Her voice breaks, and I know that she really did think I was gone forever.

"I'm okay," I assure her.

"What happened?" She straightens away from me, wiping some lingering tears away from my eyes.

"I don't really know," I confess. "Ben caught me, and then—"

"We'll talk about it later," Will interjects, and I realize Ben is done bringing everyone over to our side. "Is your mother here?"

"Yes," answers Ben slowly.

"Have you asked her about the other three fays?"

"Not exactly," replies Ben, still speaking slowly.

"What? Why not?" demands Will impatiently. "I'm glad that you've been having your sweet little family reunion here, but the clock is ticking."

"11:22," the Erlking confirms.

Ben opens his mouth then seems to think better of it. He waves in the air, conjuring up a piece of paper and a pencil, and he starts writing something on it, even as he says, "But they're preparing a feast. You don't want to miss the feast."

"Benedict," Will begins impatiently, accepting the piece of

paper Ben hands him. "You have to—" Will cuts himself off, reading whatever Ben has written on the paper. "You have two friends who are most excited for the feast," he finishes. "Five friends, actually."

"Four friends and an Erlking," corrects Ben.

Will has handed me the piece of paper. I read Ben's hastily scrawled letters. I feel the Erlking read over my shoulder. *Can't speak freely—walls have ears.* I pass the piece of paper on to Kelsey.

"Not *an* Erlking," says the Erlking again. "*The* Erlking."

Ben shrugs as Kelsey passes the piece of paper to Safford.

An awkward silence falls. None of us wants to say anything. Safford gives the paper back to Ben, who vanishes it into thin air. We stand around awkwardly.

The Erlking clears his throat eventually and holds out his hand to Will. "May I have my sword back?" he asks politely.

"Oh. Yes." Will hastily hands it over. "Well, what about this feast?" he asks Ben. "Shouldn't we go join it?"

"We have to wait for them to come to us," Ben replies.

"What do you mean?" Will asks. "Isn't that the castle right over there?"

"Yes. And you could walk until the day you are named, walk and walk and walk, and you would never reach that castle."

Will regards the castle, which looks as if it could be reached in ten minutes. "Well, that's inconvenient." He looks at Ben, and it hangs in the air, the question he's not asking. *Can't you break it?*

Ben shakes his head a bit then says, "They'll come for us soon."

We wait. It feels a bit idiotic. I want to point out that Ben seemed to have no trouble getting me to the meadow part of the Unseelie Court, but who knows what the issue is preventing him from getting us to the castle. Enchantments follow their own complicated set of rules. And I feel like there is a great deal about this whole experience that Ben has not yet shared.

Eventually, a few things hop out of the castle doors toward us, bounding over the drawbridge. They look like…

"Are those enormous dogs?" Kelsey asks incredulously.

The dogs are barking enthusiastically now as they approach.

"Corgis," Ben confirms.

"*Corgis?*" I repeat. I don't know why, of all the things I've seen in the Otherworld, I should be so completely thrown by giant corgis.

"Royal faeries always ride corgis," Ben tells me in his *obviously* tone of voice.

"*Giant* corgis?" I ask.

He looks a little irritated at that question. "Well, how would they fit on regular-sized corgis?"

"Fair point," Kelsey allows.

"I've never seen Seelies riding corgis," I point out.

"Seelies try not to *go* anywhere," Ben replies.

The three corgis have reached us by now. They loom over us, tails wagging and tongues lolling out, their corgi grins firmly in place. And faeries leap easily to the ground beside the corgis. Ben's mother I recognize. I don't know the other two faeries. One is female and one is male, and they have the unmistakable Seelie look to them. The female one walks immediately up to the Erlking.

"Hello," she says.

"Hello," he says in reply.

Then she kisses him. Very hard.

"You *hit* me at our reunion," Ben points out from behind me, as if that had not been the proper way to behave and it would have been better for me to just kiss him like *that*.

Which is annoying, because Benedict Le Fay, who left me standing on Boston Common after I'd asked him not to leave me because I loved him—not to leave because *he* loved *me*—doesn't deserve to be greeted with a kiss. And certainly not one involving tongue.

"Yes," I agree with his statement without looking back at him. "The Erlking must be better at seduction than you are."

Will, Kelsey, and Safford all swing their heads away from the show the Erlking is currently engaged in to look at me and then Ben. I would like to see Ben's reaction—I hope he is appropriately chastened by the comment—but I decide the comment's impact will be greater if I do not allow myself the moment of triumph.

I sweep over to Ben's mother. I cannot tell if she heard my exchange with Ben, and I cannot tell if it would mean anything to her anyway. "Is this how we're getting to the feast?" I inquire politely. "On the corgis?"

"Of course," she says, and then she sends that cold Seelie anti-smile around to encompass all of us. "Welcome to the Unseelie Court."

Riding on corgis is difficult, harder than it looks. It was a lot easier to ride the cave horses, even if at the time I didn't think it was especially easy. The corgis do a lot of…gamboling. That's the only word I can think of. The ride to the castle isn't long, but they do a lot of bounding about on the way there, and I have my hands twisted into the corgi's fur to keep from falling off. I could hold on to Ben, who I am sitting behind, but I feel like that might eliminate the impact of my last statement to him, which I'm honestly pretty proud of.

Our corgi leaps over the drawbridge leading to the castle, and then we are inside a courtyard, castle walls rising all around us. I slide off the corgi quickly and Ben does the same. Behind us, Kelsey and Safford are sliding off their corgi, and Will is sliding off of his. The three faeries who had ridden out to meet us had traveled back up to the courtyard, and the female one who wasn't Ben's mother had taken the Erlking along with her. The four of them are now waiting for us in the courtyard.

"What did you think of traveling by corgi?" Ben's mother asks us, smile wide on her face.

"Er," Will replies, looking dubiously at his corgi. "It was unique."

"It's the only way to travel. But maybe you have to be born to it. Come." She turns grandly, with a commanding sort of sniff, and marches through two enormous double doors into a hallway.

Ben follows her. Will and Kelsey and Safford and I all look at each other.

"Ask her," I hiss at Will.

"Shh," Will says sharply, shakes his head, and then follows after Ben.

I sigh in frustration. I mean, it wasn't like *I* asked her, but I still decide it's easier to be miffed at Will for not picking up the slack.

It is very dim inside the castle. There is some feeble light along the hallway we're walking down, but I can't really figure out where it's coming from, because there aren't any torches or lamps or orbs or anything like that. But I know there's light because Safford's red hair gleams like a beacon in front of me, picking up every piece of light there is to gather.

Safford's hair, frankly, makes me think of the sun. I decide I'm tired of being underground. I am never taking real, unenchanted sunlight for granted again.

"Here we are," Ben's mother announces, coming to an abrupt stop. She turns and smiles at us. I wish she would stop smiling; her smile is unsettling. "We are having a feast. Did Benedict tell you?"

"He mentioned it," Will replies politely.

"Excellent. Surely you wish to freshen up before the feast.

You're looking a bit…" She casts her eyes over us. "Travel weary," she finishes delicately.

Ben's mother turns to her left and throws open a door I hadn't noticed before. Then she turns to Will. "Mr. Blaxton," she says to him and indicates the doorway.

Will does not move, and I realize that, while she hasn't named him with intent, she nonetheless knows his name. Her smile grows more chilling. I didn't realize that was possible.

"Thank you," Will says eventually, after a moment of silence. He sounds smooth and unruffled, but I think it's all an act. Will, after all, has been living among faeries a long time and can lie with the best of them. He walks briskly through the doorway and then closes the door behind him. Well. I hope he closes it. I hope it doesn't swing shut of its own accord.

Ben's mother moves down the hallway, flinging open more doors. "Safford," she says. "And Kelsey."

They both hesitate on the thresholds of their rooms. Kelsey looks back at me. I flicker a little smile at her, as if I know that this is all going to be okay, when coming to the Unseelie Court now seems to me to be the worst idea that I have ever had. And then Kelsey walks into her room and shuts the door, as does Safford.

Ben's mother moves to the next door in the hallway. "And now, for the fay of the autumnal equinox," she starts, hand on the iron ring that acts as a doorknob.

"She'll stay with me," Ben inserts and takes a step closer to me in the twilight of the hallway.

I look at him in surprise and annoyance, as his mother says, sounding amused, "I suspected you would insist upon as much."

She starts walking again, and Ben places a hand on the small of my back to nudge me forward.

I resist. "I'd rather have my own room," I announce loudly, because really, that seems a little arrogant of Ben, who I am *still angry with* and who isn't acknowledging that I have every right to be angry.

His mother stops walking and turns back to us. She lifts her eyebrows at me. "Would you?" she muses speculatively. She walks slowly back to us and leans down, so that we are level. I look straight into her colorless eyes, and I suppress my shudder. "Would you *really*?"

What are we doing? I wonder suddenly. We need to get our information and leave. I blurt out, "We're looking for the other fays."

"It is the fate of so many to be looking so far and so long for so much," responds Ben's mother.

"Okay," I say, even though I could not care less about whatever that was. "But the book of power said that you know where they are because you hid them."

"Did I hide them?" says Ben's mother. "It was so very long ago. So difficult to remember…"

I think of the Seelies, of their secret power of forgetting, and I wonder if Ben's mom is suffering from it. "It was written in the book," I say eagerly, hoping it will jog her memory.

Ben's mother lifts her eyebrows at me. "You have a book?"

"I don't, but—"

Ben's mother reaches out and lays a finger against my lips. Her finger is ice-cold and I stop talking out of sheer shock. "You have not learned the lesson yet, little fay."

"Don't," Ben starts, but his mother flicks a glance up at him and says, "Shh, shh, shh."

"What lesson?" I manage around her finger. I try to jerk my head back but her finger follows, contact with my lips not lessening.

"You shouldn't ask questions before dinner. It's rude." She leans closer to me, and I am suddenly abruptly grateful for the warm barrier of Ben behind me, because it reminds me that I'm not alone. "Must I teach you this lesson? Shall we begin right now?" Her finger moves off my lips, trails over my cheekbone, tucks a piece of my hair behind my ear.

"Stop," I manage finally, harshly, and jerk out of her grasp.

She smiles an anti-smile at me. "Good. I thought you'd be a quick learner." She turns and walks away, calling over her shoulder, "You should wear the coat I got for you, Benedict. It's a special occasion."

"We'll see," Ben answers noncommittally and then grabs my hand. He pulls me into a room with him before I can react, still thrown by the phantom recall of his mother's finger on me.

"She's *awful*," I say, shaking.

"Yes, turns out she's not the most charming of faeries. Are you all right?"

"I'm fine," I answer vaguely, preoccupied by studying the room we're in.

It's perfectly round, with a bed and a desk and a chair and a round window in the wall. The ceiling is high above us, crossed over with wooden beams, and there are a few wrought-iron chandeliers hanging from it. The floor appears to be dirt, which suits the rough furnishings of the room, and the view out the window looks like the sunny meadow where we had been earlier that day, when I had first met Ben's mother.

I shake my hand out of Ben's and walk over to the window. It doesn't have any glass over it—Unseelies must share the glass aversion trait with Seelies—so I stick my head through it and look at the meadow.

"It's an enchantment," Ben says behind me.

"I figured," I say and pull my head back through the window.

Ben is on the bed, on his back, staring up at the ceiling. It's a little bit strange, because I have, technically, slept with Ben, curled close into him, but there has never been a bed involved before, so I stand awkwardly by his window. Plus, there's the fact that I'm angry with him. It's only been a few days since I last saw him, I think, if I'm keeping time correctly, but it feels as if it's been years, or it's been a few minutes. I'm so confused by the battering I feel like my emotions are taking from seeing him again. It was easier to hate him so much when he wasn't right in front of me, so familiar, and I wasn't calling up the memory of several different lifetimes' worth of longing for him. But it was also easier to forgive him when he wasn't right in front of me being so unapologetic about the whole thing.

I open my mouth to tell him to leave.

"She's very nostalgic," Ben says finally, breaking the silence.

"Who is?"

"My mother. This is the room I grew up in."

So I guess I can't tell him to leave then. I blink in surprise and look around the room with new eyes. "This is?"

"Well, I mean, not really, that room doesn't exist anymore. She's enchanted it this way. She's very nostalgic, like I say."

I look at him. "She enchanted it this way for you?"

He shakes his head briefly. "She didn't do it for me."

"How do you know?"

"I know." He turns his head to finally look at me. His eyes are very green in this room, green like the meadow outside. "Go on," he says.

"Go on with what?" I ask, confused.

"With questions. You must have a million questions. You always have a million questions. You never stop asking questions. So go on."

I bristle. "I'm sorry if my questions irritate you."

"I never said they irritate me."

"What is going on here, Ben?"

Ben considers then shakes his head. "You need to start with a simpler question than that."

"Have you asked your mother where the other fays are?"

"Yes. I get in response the sort of thing you just saw. She won't answer any questions. Which isn't exactly unusual for a faerie."

I'm frustrated. "So she doesn't want to help us? Why did she hide the fays if she wasn't going to help us?"

Ben is silent for a moment. "I don't think she's...right. She spent time in Tir na nOg. It does things to you. Faeries are terrible at plans to begin with, and then she...I don't think she..."

"So did she really forget? We can ask Will what he did with the book. Maybe it will jog her memory?"

"I don't know if she wants it anymore," Ben admits. "I think she did, once, want the overthrow of the Seelie Court. But she *likes* it here. She's told me more than once. Actually she tells me constantly: how much I'm going to like it here."

And so Ben got what he wanted, I think. Reunited with his mother. Happy ending to the story. And forget about the rest of us trying to fulfill our prophecy; he's just going to let it go, wait it out here in the Unseelie Court.

"Do you think if you stay here with her, you won't succumb to the prophecy and die?" I demand.

Ben looks at me in confusion.

"Benedict Le Fay will betray you," I remind him, "and then he will die."

Ben shakes his head. "That's not the prophecy. That's a false prophecy. That was your mother, getting into our heads. No one else has ever said anything like that about

105

the prophecy, not even a pig's whisper. I wish you'd stop worrying about that."

I am frustrated that I'm the only one who seems to be taking the threat seriously. I march over to the door and try to open it. It's locked.

"Where are you going?" Ben asks.

"Unlock this door," I command.

"Why?"

"Because I'm going to my room, obviously. I can't stay here with you."

"I need to keep you safe. I can't do it if you're not with me."

"Oh, all of a sudden you're worried again about keeping me safe?"

"When did I stop worrying about that?"

I am amazed he is asking me this question. I have never before realized how *annoying* it is that he's a faerie. "When you left me!"

"I have left you plenty of times before. We have never spent every moment together, you and I. Why, now, does my leaving you mean that I'm not keeping you safe?"

"Because I asked you not to leave, Ben," I snap at him.

He sits up on the bed, which I am glad about, because at least now it seems like he's taking this seriously. "You asked me not to leave. I disagreed with that. We never had a conversation about keeping you safe and whether I ought to worry about it anymore. You made that decision all on your own."

"What is that supposed to mean?"

"You almost died in the dragon pit. Did you not wonder why, all of a sudden, you could fall to your death if you didn't want to? My mother put her *hand* on you and you couldn't stop it."

I already know the answer to that. "Because you took the enchantment off me."

"Because you fought it off. I didn't take it off you—you wouldn't let me keep it on you. You're lucky you fell in the dragon pit where I could get to you."

"If you hadn't left," I point out hotly, "I wouldn't have been anywhere *near* the dragon pit. Not without you, at least."

Ben sighs and falls back on the bed, looking up at the ceiling.

"How did you know I was in danger in the dragon pit?"

"You're carrying my talisman," he says dully, not looking at me. "You've broken the spell, but the talisman links us. You were in distress, and I felt it."

"I'm in *constant* distress."

"Not like that."

I think of the blind panic I'd been in as I fell in the dragon pit and consider that I have not been that panicked before, not even in Park Street, because then I had options, escape routes I was planning. In the dragon pit, I had given up hope, and maybe that had been distress enough to reach out for Ben, even though I hadn't known I was doing it.

I let silence fall for a moment. My hand is still on the door-knob, still ready to leave, but I've realized there's so much I don't know and so much Ben does know. I need to ask him, I need to make myself ask him, here, now, because if I walk out of this room, I don't know if I'll ever have enough courage to face him this way again.

"Is everyone else in danger?" I ask.

"These are dangerous times. Everyone's in danger," he says to the ceiling.

"I mean Kelsey and Safford and Will."

"They're fine. They won't be harmed. They have nothing to do with the prophecy."

"The Unseelies tried to kill me at the dragon pit."

"How did you fall into the pit?"

"The bridge disappeared."

"Ah. The spell functions by itself. There isn't an Unseelie paying attention to it and deciding who should cross and who should not. It senses threats and it breaks of its own accord. It's an automatic reaction."

"Oh, great," I say, throwing up my hands. "Automatic reaction. That's fine then. Don't trouble yourself too much over the fact that I was almost eaten by a dragon."

Ben sits up again. "Of course I'm troubled over it, Selkie," he snaps at me. "But I've been trying to keep you safe, and you keep trying your hardest to thwart me at every turn, so I don't know what you want me to say here. Am I troubled that you were almost eaten by a dragon? Yes! Of course I am! But you shouldn't have been anywhere near the dragon! You should have been home! In Boston! Where it's safe!"

"It isn't safe in Boston!" I shout back. "How can you possibly think that? The Seelies are trying to get through the enchantment."

"The Seelies have been trying to get through that enchantment for centuries!"

"But they're succeeding now! The *sun* went out! And the clocks stopped and then they started back up again and now it's almost twelve o'clock!"

Ben stares at me. "Is that true?"

"Yes!"

"Then we're running out of time!"

"Exactly! And it's all nice for you—you found your mom and she made you your childhood room and wants you to stay here with her forever—but in the meantime, the world out there is falling apart and you're not *helping.*"

"I didn't know," Ben says. "I thought there'd be time."

"You would've known if you hadn't *left,*" I point out.

Ben, for once, doesn't have any kind of smart retort to that. Which I guess is as close to an apology as I'm ever going to get.

"You'd also know if faeries had thought to enchant cell phones into being at any point," I mumble and sit at Ben's desk, because I'm feeling exhausted suddenly, like if I don't sit, I might collapse.

"We'll get the information from my mother at the feast," Ben says.

I don't know what to say to that. Like, great, Ben thinks it's going to just be *that easy.* I thought it would just be *that easy* too, and then I met his mother and she wasn't like that at all.

There's a coat draped over the back of the chair I'm sitting in. A black coat with feathered epaulets and spangled over with threads of silver and gold. I run my hand over it. I can think of nothing less Ben-like.

"Where did you get this?" I ask.

"My mother. That's the coat she was talking about."

"Well." I stare at the coat and try to come up with something nice to say about it. I settle on, "It was nice of her to give you a gift."

"It's hideous," he says flatly.

"Well, it is—"

"It's *undignified*," he interrupts me.

"Ben," I point out, "you just rode a giant corgi. Hasn't the indignity boat sailed?"

He flops back onto the bed with a huff. "Corgis are royal forms of transportation," he protests.

"Were the corgis we would see on Boston Common sometimes faerie dogs?"

"Don't be absurd. Those are pygmy corgis."

"They're miniature corgis, like miniature Great Danes?"

"No, they're ridden by pygmies," he responds matter-of-factly, as if this makes perfect sense.

It's the kind of conversation I feel like we could have had before, on the Common, watching dogs and their owners go back and forth, sipping lemonade that Ben has made. We wouldn't have talked about faeries—I didn't know there were faeries to talk about back then—but we would have talked about something silly and innocuous like this. I would be worrying about the prom, and whether I wanted to go, and whether I could get Ben to ask me. Such a *silly, stupid* thing to worry about. I had been such a *silly, stupid girl*. When I should have been worrying about my world being destroyed, about my aunts and my father in a Boston that's going to pieces, about a prophecy I am baffled by at every turn.

And I am crying. Hard. I can't get myself to stop. I put my face in my hands and try to stifle my sobs so Ben won't know, because the whole thing is humiliating.

As if he's somehow going to not notice this inelegant, embarrassing, sniveling display.

"You're crying," he says from his bed.

I cry harder and bury my face harder in my hands, trying to catch my breath.

"You *never* cry," he says. He sounds amazed that this is happening.

It's true. I don't cry very much. It's probably why I feel like I'm so bad at it, like now that I've started crying I'll never stop, that I will cry for the rest of my life, here in this underground castle that makes me feel claustrophobic, enchanted window notwithstanding.

Ben's touch on the crown of my head is feather-light, and I jerk away, but he tugs me closer, and I shouldn't but I stop fighting and cry messily into his neck. The only thing worse than crying is crying *alone*, with no one there to comfort you. I need him and I can't even be hard on myself for that. Ben pulls me off the chair and we land in a heap on the dirt floor. He lets me cuddle into his lap and sob, and he holds me closer, silent and patient.

"I'm so tired," I manage in hiccupping, bursting gasps. "I'm *exhausted*. I am exhausted from being part of some stupid prophecy that everyone wants me to fulfill—but nobody knows how I should fulfill it—and everyone expects me to know how. But every time I try to do something—anything—it turns out wrong. I brought everyone here—because I thought your mother would help—but it doesn't seem like she's going to help—and meanwhile I don't know where my family is—and faeries keep getting named in the Otherworld—and it's all falling apart."

"Shh, shh, shh," Ben murmurs and strokes at my hair. It's not telling me anything useful, but it doesn't matter. It literally feels like the best thing he could do for me right now.

I do not cry forever. I reach the end of it eventually and find myself sniffling instead of sobbing, my head against his shoulder and my nose nudging at his collarbone. "This doesn't mean I've forgiven you," I tell him and sniffle again.

"Selkie Stewart," he breathes, fluttering across my skin. He chases my name with a barely there brush of his lips. And then he says, "Your face is *wet*."

And I actually laugh against him.

CHAPTER 9

There is a bathroom attached to Ben's room, through a door in the wall that is hidden until he calls it into being. There is a shower in the bathroom, and I have never seen anything more beautiful in my life. We can't do anything until after the feast anyway, so I let myself take a shower. I stand directly under the flow of the water, letting it course through my hair and over my face, and my fingertips wrinkle into prunes and I don't care. The water is hot and comforting; with my eyes closed, I could be home. I know that I am not, but I feel that the feast ahead of me is not going to be fun, and taking a shower feels like such a wonderfully normal thing to do. I don't think of my aunts and my father and all the people that I am helpless to protect right now. I focus on the water, beating down on me, flowing over me, and just don't let myself *think*.

I have no idea how long I stand in the shower before someone knocks on the door. It's probably Ben, and I know that, but I still get tense under the spray of the water, opening my eyes and looking at the gleaming, metallic tiles on the wall in front of me. They don't look like normal human tiles, which is why closing my eyes is necessary to keep up the illusion of being home.

"Who is it?" I call cautiously, although what am I going to do if it isn't Ben?

"Me," Ben calls back. "Can I come in?"

I've locked the door, but that, of course, means nothing at all to Ben. The shower curtain is dark and metallic, like the tiles around me, and there is no way Ben is going to see anything, and I trust him not to try to look anyway. It's not like Ben has displayed much of a tendency to try to take advantage of me. "Yes," I assent.

I hear the door open immediately, as if it was never locked at all.

"It's wet in here," Ben says. I can *hear* his nose wrinkling with disapproval.

"I'm showering," I point out. "Water is involved."

"It's time for the feast."

I sigh. "I figured."

"My mother brought you some clothing."

"Is it a dress with little bells?"

"No, the Unseelies don't like bells."

"Is it a sparkly black coat?"

"No. It's just a dress. I'll leave it here for you. And now I have to close this door. It's entirely too unpleasant in here." He does so immediately, ducking away from the humidity.

I take a deep breath and turn the shower off and step out into the bathroom, drying off. I towel-dry my hair as best as

I can and then pull it back into a ponytail. The dress Ben's mother has brought for me is a bright springtime yellow; it reminds me of chicks and corn and sun. All the dresses I've seen here have been sunny colors—I wonder if that's a consequence of being stuck underground. And I wonder why Ben's coat is so full of night by contrast.

I look at myself in the mirror. My white-blond hair doesn't darken much when wet, but at least it stays back, no wisps escaping around my face. The yellow dress isn't really my preferred color—I like to wear shades of blue to match my eyes—but it fits me beautifully. Probably an enchantment.

I step out into Ben's room. He is wearing his usual layers to try to protect him from ever being wet ever—Ben is actually allergic to water, which sounds weird but makes total sense when you're a faerie. This time, the layers are a deep lavender polo shirt and, peeking out underneath, a tangerine-colored T-shirt.

"Ready?" he asks.

"You're not wearing your coat?" I say to him, dropping my clothes in a heap on the chair.

"I hate that coat," he replies.

"It might make your mother happy if you wear it."

"That's a quaint notion," Ben remarks, and his eyes linger on the coat. "I don't like the coat. It makes me feel…I'm not wearing the coat." He turns determinedly toward the door and tugs it open.

"Should I wear my sweatshirt?" I ask, and I sound almost shy.

Ben pauses and looks back at me. "I don't know," he answers evenly. "Should you? That's your decision."

I hesitate then I pull it over my head, and I try not to analyze my motives for doing so.

The hallway is very dark after the brightness of Ben's room.

"If they can enchant sunlight," I ask Ben, "why don't they enchant this whole place?"

"*They* can't enchant sunlight," he responds as we walk swiftly down the hallway. "My mother can. This way." He pulls me through an open archway that appears to our right, and all of a sudden we are in a vast banquet hall. The ceiling soars over our head, with dark chandeliers dripping from it. The table is made of stone, as are the chairs, and everything seems rough and uncomfortable and barely serviceable. The table is crowded with faeries in bright clothing, tearing into food with loud enthusiasm. There is a large cluster that is laughing raucously to one side, and the Erlking appears to be in the middle of that, telling a story that apparently requires many hand gestures, not all of them respectable.

It is easy to locate Will and Safford and Kelsey; they are the silent, still ones who are watching the proceedings with a slight frown. And next to them, at the very head of the table, sits Ben's mother.

She rises as we approach. "Ah, there you are," she says in welcome. "Don't you look lovely," she purrs at me and then frowns a bit at Ben. "You didn't wear your coat."

"Maybe next time," Ben responds lightly and sits down.

I sit opposite him, and food appears on our plates. Fruit. I was looking forward to something more substantial, but fruit will definitely do.

Kelsey, beside me, has already stripped her bunch of grapes clean. She is dressed in pale pink, the color of a barely there sunrise. Her long blond hair, like mine, is pulled back into a wet ponytail.

"There was nothing else I could do, so I figured I'd take a shower," she says to me.

"I had the exact same thought," I agree. "So have we…?" I make a gesture that I hope can be interpreted as *asked Ben's mother the important question and gotten the answer so we can get out of here* and pop a grape in my mouth. It tastes like soda.

Kelsey shakes her head a little bit.

I look beyond Kelsey to the rest of the table. It is almost exactly the way dinner used to be in the Seelie Court, loud and disorganized, with wine freely flowing. The Erlking seems to be a much greater attraction than any of the other Unseelies; most of them are hanging on his every word. He is still telling a story, although he keeps pausing now to take sips from the spout of a small teapot he is holding.

I turn back to my plate. There is now cheese on it as well, and I take an experimental nibble of it. Coffee.

"Perhaps," says Ben's mother, "you are interested in the history of the Unseelie Court."

"Actually," I say, because it's time to get this show on the road—I have no idea what time the Erlking's pocket watch reads now. "We're looking for the other fays that you hid."

"We are all of us misfits here," says Ben's mother as if I haven't spoken at all, "cast out by the Seelies in their capricious rule. We welcome all who come to our door."

Will, who is sitting beside Ben across from me, looks at Ben's mother with his eyebrows raised.

"You disagree, Mr. Blaxton?" asks Ben's mother scathingly.

"Not at all," replies Will in a silky tone that means just the opposite. He holds Ben's mother's gaze and sits back in his chair, sipping his wine.

Ben's mother continues, her voice brittle now and her hands tight around her rough tin fork and knife. "It is hard for us, cast out, here below. We are creatures who crave the light. If the eternal darkness sometimes drives us to actions that are, shall we say, questionable, who can condemn us, living a life so contrary to our natures?"

I pick up one of the tin knives and slip it into my pocket. The last knife I took came in handy.

"Who indeed?" Will responds and raises his glass in a little toast. I know it is mocking, but it is mocking under the surface. Outwardly he is nothing but calm respect.

"We really need to know about the fays," I insist. "The ones you hid. If you could try to remember—"

"As if I would forget!" she scoffs at me. "I am famous for my remembering."

"Then maybe—"

"If it were time for the prophecy to be fulfilled, then the fays would have assembled together. If you are still all alone, then it is not time."

"It *is* time," says Will. "The clocks are ticking."

"That is not my concern. I do not establish the time, Mr. Blaxton."

"Don't you want to help us?" I ask desperately. "Isn't that why you hid the fays? Because you want to help us fulfill the prophecy?"

"Do you know about the prophecy, little fay?" she asks me, sounding half-amused and half-dismissive of how stupid I am.

"Yes," I say stubbornly. "I know all about it." I try to pretend that means I'm also going to know what I can do to fulfill it.

"You do not. Because if you knew about the prophecy, then you would know that I didn't necessarily hide the fays because I wanted them to overthrow the Seelie Court. There is a warring prophecy. Did you not tell her this, Mr. Blaxton?"

I look at Will, confused.

Will says, "There is always a warring prophecy. It doesn't matter."

"Oh, but it does. The prophecy you want to fulfill is the overthrow of the Seelie *and* the Unseelie Courts. Does it seem likely that I wish that prophecy fulfilled, given the home I have found here?"

I feel cold, because now that she mentions it, that doesn't seem likely. "What's the warring prophecy?"

"That one of the fays would go to the Isle of Avalon and consolidate Seelie power forever."

Which was why I had been wanted in the Seelie Court, I remember. Why I wasn't named immediately.

"So you want that prophecy to be fulfilled?" I say, because that doesn't make sense to me either.

"I don't want any prophecies to come into play at all. I like the status quo. I've done quite well for myself with the status quo. Why should I introduce interfering fays who don't know what they're doing into the equation? You know just enough to destroy everything. So I hid the others. You slipped through my fingers and fell to my son, who has all sorts of interesting thoughts about power in the Otherworld. Really, he and I have just *begun* to explore the wonder of his politics. As for the other three fays, if your prophecy was really meant to be fulfilled, you'd have found them already. After all, don't you, little fay, have a habit of collecting exactly what you need?" She leans toward me, her eyes flashing. She has eyes that at first glance are like Ben's, a swirl of pale impressions of color, but as they slice into me, icy silver, I realize that they are not at all like Ben's.

And that makes me angry. *I am so tired of being betrayed by faeries*, I think.

"So you're not going to help us?" I demand.

"*Help* you? How quaint that you thought I ever was. How very *human* of you, really." She looks to Will and Ben. Will is frowning at her, but Ben is staring at the food in front of him, his face a mask. "That is your fault, you know. The two of you hid her too well. She is unused to such delicate and intricate creatures as we. We are not your usual coarse ogres or goblins."

I take offense at the ogre dig, but Ben's mother is no longer looking at me. Her focus seems to have shifted to the Erlking down the table. The rest of us glance at the Erlking as well. As if sensing all of us, he looks up and winks in our direction.

"He's insufferable," proclaims Ben's mother.

"Isn't he just?" Will agrees, studying his wine. He is no longer frowning. In fact, he looks very calm and at ease.

Ben's mother rises suddenly, startling me, and I think that she is going to do something to Will. I tense for it, but she merely sweeps by us and then settles next to the Erlking, listening as raptly as the rest of the other Unseelies.

"Insufferable," Will murmurs at his wine, "but so very useful to have around." He takes a sip. "A creature whose talent is seduction."

"Well, now he's just showing off," comments Kelsey.

I glance back over at the Erlking, who appears to be on the verge of outright making out with one of the male Unseelies.

"How did he get involved?" Ben asks. He sounds impatient and annoyed.

"He's a friend of Will's," Kelsey answers.

"*Will*," says Ben. "Are we never going to come to the end of your conquests?"

Kelsey and I both look from the Erlking, murmuring now in Ben's mother's ear, to Will.

"He—I—It's—" Will stammers. "He's *very* good at— Never mind." Will clears his throat and puts his wineglass on the table. "He got us into the Unseelie Court, didn't he? And he's got everyone distracted. Enough that I've got their listening charms blocked and they haven't noticed. So let's stop talking about the Erlking and start focusing on the fact that we need to get out of here. *All* of us." He looks at Ben meaningfully, the emphasis not subtle. Ben doesn't protest that he's coming with us, and I can't tell if I'm surprised or not. I thought before that maybe this had all been a happy reunion for him, but it doesn't seem like it is now. "So how are we doing it?" asks Will.

"I don't know," Ben says. "I especially don't even understand how you got in here."

"We *walked*," Will informs him flatly. He seems to be losing his patience.

"Then I would suggest you try walking *out*," remarks Ben.

"That's your plan? We just get up and start walking?" drawls Will.

"I don't have a plan," Ben snaps at him. "I'm a faerie, remember? And I especially don't have a plan for *this*. None of you were ever supposed to be here. You're the ones who showed up. No one asked you to come. I was perfectly fine."

"We need you for the prophecy, Benedict," Will clips out at him. "And the Seelies are closing in. We don't have time to sit around waiting for you to be done with your foolish, headstrong *lark*."

"I don't understand why the prophecy can't be fulfilled without me. What more can I do? I kept a fay safe for as long as I could. I believe my obligations are completed."

"Oh," I say hotly, "your *obligations*?"

"You know what I mean—"

"And you know that prophecies don't work like that," Will interrupts him. "The prophecy is a mess right now, because *you've* made a mess of it, but when it was readable, you figured into it. Four fays, and you. We don't have the four fays; let's at least have you. Give us a bit of a fighting chance here?"

Ben looks uncertain. It is not a look I see often on Ben, and honestly, it's not one I like to see. Especially not now. He licks his lips and his eyes flicker to his mother, still hanging on the Erlking's every word.

"Will," he says slowly, "is your blocking enchantment firm?"

"Yes, the Unseelies are distracted." Will looks toward the Erlking, and I look in that direction instinctively. The Erlking briefly meets Will's eyes and then abruptly leans over and kisses Ben's mother passionately. "Your mother most of all," says Will. "Talk quickly."

Ben takes a shaky breath. He looks terrified abruptly, and answering terror squeezes coldly around me. "I don't think I can get out of here," he says, staring at the empty plate in front of him.

"What do you mean?" asks Will.

"I haven't tried. Actually, I don't want to try. I don't want her to get suspicious or think I'm trying to leave, but I feel like I can't travel away from here. I feel like I'm *damp*, all the time."

I stare at him. "That's why you were unsure about getting everyone on the other side of the dragon pit," I realize.

He meets my eyes and admits, "I wasn't sure I could get over there. I'm honestly amazed I could even save you. I can move around the Unseelie Court fairly freely, but I don't think I can leave here, not even the conventional way, not even if I walk."

"But we have to get you out of here with us," I say. "This *was* a trap. Your mother did this to lure you away from us. She wants to thwart both prophecies. As long as you're here, we can't bring down the Courts. We're stuck."

Ben doesn't look at me. He looks up at the ceiling high above us and fiddles with his fork. "I didn't think it was a trap," he says. "I wouldn't have come if I'd thought…"

"It doesn't matter now," Will inserts impatiently. "Benedict, she has you pinned."

Ben looks at him. He looks exhausted. "I don't know what you mean."

"She's pinned you into place. And it's Le Fay magic, so it's your own energy turning against you. That's why you're feeling damp; she's using your energy to hold you in place."

"Clever," allows Ben, sounding bitter. He fiddles some more with his fork.

"No." Will leans toward him urgently. "You're missing the point. *You're* keeping yourself here—this is your energy being stolen. *Break* it."

"It isn't my energy, Will. It *was* my energy. She's commandeered it."

"Listen to me," Will says to him, speaking very firmly and clearly. "Listen to me, and *believe* this, because you never have, and you've always needed to: you are stronger than her. You've always been stronger than her. Stop letting her enchant you and *break* it."

"I'm not *letting* her do this, Will," Ben snaps. He looks furious now, his eyes sliding into silver as he glares at Will, the resemblance to his mother just that tiny bit stronger, and I might shudder without meaning to.

"Yes, you are," Will insists. "You don't even realize it. Benedict, they have been planning this from the moment of your birth. Do you know the only way your mother can beat you? It's the only way any faerie in the Otherworld can beat you: by making you *believe* that they can. And she's done it your whole life, her and your father and *everyone*, spinning the tale and winding it into the heart of you, the legend of your mother, the greatest enchantress in the Otherworld, the great traveler, who you have been chasing your entire life. She never existed, Benedict. She's a grand myth to trap you in."

"That doesn't make sense, Will. She hid one of my names from them; she's protected me my whole life. They could have killed me long ago to stop this prophecy before it began. Why would she protect me only to do this to me instead?"

"I don't know. I can't answer that. But I know I'm right about one thing: if you fight her, you will win."

Ben is silent. He still looks terrified. He glances toward his mother, but I keep my eyes on him. Will's story is astonishing, and I'm not sure if he believes what he's saying or if he's just trying to give Ben a pep talk.

Ben looks back at Will. "She knows my name, Will. All of it. She's the only being in creation who can name me. Do you know how easy it has always been for me, knowing that no matter what I did, no one could ever really get to me? They could hurt me, yes. They could weaken me and torture me and bring me pain, but they couldn't dissolve me. I've never had to be brave, Will. And the truth is that I don't know if I am. She could name me, and I don't want to cross her. I don't know if I can take that risk." He takes a deep, shuddering breath. "I'm terrified."

I feel for him. I don't want to feel for him now that he's getting a taste of how the rest of us live. But he looks so lost and scared and very young in the grips of it. I have always thought of Ben as older than me, by some indiscriminate amount of time, but he seems now much younger. This is experience I have, living with the looming, suffocating feeling of fear.

And I realize now that Will is right. The Ben I know—confident and secure in his own abilities—would have walked out of the Unseelie Court long ago. He would have found a way. We may not get out of here alive, but it isn't even worth the effort unless Ben *believes*.

"All anybody ever tells me," I remark nonchalantly, "is how

you're the best at everything." Ben looks at me in surprise, and I tick things off on my fingers. "The best traveler in the Otherworld, the best enchanter in the Otherworld, the best kisser in the Otherworld." I look at him, meeting his eyes firmly. "You're Benedict Le Fay," I remind him. "She's been here this whole time, Ben. She could have named you whenever she wanted. You said it yourself—she could have done it so easily. And she hasn't. You know why? She doesn't think she can beat you. She can't even keep you here without using your own energy to do it."

Ben shakes his head a bit. "All she'd have to do is—"

"*She doesn't think she can beat you,*" I repeat firmly, keeping my gaze locked on his.

I see Will out of the corner of my eye, watching Ben's expression avidly. He looks as if he barely dares to move.

Ben breaks my gaze after a long moment of tense silence. He shifts his eyes toward his mother and then looks over my shoulder. I glance in that direction, at the archway we entered through. There is a door in that archway now, heavy and oak, whereas it had been wide open when we'd walked in.

I look back at Ben. He is frowning. His frown deepens. He shifts in his seat.

"Will, I need you to drop the blocking enchantment. You're blocking *me*," he says suddenly without taking his eyes from the door.

It is less than a second after he says this that a chair topples over at the Erlking's end of the table. Ben's mother's chair,

I realize, and I am busy looking in that direction when, less than a second after that, there is a loud crash as the door to the banquet hall flings itself open and collides with the wall. A gust of wind sends wineglasses tumbling over up and down the table, splintering against the stone, wine spilling over the table, red as blood. The wind whips at the hair in my ponytail and at the flowing material of my gown. There are exclamations of surprise and rising panic from Unseelies as they hasten to avoid the streams of wine and try to duck away from the howl of the gale.

I look at Ben, pushing my hair out of my eyes. He is sitting calmly in his seat, regarding his mother, his eyes pale as a windowpane.

When I look down at his mother, she is still in a heap on the floor, staring at him in astonishment. And something else, which looks to me like fear.

"I think," Ben announces clearly over the groan of the wind as it slaps against the walls of the banquet hall, "that we are going." He rises and starts walking, and the rest of us scramble out of our seats to follow him. He pauses only once, in the doorway, to throw over his shoulder, "Come along, Erlking. That means you as well."

The Erlking is already striding over to us. His black velvet cloak looks very dramatic in the strong wind. "How very gracious of you, Benedict," he says cordially as he walks through the doorway with the rest of us.

"I am nothing if not gracious," Ben replies lightly, and then watches the door to the banquet hall slam shut behind all of us. The wind immediately dies down. We stand in a calm and deserted hallway, staring at the closed door.

"She's strong," Ben says after a moment. "I'm not going to be able to hold her in there for long. And she's probably going to name me as soon as she gets out. So we should get going."

"Excellent," the Erlking agrees. "Do you have any suggestions?"

"Yes," Ben answers. "We're going to take the corgis. This way." He takes off down the hallway.

"We're going to ride giant dogs to save the world," says Kelsey. "My grandkids are never even going to *believe* this story."

And then we take off after Ben.

CHAPTER 10

We are running for only a few seconds before Ben abruptly skids to a stop and turns around, making a motion with his arm as if he is flinging something. He turns again just as quickly, picking up the run again.

"Hurry up!" he calls to us without even looking behind him, and there comes the sound of a small explosion behind us.

"What was that?" Kelsey asks, panting as we run.

"Never mind," Ben responds. He is gasping for breath too. "Keep moving."

Thunder rumbles, which is startling, since we're not outside. I glance up, watching clouds gather over our heads, curling along the ceiling above us. Ben looks up too.

"I've got you covered," Will calls to him, and indeed, when the rain opens up, while it soaks the rest of us, it doesn't even touch Ben. He turns back and flings something again before resuming his flat-out run, and there is another small explosion. Then, abruptly, in front of me, he stumbles.

I'm running so close to him that I knock into him, and I'm worrying that I've gotten him wet, but he regains his balance, moving off at a dead run again. The Erlking is ahead of us, his cloak billowing as he wheels around a corner. I wonder how he knows where to go, but Ben turns around the same corner, so he must be going the right way.

Ben stumbles again, reaching out and grabbing at the wall to keep his balance, and I realize then that he is not okay. He is gasping for breath, but it's not from running. It's from something else; there is a tearing edge to it.

"What's wrong?" I ask, drawing next to him. I don't dare touch him, because I'm soaking wet.

He shakes his head. "Keep moving."

Will has caught up to us and is looking at Ben in concern. "What's the matter?"

"I can't sever the connection between us. She's trying to turn my enchantments back on me."

"She's purposely draining you," says Will.

"*Benedict Le Fay.*"

His name, shouted along the hallway, reverberates. Ben winces a bit but says, "Well, you were right about that. She's not especially good at naming."

Will is looking down the hallway. "We have to keep moving. Keep going."

Ben nods and straightens and moves forward but then snaps backward. Will and I turn back to him. He takes another step, pushing as if he is swimming through pudding or something.

"What's going on?" I ask. Safford and Kelsey have turned back. I sense them come up behind us.

Ben takes another step, frowning. "I'm going to have to just fight it out with her," he decides. "She's literally pulling me back."

"What's her name?" I ask. "I'll name her."

Ben gives me a look. "Do you think I know her name? Do you think *anyone* knows her name?"

"Then say my name," I say quickly. "Say it."

After a moment, Ben says, "Selkie Stewart," and we are able to take a few more steps before he hits another block.

"Say it again," I tell him.

He looks annoyed. "We can't keep—"

"You need to find the talisman," the Erlking interjects.

I look at him in surprise, because I hadn't realized he'd turned back too.

Ben regards him blankly. "The talisman? What talisman?"

"You have to break her enchantment. You need the talisman to do it."

Ben looks displeased. "I'm a faerie. I don't need the talisman to break an enchantment—"

"Yes, you do. He's right," Will interrupts. "He's absolutely right, because you're fighting your own magic. You can't break it completely without draining yourself. That's really very clever of her."

Ben glares at him. "You could have realized this before you told me to run."

Will has the good grace to look sheepish. "Sorry."

With a roar of pure fury, Ben's mother rounds the corner

and draws to a stop. It is clear she did not expect us to be standing there, but she recovers from her surprise and sends us one of those anti-smiles powerful faeries seem to specialize in. "You're trapped," she announces confidently.

Ben straightens away from the wall and sweeps his hand toward his mother, pushing the rain in her direction. It splashes over her and she shrieks. A tongue of fire races from where she's standing, hissing as the rain hits it, licking out toward us until the moment when it fizzles out entirely, and judging from the rage on his mother's face, that was Ben's doing too.

"This is ridiculous," says the Erlking and pulls me to the left, tumbling me into a dark room. Kelsey and Safford follow us, and Will pulls Ben in and then closes the door.

"Lock it," he tells Ben.

"Done," Ben says.

"But she's a traveler too," I point out. "Won't she just be able to unlock it?"

"Not if I can hold it for a bit," Ben responds grimly.

I want to ask what good it's doing us to be trapped in a room instead of out in the hallway where we can run, but Ben's breaths have evened out a bit and he seems to be in less distress, so maybe he really did need a breather.

Will sends up an orb of light.

We are in a decent-sized room, but it is entirely empty except for a single purple orchid sitting in a pot on the other side of the room. It looks completely incongruous, there in the middle of the floor.

"What the hell is that?" the Erlking asks.

"It's a flower," Will answers.

"Why is it in here? I don't like it."

Will walks cautiously over to it and looks down at the pot. "It says here its name is Larry."

"The plant has a name?" Kelsey asks.

"Yes," Will confirms.

"The plant's name is *Larry*?" she asks.

"Yes," says Will again and turns away from the orchid, walking back toward us.

I turn my attention to Ben. He is staring at the door. There are alarming thumps coming from the other side of it.

"Will it hold?" the Erlking asks him.

"Yes," Ben responds confidently.

"I suppose that's something, but it means we're trapped in here," remarks the Erlking, echoing the thought I just had.

"Better than being trapped out there." Ben turns away from the door. "It gives us time to think. What would she have used for the talisman?"

I am relieved that he seems to be trying to put together a plan. He seems much more like the old Ben. I turn to watch him pace into the room, and that is when I realize that the orchid has tripled in size. I stare at it.

"Was the plant always that big?" Kelsey asks, also staring at it.

Will stares at it too, standing very still. "No," he answers slowly.

Even as we watch, the orchid grows another foot, leaping into the air.

Kelsey takes a step back, and I don't blame her. "Make it stop," she says.

Ben has also taken a step away from the orchid. "I can't," he replies. "I need to keep my focus on the door. Will?"

"I'm trying," says Will, even as the orchid grows another two feet.

"It doesn't seem to be working," Kelsey points out.

"I can see that," Will bites back.

The orchid hits the ceiling.

"Forget about the orchid." Ben turns away from it. "We need to get the talisman. If we can get the talisman, then I can get away from here. Until then, we're just trapped."

"So what's a talisman look like?" I ask.

"It could look like anything," the Erlking replies. "It's whatever the faerie casting the enchantment chose to imbue with the power. Is there anything your mother is especially fond of, that she keeps by her side, especially when you're around?"

"Anything she keeps by her side." Ben looks perplexed. "Not that I can think of."

But I am focusing on a different part of what the Erlking said. "Anything your mother is especially fond of," I repeat. "Ben. Your coat."

"My coat," he echoes. "You think it's my coat?"

"Is this the talisman of your enchantment?" I indicate my sweatshirt.

"Yeah," he affirms.

"You gave it to me. You didn't keep it for yourself."

"Because the enchantment is yours to control."

"Right. And that's what she did to you. Will said this is *your* enchantment. She gave the talisman to you."

"Oh, that *is* clever," breathes the Erlking.

"That means *I* can't really break the enchantment by stealing the talisman. I already have the talisman," Ben realizes.

"You have to give the talisman to somebody else," Will says. "Someone the enchantment wasn't intended for. It will break it."

"Me," I say and look at Ben. "I'll take the coat."

"Anybody can take it," Will interjects. "It doesn't have to be you."

Ben looks at me and then nods briskly and turns to Will. "No, it has to be Selkie and me. If we go, my mother will chase after us. We're the ones she cares about. The rest of you will be free to get to the corgis, and Selkie and I will break the enchantment and we'll meet you."

"Uh, guys?" ventures Kelsey from behind us.

"Where are the corgis?" Will asks. "How do we get to them?"

"I know how to get to them," the Erlking interjects confidently.

"Guys, seriously," Kelsey says, but I'm distracted by the Erlking's statement.

As is Ben. Ben looks at him. "How do you know so much about the layout of this place?"

"I'm just very clever," the Erlking responds mildly.

Ben frowns, and I get the impression he doesn't really approve of the Erlking being clever on top of everything else.

Something brushes against my shoulder, and I think it's Kelsey, trying to get my attention, and I turn toward her just as she shrieks. I realize immediately why she shrieked, because it wasn't Kelsey brushing my shoulder—it was the orchid, which has now grown so that it stretches across the room. I have a flashback to the tulips that nearly strangled me during my first time in the Otherworld. Larry the orchid is growing so quickly that I find myself staring at a branch shooting toward me. It doesn't poke my eye out only because Ben grabs me out of the way.

We are crowded together against the door as the orchid encroaches upon us. It snakes out a tendril that curls around Kelsey's wrist.

"Get it off!" Kelsey exclaims in a panic, but the orchid tugs, tumbling Kelsey forward, and she lands straight in one of its enormous blossoms, sending up a puff of pollen.

Safford lunges for her, pulling her out, and then the Erlking unsheathes his sword and begins hacking at the orchid. I remember the knife that I stole from dinner and pull that out as well, but it's hardly effective against the onslaught of the orchid.

The orchid named Larry.

The orchid *named* Larry.

"*Larry!*" I shout, throwing all of my intent behind it,

hoping that naming works on supernatural plants as well as supernatural creatures.

It does. Larry shrivels up until it's back to the size it was when we first entered the room.

I breathe a sigh of relief.

The Erlking sheathes his sword, breathing hard, and says, "Well done. Will it stay that size now?"

"I have no idea," I say. I love that the Erlking thinks I know about any of the craziness going on around us. My only idea was to take us all here in the first place, and look how well *that* turned out.

Kelsey is in a terrifyingly still heap on the floor with the orchid detritus all around her.

Safford and I lean over her in mirrored desperation. She's breathing; she just seems to be thoroughly unconscious.

"What's wrong with her?" I demand, looking up at Ben.

"It's an enchantment," Ben says grimly.

"Well, break it," I order him.

"I can't, I—"

Kelsey sits up abruptly, coughing.

"Kelsey!" I exclaim and give her a hug. "Are you okay?"

"Yes," she manages around her coughs. "What happened?"

"We were so worried," I tell her. "You fell into the orchid blossom, and then you just…collapsed."

"So I was almost killed by an orchid," she concludes flatly.

And then, startling me, Safford pushes me aside and catches Kelsey in a fierce and desperate hug. Kelsey makes a little exclamation of surprise, but she hugs him back.

I look to Ben, to thank him, but he shakes his head. "It wasn't me. It was Will."

I turn to thank Will, but he's frowning toward Larry the orchid, and when I turn back there, I realize that it's started growing again, that the Erlking is once again hacking at the branches, but they are growing more quickly than he can cut them off.

"*Larry*," I say again, and it works again, but only briefly before it starts growing again. I can't just stand here and keep repeating its name constantly. We need to do something else.

Will clearly has the same idea. "You two need to go," he says without taking his eyes off the orchid. "Right now. We have to get out of this room." He looks at Ben. "We'll see you later."

I don't even have time to say good-bye to them before Ben grabs my hand and the room vanishes.

We are back in his bedroom, which seems very quiet and empty, given that it does not have a killer orchid in it. We are standing right by the chair on which I placed the coat before we went to the banquet. We both look down at it for a moment.

"Do I just…take it?" I ask uncertainly.

I hear Ben draw in breath to respond, and then his mother, out of nowhere, knocks him over with a physical blow. I have never seen a faerie actually *hit* another faerie like that; they seem to fight mostly through their magic. I am momentarily so shocked as Ben staggers backward that I can't even react.

I think that fighting this way must be unusual, because Ben can't seem to gather himself. He is so caught off guard that he is just retreating, trying to duck away but not succeeding as his mother keeps planting slaps and shoves and kicks on him.

I launch myself into action, just as Ben finds himself backed against the bathroom door. There is a moment when he looks at his mother, and his eyes are narrowed. He doesn't look the slightest bit afraid—he looks furious and also thoughtful, as if he is already planning some kind of retaliation.

His mother seems to pause at his expression too. "You—" she begins, but we never get to hear what else she was going to say, because I lunge and close my hands into the fabric of her gown. The thing is, her gown looks soft and gauzy, but touching it is like closing my hands into a bramble of thorns. I gasp in surprised pain, and I see Ben's narrowed eyes shift to me, worried for a split second of distraction, before I shake off the pain, pretend it's not there, and tug backward.

His mother isn't expecting it, and she stumbles away from him, giving him enough room to duck away. She keeps trying to pull her dress out of my grasp, but I am hanging on grimly. My hands feel as if they are on fire, but I refuse to let go, and she tries to whip me around. I collide painfully with the wall, and for a moment, the room spins around me.

Ben throws his mother aside. At least, it seems to me that's what he does, in the hazy spinning of the room. Her dress rips, my hands still caught in a tangle of vicious fabric that is no longer connected to his mother. He thrusts his coat at me, and I realize that he went to retrieve it. I drop the fabric and grab the coat automatically.

"Selkie Stewart," he says hurriedly, under his breath. "I renounce this coat and give it to you. I want you to have it. Will you take it? Say yes."

I don't need the prompting. I am already saying yes and nodding my head for extra effect.

Ben gasps, and I wonder for a second if I've done something wrong. I hear an answering gasp from his mother, and then Ben takes the most enormous breath, closing his eyes briefly. When he opens them, they are a light and clear blue, pale like the trickle of a brook. He sends me a brilliant smile, and his hands find mine underneath the coat I am clinging to, and then we are gone.

CHAPTER 11

We are outside, sitting on hard, unforgiving ground. The sky overhead is a brilliant blue, but the temperature is crystalline cold and I am shivering almost immediately.

Ben tugs the coat out of my hands and pulls it around me then stops, staring down. He looks…horrified.

"What…?" I start to ask—and then look down myself. My hands still hurt, but I hadn't *looked* at them. They're covered in blood, streams of it running down my wrists, dripping onto the dirt, and they are swollen and almost purple.

"What *happened*?" Ben asks, his voice low with concern.

"Your mother's dress…" I start to explain.

Ben takes my hands carefully in his, holding them gently, and I find myself holding my breath. The look on his face is so intimate and loving. I am feeling light-headed and a little bit dizzy, and Ben seems utterly capable of taking care of me for a moment. I want to just let him, the temptation sweet in my mouth.

I study his face as he looks at my hands, the bruise of his dark eyelashes against his pale cheeks, the concentrated bow of his mouth. He is absurdly beautiful, and I had forgotten. It's not like I've had much time to sit and admire Ben recently.

My hands stop throbbing, and he looks up at me from underneath his eyelashes. "Better?" he asks. His thumbs are rubbing soft circles over the pulse points in my wrist.

"Much," I croak breathlessly, because it's all I can get out.

His lips curve crookedly, and I figure he can probably *feel* my pulse increasing under the brush of his thumb. "Good." He glances around us. "Oh, St. David's Ruin. Cottingley. Not quite where I was aiming, but I *was* under a bit of duress." He looks back at me. "And my favorite part of Cottingley, actually." He beams at me.

I can't tell if he means it's his favorite part of Cottingley because he kissed me here, or if he means nothing by this at all. "Did you use some of my energy to make that jump?" I ask instead. His thumbs are still tickling at my wrists. I wish he'd stop. I wish he'd never stop.

"Yes. I had to. We'd never have gotten out of the Unseelie Court alive if I hadn't. Why?"

"I feel a little bit dizzy," I confess.

His smile widens, and he ducks his head closer to me. "That could be an energy drain," he says, his eyes filling my vision. "It could be other things too."

I am struggling to maintain some logic and sensible thinking. "Can we get back to Boston?"

"Yes," he responds. "I need a minute to breathe." He drops my hands, and I hover between relief and disappointment, but not for very long, because then he lifts his hands until he is cupping my head in them, his fingers in my hair and along the back of my neck, rubbing into the skin behind my ear and shivering at my jawline. "Or a century," he murmurs. "Depending on the time you're keeping."

I stop thinking, and then he kisses me.

Which doesn't help the thinking thing.

My thoughts are all scattered, but somewhere in there, I have the vague idea that even though I've been denying it, I really have been sick with worry over him. I thought it was possible I'd never see him again, never mind kiss him, and I told myself I would have been fine with that, but now that he's kissing me, I know that was all a lie, and I find myself kissing him back.

Kissing Ben is almost like being blindfolded, turned three times in a circle, and then being told to try to figure out where one particular person is sitting in a crowd of thirty thousand scattered all around you. It's *that* disorienting. Although far more pleasant. But that is the only excuse I have for the fact that when Ben finally draws back, panting for breath, I am somehow flat on my back and he is leaning over me.

When did that happen? I wonder dizzily, looking up at him.

"Thank you," he says and draws a finger down my nose, which shouldn't be sexy yet somehow manages to be.

I want to draw him back in for another kiss, but now I'm confused, so I say, "For what?"

"For saving me. Again." He brushes his thumb over my

145

lower lip, which feels heavy and wet from Ben kissing all rational thought out of me, and I freeze up as it crashes down on me, *saving him, again.*

I think of the tidal wave of ice that had poured into me on Boston Common when he left me standing there, left me without a second thought. *Stay because you love me,* I'd begged, and he had looked away, and he had left. And after all that, I still rescued him. Again. Yes, I had wanted to get to his mother and ask about the fays, but really, underneath it all, if I'm totally honest, wasn't I just trying to save his life? What is *wrong* with me?

I make a noise and squirm incoherently, pushing at him. He gets the gist of what I'm trying to communicate, letting me up, but he looks bewildered.

"What—" he begins.

I hold up a hand to cut him off. I am dizzy again, and it takes a second for the ruined building to stop swimming up and down around me. I wonder exactly how much of my energy Ben had to use to get us out of the Unseelie Court.

"Don't do that again," I tell him.

He continues to look puzzled. "Thank you?"

I give him a look that I hope is withering, swaying to my feet. "Kiss me."

He looks surprised. "Oh, I…oh. I thought…" He looks even more confused now.

I am furious with him, sitting there on the ground, looking quite at home and quite delicious and oh, yes, I am *furious* with him. "You think I'm going to forget that you left me, and I'm not going to."

"Selkie," he says warily. "I didn't mean to—"

"Oh, you meant to," I spit out. "You left *very deliberately*. You left even though I begged you not to go."

"Selkie," he says. "I had to—"

"It was a *trap*, Ben. You walked right into a *trap*."

He looks rueful. "I know. And if I had listened to you—"

"*You should not have listened to me because it was a trap!*" I shout at him, and my words ring around the ice-encrusted surfaces of St. David's Ruin.

Ben gapes up at me. He is very plainly shocked. It is clear he expected nothing like this from me.

"You thought you would leave me," I accuse, "and then you'd come back, and I'd still be here waiting for you, this lovesick little girl who's loved you her whole life."

"Selkie." He finally scrambles to his feet, looking anxious. "That's not what I thought. I thought, when I left you that day, that I was giving up every chance I might ever have with you. I never thought…I never thought I'd be able to fix it."

I have put the coat on fully, and it feels like protective armor as I cross my arms and take an insulating step away from him. "And you went anyway."

"I had to go. Don't you see? I *had* to go."

"I do see. If Will's right—and I think he is—you were manipulated your entire life to that moment, and you could have saved us so much trouble if you'd just kept your promise to me. We'd still be in Boston right now. Nothing would have gone awry. There'd be no pieces to pick up. We'd be with my aunts and sure my father was with us and okay. We'd be planning our attack, and we'd be *happy*. But you couldn't."

"Selkie," he says firmly. "I'm sorry. I am. I'm very sorry. But we'll fix it, okay? We'll go back to Boston, and we'll find your aunts and your father, and we'll plan our attack and—you came after me. You came…You came to *save* me. You're the only being I've ever met who ever wanted to *save* me before, Selkie."

He looks amazed at this, amazed at *me*. I want to weep, half from sorrow and half from sharp and painful anger, because he's looking at me like he loves me, like I am the most astonishing creature in the Otherworld or beyond, like he really does think it's true that no one other than me would ever lift a finger to save him. And I don't want to think that that might be true, because then I would forget about the fact that he lied to me and betrayed me, and I would just cuddle him and tell him that *of course* I would always save him.

And it's true, I think with a sinking feeling of inevitability—I would, much as I should no longer feel that way. Even with everything he'd done to me, there was a part of me that could so vividly imagine the idea of raw pain in Ben's starlight eyes and no one being there to comfort him, no one there to push his unruly curls off his forehead and hug him close and make him feel better.

The unerring, shameful truth about me is that I have

always wanted to be there for everything about Ben. I lived a life without him, when he enchanted me into forgetting him, and I remember how much I missed him without even knowing who he was, how much I wandered through Boston Common looking for him without knowing what I could possibly be looking for. I never stopped looking for him, everywhere I went, and that was before I *knew* him.

And yet, together with all of that, I can't help but remember that he *left*. We could have been perfect, he and I. We could have been our own little faerie tale. And he *ruined* it. "You promised me that you would never leave me." I am so annoyed that my voice is choked up when I say it. "You promised me. And then you did. As if it was nothing. As if that promise meant *nothing* to you. Those were just words you told me, to keep me near you a bit longer, to manipulate me."

"That's not true," he interrupts swiftly, but I interrupt him. I refuse to stop now that I've started.

"And I trusted you, Ben. All anyone ever told me was that I shouldn't; *you* told me yourself not to do it, and I did. And then you…then you…" I can't even say it, because I'm scared if I do, I'll start crying.

Ben stands across from me, the vision of him swimming a bit in front of my eyes. I don't know if it's because I'm crying or because I'm so dizzy. His eyes look…*hurt*. Which isn't fair, because he hurt *me*. He hurt me worse than anyone ever has before, Seelies and Unseelies included. He is not allowed to be hurt.

"Selkie," he says, and what he says next almost makes me hate him. "I love you. I do. And I love that you trust me. I've never had anyone—that's not something I—we're not very good at it, not naturally. I'm sorry, I didn't mean to—"

"I *trusted* you," I correct him, and I hope I sound cold and overbearing about it instead of small and wounded. "I *trusted* you, more than I've ever trusted anyone else in my life. You were my constant. You were the one who was always there. You made me feel safe and protected, and you were…" I admit it then. "You were *mine*. But you weren't. You're not. I trusted you when everyone told me not to, and then you left, and you made me feel insignificant and *stupid*."

"Selkie," he says desperately. He takes a step toward me, but he must see me tense, because he doesn't come any closer. "Selkie, I handled it poorly. I'm *so* sorry. Please, I just—I handled it poorly, I can—"

"Never trust a faerie," I remind him. "You told me that I was appallingly bad at remembering that. You told me that right here, right where we're standing. When I said that the only faerie I trusted was you, you told me that's why I was so appallingly bad at it. Do you remember?"

"I—"

I don't give him a chance to respond. "I don't know why I didn't listen to you then, but I've learned my lesson now. I'm sorry, Benedict." I use the name very deliberately, and I see the blink of reaction in him, a small flinch, even though I haven't really intended to name him. I just wanted to put distance between us, have him not be, for a second, the familiar *Ben* of lazy summer days on the Common. "I think you could promise the world now, the moon and the stars and your undying love. And how could I ever believe you?"

He looks stunned, too stunned to manage to say anything.

I feel very tired now that this conversation seems concluded. I wonder if I meant any of it. I feel like I did, but I also feel like, if Ben would like to hold me right now, I would be okay with that. If Ben would like a second chance, if he would like to beg me for one, it probably wouldn't take me long to change my mind and give it to him.

It would've been nice if I could've fallen out of love with him the minute he broke his promise to me.

I feel as if I am swaying on my feet. I actually stretch out a hand to steady myself on something, but there is nothing there to serve that purpose.

Ben's eyes are no longer stunned; they are concerned. "Are you okay?"

"I'm fine," I lie. "I mean what I'm saying."

"Yes," he clips out, frowning. "I've grasped that."

"I'm happy you're safe. I am. I'm glad we were able to save you. I don't want you to *die*."

"Good to know," drawls Ben.

"Just don't kiss me again." I turn away from him, and I want to be able to walk off grandly, head held high, showing how very okay I am with all of this.

Up is down and down is up. It's like being kissed by Ben. It's like being…it's like…falling over. Or it is falling over. I don't know. Am I on the ground? Am I in Ben's arms?

"Selkie," he says and shakes me, hands on my shoulders. "*Selkie*."

"Don't kiss me," I manage blurrily.

"Would you stop it with that?" he snaps. "Tell me what's wrong with you. I can't fix you until we figure it out. Selkie." He shakes me again.

"I feel sick," I inform him and tip forward against his shoulder. I am shivering violently, but I am burning hot, and the world rocks around me, making me queasy. I close my hands into Ben's shirts. "Stop moving," I beg him. "Stop moving."

"I'm not," he says. His arms go up, holding me to him, and I should tell him to stop that. "I'm not. Selkie, darling, you're wearing my sweatshirt. Let me put the charm back on you. We need to push this off—"

He is probably making sense, and I am willing to listen to what he has to say, but first he has to stop twirling me around. "Stop moving, *please*," I plead.

He is gone suddenly, I am crumpled to the ground in a heap, and the ruin spins around me like a carousel. Then Ben is pushing at my coat. Is he *undressing* me?

"Don't," I try to frown at him.

"I have to get this coat off you. I think it's killing you," he responds. His voice sounds frantic with worry. I wish I could understand what he's worried about. Maybe if he stopped touching me, I could pay attention to him. "Selkie, *help* me, come on, darling, *please*." He keeps tugging at my coat.

"It's cold," I tell him. "I'm not having sex with you here."

He rolls me, still tugging at my coat. He is practically manhandling me, and I am trying to resist but I am doing a terrible job of it.

"Plus," I continue, "I feel sick."

He seems to have succeeded in getting my coat off me. Now I am shuddering even more violently, and he gathers me up in his arms, pulling me close, and I am grateful for the warmth. The world looks like twilight; it is a swirl of violets. I can barely make out Ben, and I blink, trying to clear my vision, but the dimness is better. I can no longer really see the world whirring by me, and that's better.

"Selkie." Ben's voice is low and urgent. "Selkie, listen to me, *please* listen to me." He presses his forehead against mine. "Love me, just for a little while, the way you used to, *please*. Love me and let me in. I can't fix this with you fighting me this way. We'll finish this fight later, I promise. Love me now. Love me the way you used to."

"Don't kiss me," I tell him. I seem to remember that this is important. I close my eyes and lean into the press of his forehead, to the solidity of his body. He is the only thing in the universe not spinning. He is the only fixed point I can find, and I am half-annoyed at that, for reasons I can only half form. *Must he always be my fixed point?* I think. *Must he always?*

"I'm not going to kiss you," he assures me. "Just tell me you love me. Tell me it once, Selkie, just this once. Just whisper it in my ear and I'll pretend I never heard it. Just *tell* me."

What harm can it do? I think. *Maybe I'll tell him, and then he'll leave me alone, he'll put me down, and the world will be right side up again.* "I love you," I say. And then I figure he might as well know the rest of it. "And I'll always save you. Don't worry."

For a split second, the world is finally still. I hear Ben take a breath that is more like a shudder, and then he presses a kiss to my forehead. I want to remind him that he promised not to kiss me, but then I think that maybe he meant kissing my *mouth* and so maybe I'll let him off on this technicality and be more specific next time.

"Likewise," he says shakily into my ear, and I don't really remember what he's *likewise*-ing.

I'd think harder about it, except that the world finally spins itself out and I find myself in blackness.

CHAPTER 12

The world is loud and it is soft. Sometimes there are people shouting all around me, and sometimes there is nothing but the whisper of a breath beside me. Sometimes I am so hot that I feel that my skin is on fire and I push at everything near me in an effort to find some relief, and sometimes I am so cold that I shiver until it hurts and it doesn't matter how many things are wrapped around me.

It is lonely and I am all alone, although it seems to me that whenever I think that, Ben's voice drifts through my head, a low murmur. *I'm here. I'm right here.*

And he is.

I open my eyes, and I am in my room. My own bedroom, at home, on Beacon Hill. It is dim in the room, twilight, or else early morning, just before dawn.

I feel hollow and fragile, like if I move I might be ill, so I stay in exactly the position I'm in, concentrating on breathing and trying to remember how I got here. Because I wasn't here. Was I? I don't think I was. My mind is a massive tangle; getting a handle on the recent past is like trying to stagger my way through brambles.

So instead I try to focus on as many present sensations as I can—the slide of the sheet against me and the cradle of the pillow underneath my head. I am on my side, tipped toward my window, and my hands are…caught up in something I know I should recognize…

I close my hand into fists, and someone sighs, the mattress shifting a bit under me.

I look down. Ben is in a chair next to me, and he is clearly sleeping, leaned over, his head on the bed next to me. It looks as if it should be uncomfortable, but after he finishes stirring, he seems to fall back into a deep sleep. I look at my hands, closed into fistfuls of his hair, and then slowly, carefully, I uncurl my fingers and disentangle them. Ben sleeps on.

I stay very still, no longer just because I don't want to get sick but because I don't want Ben to wake up. Although it appears to me that I've been sleeping for many hours, if not days. Honestly, I feel exhausted, and I don't feel up to another argument with Ben. The truth is I can't quite remember how we left things. Everything from the moment he gave me the coat is a vague blur. There were kisses, but there was also… there was…I told him, didn't I? That I couldn't trust him anymore? Did I make him understand that? I am too tired to try to untangle the complicated interweaving of heartbro-ken devotion.

I am concentrating so hard on trying to remember how the conversation with Ben ended that I'm not sure how long

I lay there staring at him before I realize that he's awake. He has turned his head, still resting on my mattress, and is regarding me calmly, his eyes pale, barely a hint of color, and inscrutable.

"You're awake," he says eventually, after we look at each other for a long moment.

I feel too weak to even speak to him. I manage to nod.

"Really awake," he says. He reaches out a hand and presses it against the curve of my cheek. I close my eyes, even though I don't want to.

He takes his hand away and makes a curious shuddering sound. I open my eyes, since that's not what I expected, and he's buried his face in the bedspread.

I want to say something to him, although I don't know what, and he lifts his head before I can decide. I realize for the first time that he looks awful, pale and drawn, dark smudges under his eyes. His hair is not the good kind of unkempt. I wonder if he's been sick too.

"I'm sorry," he tells me. He leans back in the chair. "I didn't realize the coat was cursed."

This feels like the precursor to a serious conversation, which I do not have the energy for. I am dying for a glass of water, and I wonder if Ben is the right faerie to ask to find me some.

But there is no need, because then the door is flung open and both of my aunts scurry through and fall upon me, a mass of hugs and kisses and exclamations from them, until finally somebody thinks to give me some water. When I am able to take stock of things again, every person is in the room—my aunts and Will and the Erlking and Kelsey and Safford—except for Ben, who is nowhere to be seen.

Kelsey and my aunts are clustered by the bed, looking at me in concern. They look as if they might never stop looking at me in concern.

"How do you feel?" Kelsey asks me.

"Fine," I lie, because I feel terrible, but I'm not delirious or semiconscious, so I suppose that I am fine in comparison to that. "What happened?"

"We weren't there…" Kelsey begins, looking to my aunts.

"We don't know," Aunt True says with a sniff of disapproval.

"Well, we know what Benedict *said*," Aunt Virtue contributes.

"He staggered through the door with you unconscious in his arms and started babbling about cursed coats," Aunt True continues.

"You've been sick for *days*, sweetheart." Aunt Virtue reaches out and tenderly brushes my hair away from my face.

I feel, in that moment, very loved.

I look at Kelsey. "But where were you?"

She looks alarmed. "Getting back from the Unseelie Court. Remember?"

I do, now that she mentions it. I feel like my memory is awakening slowly. "Oh. Right. That's right. Ben and I went to get the coat. The coat that was cursed. Right."

"Only it took Benedict an extraordinarily long time to figure out the coat was cursed," comments Will. He is leaning against the wall at the foot of my bed. He sounds and looks casual, but I can tell he's anything but.

"I…" I can't quite remember what happened. "I was wearing the coat, and I was…" We'd been arguing. That's what we'd been doing. We'd both been distracted. I don't want to say that. I clear my throat and take another sip of water.

The sip of water is a good idea, because it gives Aunt Virtue the opportunity to turn to Will and spit out accusingly, "Don't upset her. She's still very weak."

Will looks unperturbed at being yelled at. His eyes stay on me. "That assessment I agree with. You need to sleep."

"I've been sleeping for days apparently," I respond, but I don't know why I'm arguing. I'm so tired now I feel like I could fall asleep immediately.

"That wasn't useful sleep." Will shakes his head.

"Can you enchant her?" Aunt True asks him.

"I don't want to be enchanted," I protest. I am tired of being enchanted. I want to be *not* enchanted, fully and utterly. I want the world to be a real place, a place that makes sense, a place that is *true*.

"It will help you get better," Aunt True informs me anxiously. "Will can give you a deep, dreamless, healing sleep. You'll feel so much better when you wake up."

"Where's Ben?" I ask. I don't want to ask it but I feel like

I have to. The story makes no sense to me—we were in Cottingley, weren't we? Not Boston. Right?—and he is the only one who was there, the only one who can tell me.

"He's sleeping," Will responds, which I think is so strange. He was just sleeping in here.

Aunt Virtue snorts. "More like collapsed."

Will doesn't look at her as he replies. "He's fine. Everyone's just going to sleep this whole thing off, and it'll all be behind us by tonight."

"It *is* nighttime," I point out, confused. "Isn't it?"

"That's just what it looks like when the sun has mostly gone out," Will replies grimly and then moves over to my bedside. "Just let me," he says. "You'll feel so much better when you wake up again."

I must have told Will yes, nodded, or something, because the next thing I know, I'm wide-awake, sitting straight up in the bed, and the room is empty again. That same hazy half-light is filtering through my window. And the room is not entirely empty, I realize. The Erlking is sitting in the chair by my bed that Ben had been in. He blends into the darkness around him, except for the sword swinging by his side, the jewels on its hilt gleaming dimly in the light.

"Ah," he says to me. "You look *much* better."

I am staring at his sword. "Why isn't your talisman cursed?"

"Because Benedict's mother is apparently *extremely* charming," the Erlking replies sarcastically. "It wasn't enough for her to work at cross-purposes against every prophecy the stars have written. She had to use a curse too."

I shudder.

"Are you cold?" he asks.

"No," I answer truthfully. "I'm…" I shrug and adjust the pillow underneath me so I'm sitting up against the headboard. "Where's everyone else?"

"Sleeping. It's the middle of the night. We've been taking turns watching you."

"Well," I remark dryly. "You're a much better watch than Ben."

"Why do you say that?"

"Because he was sleeping on the job when I woke up before."

"Oh. No, we weren't taking turns then. We couldn't. It had to be Benedict."

"What do you mean?"

"Selkie." The Erlking looks confused by me, but in a kind way. "You just survived a curse. A curse placed on you by what was previously believed to be the most talented enchantment faerie in the Otherworld. How do you think you did that?"

"I…I have no idea," I admit.

"No. Neither do I," agrees the Erlking. "But whatever Benedict did to get that curse off you was cleverer than anything I've seen before in a very long life full of clever things. I revise what I said to you before."

"What's that?"

"When I told you never to trust a Le Fay. You can apparently trust *that* Le Fay."

The irony is not lost on me. "No, I can't."

"You've absolutely bewitched him. Your talent must be seduction as well. Why didn't you tell me?" He is smiling at me, as if this is all teasing good fun.

I don't want to talk about Ben anymore. "How did you get out of the Unseelie Court?"

"We took the corgis."

"And?"

"And then we left the Unseelie Court."

I stare at him. "That's it?"

"That's it. Apparently, all the drama was centered around you. Will says this is a quality you have."

"It's not a quality I *want* to have," I grumble.

The Erlking looks amused. "We have very little control over most of the qualities we have. Anyway, their control is diluting."

"Whose control?"

"The Seelies and the Unseelies. We got out of the Unseelie Court because they couldn't stop us anymore. They're losing control. Things are happening all over, things that they don't want to happen. The prophecy is already moving."

"What time is it?" I ask anxiously. *How much time have I wasted here?*

The Erlking holds out his pocket watch. I can see it only dimly. 11:31.

"Past the half-hour mark," I comment weakly.

"Indeed." The Erlking replaces it. "So perhaps better that we get moving again as quickly as possible."

"How did I get back here?" I ask.

"You'd have to ask Benedict," the Erlking answers, "which means you need to wait for him to recover."

"Recover from what?"

The Erlking looks a bit irritated with me. "Didn't you hear me? He's recovering from saving *you*."

I don't know what to say in response to that, so instead I say that I'm starving, which I am. We go to the kitchen.

I hunt through the cupboards. The Erlking sits at the kitchen table and watches me.

I glance over at him as I find some bread. Toast sounds like something I can handle eating. I stick two pieces of bread in the toaster, and Will walks into the kitchen.

"I thought I heard you up," he says to me. He is fully dressed, brown corduroy pants and a dark green sweater. I remember how absentminded professor I thought he looked so long ago, when I first met him at the Salem Which Museum. I wonder how we got to this place from that place. The thing is, I *know* how we got here, and even I don't believe it.

"She was hungry," the Erlking tells him.

"Good. You're looking much better." He sits at the kitchen table.

"Your dreamless sleep thing really worked. Thanks."

"I'm not the one you should be thanking. This was all

Benedict. At least the one of us foolish enough not to notice a curse until it had already imprinted on you was also the one of us capable of saving you from it."

I don't want to think anymore about any of that. My toast pops up, and I grab it and put it on a plate and assemble butter and jam. Then I sit at the table and prepare my middle-of-the-night breakfast.

"We need to discuss what we're going to do next," says Will.

I know that we do. The clock is ticking. But I am tired, and I apparently almost died not long ago. I want to have my toast and then go back to bed and sleep for a thousand years. Or a few hours. Depending on what time you're keeping.

I want all this never to have happened, really, and that's something I know I can never have.

I ignore the fact that Will is talking about the prophecy's next steps. "Where's my father?" I ask. "I haven't seen him."

Will looks a bit shifty eyed. Which is not good. I slowly push my toast away. "Where is he, Will?" I demand.

"Your aunts couldn't get to him. The train stopped running."

"They were on a human train," I point out. "They were on the Red Line."

"It shut down," Will says. "They couldn't go to your father's."

"So they could have taken a taxi."

"Selkie. They *couldn't*. We're keeping the core of Boston together through an effort you can only guess at. It would have been too risky for your aunts to—"

I round on the Erlking. "You were supposed to protect them. Your people were supposed to go and get—"

"They couldn't," the Erlking cuts me off icily. "We have been restricted to Boston, and your father is outside of Boston. We can't get there."

"That's you. What about me? Can *I* get there?"

"Selkie, you're not going anywhere," Will tells me, which as good as saying *yes* to me. "You have to remember the prophecy."

"The prophecy isn't very helpful, Will," I snap. "My only remaining idea about how to find the other three fays is to just walk out the door and start asking people randomly."

"We got Ben back—" Will begins.

I am frustrated enough to say, "And what? What good does he do us without the other fays? And in the meantime, my father is a sitting duck—"

"There's going to be a battle, Selkie," Will cuts me off sharply.

"What does that mean?" I ask, because my mind shies away from what it probably means, from the thought of there being an actual *battle*, with all that implies, as if everything we've been going through so far has been nothing, just the opening act.

"Just what you'd think," Will says flatly.

"Will," I begin and take a deep breath, trying to organize my thoughts. "We can't have a *battle*."

"We either have a battle or the Seelies win, and everything goes back to the way it was before Parsymeon, everyone living in secrecy, trying to stay out of the way because you never know when the Seelies might show up and destroy you without thought. Everything in the Otherworld just wants to live. We have to fight for them."

"I don't know how to *fight*," I say. "I can't fight in a *battle*. You've lost your mind."

"Selkie, you've escaped from both the Seelie and the Unseelie Courts," Will reminds me impatiently. "There's very little you *can't* do. Haven't you figured that out?"

"That wasn't me," I protest. "None of this has been *me*."

"Then who has it been?"

"The prophecy. Or…I don't know. I'm not actually…" I realize even as I say it that it sounds absurd. It's true, in my head, in my perception of myself—I am not actually this person that I am. But it appears that I actually *am* this person. I am no longer the girl on Boston Common reading to Ben over freshly made lemonade. I am, apparently, the fay of the autumnal equinox. "But don't we need the other three fays? How are we going to have a battle with just *me*? We can't. Can we?"

There is a moment of silence. "The battle is coming whether we like it or not. Selkie, the *sun* is gone. And it's 11:31."

"11:32 now," the Erlking inserts quietly. "We lost another minute."

"11:32. Time is running out. At any moment, the clock could start ticking faster and faster. Finding the other three fays would be ideal, but there's going to be a battle, whether we're ready for it or not. And I'd rather we go down fighting if we're going to be named either way. Wouldn't you?"

"Can Ben find the other three fays? I know that his mother hid them, but you said he should be able to recognize Le Fay magic."

Will is silent for a second, looking at me. Then he snaps, "Possibly. Maybe. If we're lucky. Which I'm not sure I'm willing to count on anymore. And anyway, he can't, can he?"

I blink in surprise. "Why not?"

"Because he's *sleeping*," Will spits out.

I don't know what to make of that. "We can't just…wake him up?"

"Selkie. You need to understand that you should be dead. You're not, and we are all very grateful for that, but I don't know how Benedict accomplished that, and I don't want to know." He seems furious, and I have no idea what to say in reaction. "He's sleeping. When he wakes, we can ask him if he can help find the other fays, now that he knows his mother has hidden them. But I don't know when that's going to be, and it's 11:32."

"11:33," the Erlking adds quietly.

Will swears and says, "You see? I think we need to get ready, don't you?" Then he stands up, scraping his chair back, and marches out of the kitchen. Stomps, more like it.

I stare after him with no idea what just happened.

"You must forgive him," the Erlking says to me, looking awkward. "He was…worried."

"We're all worried," I say, disinclined to allow Will to be more worried than the rest of us.

"When Benedict arrived here with you…it was bad. They had an enormous disagreement."

"Who did?" I ask, because I'm having a difficult time following this conversation. Maybe it's because I've just recovered from what was apparently a severely life-threatening illness.

"Benedict and Will," he answers.

"Over what? Over me?"

The Erlking looks at me, his navy blue eyes glittering hard. "You were very bad off. You were absolutely delirious. Will was furious with Benedict."

"But why?" I'm bewildered by this. "Ben didn't curse me."

"He should have noticed, Selkie. It was inexcusable for him not to have noticed until it was too late. His delay could have killed you. It *should* have killed you."

I know that I've been told this, but for the first time, it really seems to sink in, as if it was all too much for me to take in at first and only now can I start to comprehend it. I think maybe I'd assumed people were exaggerating, the way girls at school might say they were going to die upon finding out their mascara had clumped their eyelashes together. I feel myself turn cold, and the toast I've managed to eat sits uneasily in my stomach. "Will really thought I was going to die?" I say, unable to get my voice louder than a whisper.

The Erlking just looks at me until I have to drop my eyes and look away, because you can't truly absorb the news that you almost died while staring at someone else. "Anyway," the Erlking continues after a moment, as if we are having a perfectly normal conversation. "Benedict finally slammed shut your door and locked it, and then none of us could get in until…well, until you woke up."

"How long was I out?" I ask fearfully.

"Three days. And in the meantime, we've moved ever closer to the twelve o'clock hour. And now we have to wait for Benedict to recover on top of everything."

We are silent for a moment. I look out the window, where the light is still the color of a dawn without a sun. It reminds me of Ben's eyes. I think of Ben sleeping, trying to recover from saving my life. I think of the prophecy.

"We're not going to survive the battle, are we." It's not a question.

The Erlking answers me anyway. "Selkie. It's a *battle*."

CHAPTER 13

Ben is sleeping on the couch in the study. We almost never use the study because it belonged to my father. My aunts have always avoided it, and I have always followed their lead. But now that Ben is in there, I have no choice but to go in. I feel like I need to talk to him. Everything is such a blur in my head, and we're barreling toward a battle. We don't know where the other fays are, and my father is trapped outside of the city. It's 11:33 now—possibly 11:34, for all I know—and Ben is prophesied to die, and I have to talk to him. I have just always had to talk to Ben when life gets overwhelming, and even after everything, apparently that hasn't changed. Or maybe I just have to wait until things calm down before I start to break my Ben habit.

Then again, are things ever going to calm down?

Ben is nothing but a heap on the couch, covered with a blanket and curled into a ball. I walk over and look down at him. He looks both more boyish and more dangerously attractive than I would like. He has the blankets tight around him, and he looks surprisingly tense, his lips pursed tightly together, his brow furrowed, as if his sleep is taking effort. Some of the things I would like to do to Ben are things I'd rather not admit, but I'd like to smooth the dark curls of his tumbled hair off of his pale forehead. I'd like to kiss his mouth until he forgets to frown and starts smiling. I'd like to unfurrow his brow with brushes of my lips and flutters of my eyelashes.

When I first fell in love with Ben, on Boston Common, he was playful and charming. He laughed and made me laugh. He brought me lemonade and sweatshirts, and asked me inconsequential questions. When I fell in love with Ben for the second time, in Tir na nOg, he was sick and vulnerable. He shivered and clung to me. I brought him blankets and the power of my name, and the questions we should have asked each other went mostly unsaid. When I fell in love with Ben for the third time, in Cottingley, when he kissed me in a fake ruin, he was focused and deliberate, seductive and seducing, and I really thought I knew him, after all of that.

I stand and listen to his breaths, breaths that belong to Ben.

It occurs to me that I may never know Ben. It occurs to me that I am never going to stop falling in love with him either. That he will show up in an endless number of new guises, new facets, new puzzles to solve in his personality, and I will fall in love with every single one of them. And what will stay constant about him will be his quicksilver, fickle nature. The *faerie*-ness of him. I will always be his, but I am not sure he will ever be entirely mine. I am not sure he is even capable of it. I am not sure I could even get him to understand what it is I want from him.

172

I should leave the room, I think. He's fine. I've verified it for myself. Sleeping. Recovering from whatever it is he did to save my life. Something even Will doesn't want to know about. I shudder.

And then I kneel next to the couch.

Ben opens his eyes. They are the color of the mullioned windowpanes behind the couch. We look at each other for a long moment. He is still frowning.

"How do you feel?" he asks eventually.

"Fine," I answer honestly.

And it happens then. His brow unfurrows, he relaxes, and his lips curve into a smile. His eyes flutter back closed, and he seems to nestle more deeply into the couch, as if settling himself back into sleep. "Good," he murmurs. "You look *wonderful*."

I hesitate. "Ben," I venture.

"Mmm," he says.

It is clear to me he is on the verge of falling asleep. I am torn between letting him and needing to know. "What did you do?" I whisper.

"I saved your life," he responds, sounding pleased.

"How?" I ask in another whisper.

There is a pause. He opens his eyes and looks at me for a very, very long moment. "By saving your life," he whispers back.

"Ben…"

"You've been talking to Will." He closes his eyes again

and speaks slowly, evenly, matter-of-factly. "You came into Tir na nOg, where your death seemed certain and assured. You went there for me, and you wouldn't leave without me. And you followed me into the Unseelie Court when you shouldn't have, when I'd just betrayed you. You've allied with goblins, stared down Seelies, endured church bells, tumbled into a dragon pit, and been cursed. And you did it all for me. I saved your life. We leave it there, you and I. That is all that must be said: I love you, and I'll always save you. Don't worry."

I watch him as he falls back asleep. *I love you, and I'll always save you. Don't worry.* The words sound vaguely familiar to me, like words said in a dream, or words I learned once to a song whose tune I've forgotten, or words in a book whose plot I've lost. *I love you, and I'll always save you. Don't worry.*

And *Benedict Le Fay will betray you. And then he will die,* I think. Has Ben fixed that by saving my life here? Is the betrayal no longer as sharp, as deadly?

I have no idea what to think.

I lay my head on the couch next to his, because I can't seem to help it. Even though I thought he was sleeping, he murmurs, "Oh," sounding both surprised and delighted. He snuggles his head closer to me, forehead against mine.

"You're burning up," I say in alarm, because he is, now that I can feel him. His skin is scorching hot, and that is not normally how his skin feels. I almost shrink away from him.

He makes a noncommittal noise.

"Ben." I sit up and look down at him, worried. He doesn't look feverish or flushed—he's as pale as always. Maybe more so. "Ben, are you sick?"

"Just tired," he replies. "Very, very tired."

I lean over him. It is more than that, but I feel he will never admit that to me. I settle for a question I think he may answer. "Will you be okay?"

He looks up at me, his eyes very clear. He really doesn't look feverish; he looks more…*heightened*. "Say my name," he says to me. "Say it now, without being angry with me. Say it now, just now that you like me."

"I always like you," I protest.

"You always *love* me," he corrects. "There is an important difference."

I feel that I shouldn't let him think that's true. And then I feel that it's ridiculous of me to deny it. I push back the hair on his forehead—he is blisteringly warm—and I say instead, gently, tenderly, "Benedict Le Fay."

He smiles at me, a brilliant, blinding smile. I don't think I have ever seen him smile just like that. It takes my breath away. "Everything is quite perfect," he tells me.

"You ridiculous faerie," I respond around a stupid lump in my throat.

He hums in evident agreement and closes his eyes and snakes a hand out of the cocoon of his blankets to tug at me. I put my head back next to his, listening to him sigh in contentment.

"I don't trust you, you know," I say, because it's true. I *love* him, but I don't trust him. I'm not sure if I ever will again. I wonder if I will live every day tense, bracing for the moment when he breaks my heart.

"Mmm," he says and pulls me closer. "That just means you're learning." There is a beat of silence. "I'm going to work on the trust thing when I get better," he adds.

"I thought you weren't sick," I point out.

He snores in my ear.

CHAPTER 14

I leave Ben sleeping in the study and move back out into the house. It is silent, everyone still sleeping. I don't know where the Erlking has gone or where Will is. Safford is sprawled on the couch in the living room, and Kelsey is on the bed in the spare room where she and I used to have sleepovers a lifetime ago. I assume that my aunts are in their rooms.

I stand in the front foyer and I look at the front door and I think of my father.

And then I open the door and step outside.

Boston seems so perfectly normal to me. I mean, granted, the day is gray and hazy, but it just seems like a cloudy day. The earliest part of rush hour is underway, commuters heading briskly along the sidewalks, dodging each other and darting out to cross the street between cars. I am seized by a fierce, sudden fondness for this place that I have called home all of my life. I have no desire to lose it or to see it destroyed. Honestly, I *love* it here.

I swallow back all the emotion, because it's not going to do me any good right now, and I cross Beacon Street and walk onto the Common, heading toward Park Street. I glance over my shoulder every so often, convinced that someone is going to step out of the house and shout at me to come back inside, that this is a stupid thing for me to be doing. But I can't help it: I know that people tried to get my father and failed, but *I* didn't try, and I've been a little bit successful with rescues lately. (Even if the last rescue was apparently a really close call, and even if I've always had help with my rescues; best to ignore those little facts.) And anyway, my father is the only parent I have who isn't trying to kill me, and he literally went insane because he wanted me so much, demanded me against all wisdom. How am I supposed to abandon him now?

I keep expecting something—anything—to happen. But nothing does. I get on the Red Line at Park Street and I take it all the way to the end at Alewife and leave the confines of Boston. The T doesn't stall. Goblins don't appear and neither do Seelies. Everyone bustles past me as if I am completely unremarkable. I wonder wildly if I should start asking them questions: *Do you think you might be a supernatural creature? When is your birthday? What is your name?* The idea makes me want to laugh hysterically. What is my *life?*

I am so keyed up by the time I reach the small, nondescript, charming-looking building where my father has lived all my life that I am practically jumping out of my skin at every movement. But I'm almost there now, and all I have to do is figure out how to get my father out and back into Boston…

I have not one inkling of a plan. I guess this is very faerie of me.

The nurse at the front desk is one I know, who has greeted me for countless visits to my father. Her name is Deb and she has two kids who are around my age and both play soccer in the autumn.

But when I go up to the front desk and smile at her, she just looks at me blankly in response. "Can I help you?" she says.

Fear begins to close around me, but I don't let it. I fight off the dark raggedness of its edges. "Is my father here?" I ask. I force myself to keep smiling.

"Who is your father, dear?" she responds. She looks mildly concerned, as if she thinks I might be the one who needs to be institutionalized.

"Etherington Stewart," I whisper. I clear my throat and repeat his name more clearly.

She frowns. "I don't think we have a patient here by that name." She taps on her keyboard and frowns some more at the computer screen. "No. No one here by that name. Are you sure you have the right place?" She looks up at me.

I look around at the vestibule I have stood in more times than I would ever be able to remember, from when I was a toddler taking my first steps to the day I had shown up asking about the possibility of having immortal aunts and was warned not to tell Benedict Le Fay my birth date. It is almost worse than hearing that my father has died, to hear that he seems to never have existed at all, that he is lost somewhere between this world and the Otherworld.

I move through the shock of the sorrow and coalesce into

rage. Wherever my mother is, I hope she can feel that I will not rest until I make her tell me what she has done with my father.

"I'm not even sure this is the right *world*," I tell Deb honestly with a bright and frigid smile. Then I turn and march out into the human world. I walk to the T station, dodging all the other pedestrians automatically, my mind on the Otherworld, on wherever my mother is, on how soon we can assemble an army that will attack her.

I swipe my T pass and get on the train that pulls up as soon as I enter. I sit and look out the window opposite me, at the darkness of the tunnel as it whizzes by. We are through Porter and almost to Harvard when the subway car begins to flicker. At first, I don't know what I'm seeing, and then I place it: the dance of flames in a fireplace out of the corner of my eye that disappears when I turn my head; the sensation that I am sitting in a cozy rocking chair, even though, when I look down, it's just the regular no-nonsense subway seat.

It's the Otherworld, I realize. The Otherworld is bleeding through. Or I'm somehow sliding into it. I don't know which.

I stand up hurriedly. We are between Harvard and Central, not yet at a stop, so I get some curious looks from people. The truth is I have no idea what I'm going to do. Can I get it to stop? *Should* I get it to stop?

I feel like I am driving in a car, trying to get reception on a radio station just out of range. Sometimes it feels like I'm standing fully in an Otherworld train, and then I blink and the static of the human world T reasserts itself. The T squeals to a stop at Central, and normal, everyday people all around me get on and get off, and I stand where I am, trying to keep my balance as the world swerves all around me.

The human T pulls away from Central, but I am no longer on it. I am now standing firmly on an Otherworld train, and across from me is my mother. She looks furious.

Which is good, because so am I.

"Where's Dad?" I demand.

"Where is Benedict Le Fay?" she demands. I don't even think she hears my question.

"What's the matter?" I drawl. "Can't you find him?"

She looks even more furious and waves her hand, which sends the china tea set on the marble end table next to the fireplace whirling through the air at me. It tumbles to the ground just before reaching me, shattering with a terrific noise that is nothing compared to the roar of frustration that my mother lets out.

I look down at the ruined remains of the tea set. "Ah," I remark. "Ben's enchantment. Of course. And you can't do anything about it, because you can't find him, so you can't name him." I look up at my mother and smile. I hope it is a perfect anti-smile. "What did you do with Dad? Where is he?"

My mother's expression shifts from rage to satisfaction. She sends me one of her own anti-smiles. "Wouldn't you like to know?"

"Yes," I snap. "Yes, I would. Give him back."

My mother smirks some more and walks toward me. I swallow and hold my ground, thinking about how she can*not* touch me. I do *not* want her to touch me. She stops just in front of me. She does not try to touch me.

She says, "You can come and get him."

"Come and get him where?"

"With me." She lifts her hand, offering it, as if I am supposed to reach out and take it. "You can come with me. I will take you to your father."

I stare at her hand. The thing is that I know she knows where he is. And she probably won't take me to him. And I remember that there is a warring prophecy, one about a fay going to Avalon and cementing the Seelie power forever, and if I go with her…But she might bring me to my father. She *might*. And if she *might*, if there's even the slightest chance that I can try to—

There is an explosion of white light. My mother whirls away from me, her mouth a round *o* of surprise, and the train splinters around us, sliding away in a dizzying confusion. I scramble for purchase, thrown off balance, and find myself on the cold concrete floor of a subway station. I watch as my mother, on the opposite side, across the tracks from me, slams hard into the tile wall lining the station.

I sit, stunned, on the floor, trying to figure out what happened, until Ben steps in front of me. And then I realize what happened: *Ben* happened.

"Hello," he calls across to my mother, who is holding her

head in her hands. I'm guessing that she cracked it against the tile wall. "There's a rumor you're looking for me."

My mother roars again, and Ben ducks, grabbing my hand and pulling us out of the way. A gaping crater appears in the place where we had just been standing.

"Get out of this station," Ben gasps at me. "Do *not* take the T. Get in a cab and get yourself home and lock all the doors."

"What? What will you be doing?"

He shoves me away, shaking his head as if that's an answer, and sends fire licking over the train tracks toward my mother.

She dowses it with water, some of which she sends Ben's way, although he pushes it away with a burst of magic.

"Where are all of your friends, Benedict?" He winces at the name and leaps away from the lightning strike she aims at him. "No one to rush in to save you now? Just a girl who was on the verge of betraying you? All of that effort to keep her alive and safe, and she would have come with me if you'd been just a pig's whisper later, Benedict Le Fay."

Ben winces again, and he gathers some effort to do something. I can feel the charge of it in the air around us, but I'm no longer paying attention to them, because I am looking around for a weapon, anything I can use, as ridiculous as it might seem. Why can't I do amazing things like fling tea sets through the air and throw fire and make bursts of blinding, explosive, destructive light? I don't care what nonsense the Erlking and Will said about the importance of being me—being me is *useless*. I hate them for having me raised human so that I never developed any faerie powers.

"Is that the best you can do?" I hear my mother taunt Ben. "Really? Is this really what you will use to fulfill your prophecy?"

Some scraps of litter, I think desperately, looking around on the floor. That's all I have. What am I going to do with that?

"Benedict," I hear my mother say behind me. She pauses for effect. "Will o' the Wisp."

Names, I realize. I have *names*.

"Cel—" she begins, but I don't let her get it out.

I whirl toward her, intent flowing through me in a wave I can feel. "*Mother*," I say scathingly.

She gasps, and then Ben collides with me, knocking me down. I feel the rush of air over us, and the wall behind us explodes, showering us with pinpricks of concrete and ceramic tile.

"I told you to *go*," Ben snaps into my ear.

But I am not listening to him. I have fallen onto my side, farther up the platform than I was, and I am staring at the art installation that runs through the center of Kendall Station. We are in Kendall, I realize, and those metallic tubes that look like elaborate decoration, I know what those are: they are *bells*. Not chiming bells. Deep, gonging, Seelie-hating bells.

"Ben," I say, shoving at him, wriggling and squirming about.

"You have to go," he insists.

"I'm going," I lie breathlessly. "I'm going." He releases me and I stumble to my feet, throwing myself at the gear crank on the wall that rings the bells.

"How *dare* you name me!" my mother shrieks behind me.

I ignore her, grabbing the crank and pulling at it.

"Selkie," she says, and I gasp with the pain of it, but I don't let go of the crank. I pull it harder.

Behind me, the bells start to ring. I hear my mother scream, and I feel myself start to fall, dizziness spreading through me, the bells vibrating in my skull.

Someone pushes at me. Ben, I realize. Catching me as I fall. Always catching me as I fall. I rest my cheek against the fleece he's wearing.

"You're a genius," he tells me. "And now, I'm sorry for this, but you've found me church bells. I've got to use them."

He reaches past me, and he turns the crank. The bells ring louder.

CHAPTER 15

I wake in a bed with the sensation of being watched. *This,* I think, *is getting old.* When I open my eyes, I am in my own bed, and I *am* being watched, by Ben, who is stretched out next to me, his eyes steady on me.

"How are you feeling?" he asks me.

"Okay," I tell him, which is true. Tired, but okay.

"You found us bells."

"I did."

"I'm going to overlook the fact that you snuck out of the house and focus on the fact that you found us bells."

"Ben," I say, frustrated. "You don't understand. I had to—"

"We'll find your father. You can't go off on your own. We'll find him *together*."

"She has him somewhere, Ben, and it's all my fault—"

"It isn't your fault. Stop that. And there is no place she could hide him that we wouldn't find him." He ducks his head down, forcing me to meet his eyes, pale as tears. "We are Selkie Stewart and Benedict Le Fay. Try and stop us. Right?"

I wish I felt like he was right about that. "Until you decide we're not anymore," I point out scathingly.

He blinks, his eyes shuttering a little bit.

I want to shove him off the bed, but instead I settle for rolling myself off the bed. "What time is it?" I say, but even as I finish, the grandfather clock starts chiming. The three-quarter hour.

I run to my bedroom door and pull it open, and I am dimly aware that everyone else in the house has gathered in the foyer, all of us looking at the grandfather clock on the landing. Which is showing 11:45.

"Is that the right time?" I call.

It's the Erlking who answers. "Yes."

Great, I think. And we're no closer to getting anything done.

I go downstairs, and the air feels thick, like syrup I am pulling myself through.

"Selkie!" Aunt Virtue thunders at me, drawing herself to her full height (which isn't very much). "How *dare* you disobey us and leave this house?"

"I had to find Dad," I defend myself. "I *had* to."

"Did you think we didn't try hard enough to find him?" Aunt Virtue continues. "Did you think we gave up on him so easily? Do you really think that nothing can be accomplished unless *you* do it personally?"

Said like that, she has a point. I feel like a risk-taking idiot for having gone out there. "I just wanted to…" I trail off, realizing that I really don't have anything I can say to make things better. There *is* no way to make things better. "They took Dad," I say. "They *took* him." I can feel tears coming close, so I push them back. "We need a plan," I announce firmly.

"What a refreshingly unfaerie thing to say," says the Erlking.

"We've been trying to come up with a plan and getting nowhere," says Will.

I only have one idea for a plan, so I say it. "I think I should go outside and start asking people for their birthdays."

Will blinks at me in astonishment. "That's your plan?"

"Isn't that the key? The birthdays? When I said my birthday, it started this whole thing in motion. Maybe it will work for the others."

"The birthday question isn't the weak part of your plan," snaps Will. "Do you know how many people there are just in Boston? Just on *Boston Common*? You think you're just going to randomly stumble over the right ones?"

"Ben's mother said two things that she's right about," I begin.

"Ben's mother who's been trying to stop this prophecy from the very beginning?" Will mocks, eyebrows lifted.

"Yes. If the prophecy's going to be fulfilled, it's got to start helping us out a little bit. And I'm good at finding and collecting just the right things that come in handy later."

"This is the most ridiculous plan," Will says dazedly. And I know it is. It's not a plan—it's a *joke*—but it's all I've got.

"All respect, Will," remarks the Erlking frankly, "but we haven't come up with a better one."

"A better one than *that*? I feel like trying to negotiate with the Seelies would be a better one than *that*."

"What time is it?" I ask the Erlking.

He looks at his watch. "11:46."

"We're wasting time," I say, marching over to the front door, and tugging it open. The air outside seems even murkier than the air inside had been. I can't tell if this is because my head is still fuzzy from the church bells at Kendall or because the actual air has shifted into something more viscous.

Standing on the sidewalk at the base of our front steps is a girl with pale blond hair with the tips dyed all the colors of the rainbow, braided in six different braids on top of her head, and a boy with a thick patch of messy straw-colored hair and a heavy smattering of freckles. The girl is in the process of shaking salt and pepper over the sidewalk. The boy seems to be sifting in some sugar as well. Boston has gone *crazy*, I think.

The boy and the girl look up at me, and just to prove to Will how serious I am about my plan, I say, "What are your birthdays?"

Astonishingly, the boy and girl exchange a look, and then the girl says, "We're the winter and the summer solstice. Which one are you?"

I blink. And then I turn to Will. "My plan worked," I say smugly.

CHAPTER 16

The girl and the boy come inside and the girl says, "I'm Merrow and he's Trow, and the moon was in its second house and then Virgo was moving toward the horizon and anyway, the stars said we had to come here."

"The stars said?" Will echoes.

"Yeah. Exactly. And Virgo and the moon too, but mostly the stars," answers Merrow.

"I know she sounds crazy," says Trow, "but she's weirdly persuasive, right?"

She is, actually. Merrow says everything with such conviction that you can't help but be carried along with her.

"So you're fays too?" Kelsey clarifies.

"I think so? Fays of the seasons? That's what Roger Williams said anyway," Merrow replies.

"Roger Williams?" asks Kelsey. "The founder of the state of Rhode Island?"

"Yes, I know it sounds crazy—" begins Merrow.

"Crazy is actually very difficult to sound to us," drawls the Erlking at her.

Merrow says, "Well, you're dressed in a black velvet

cape and wearing a huge sword, so I guess you've got a point."

I look at Will. "Do you know Roger Williams?"

Will looks offended. "Of course I know Roger Williams. I just don't…talk to Roger Williams."

"If you had less messy breakups with people," Ben tells him scathingly, "we would have gotten this figured out so much more quickly."

"Maybe if *you* hadn't taken a field trip to the Unseelie Court," Will retorts, "we would have gotten this figured out so much more quickly."

"It's 11:47," the Erlking says.

"We don't have time for this," I cut them off and turn to Merrow and Trow. "I'm Selkie, and I'm the autumnal equinox. I'm hoping you know where the other fay is."

"The only guess I have on that is Iceland," says Merrow. "We have to go to Iceland."

"Did the stars say that?" asks Kelsey.

"No, that was the honey and the ketchup, when we mixed them together in the diner while we were waiting for the train. The stars keep changing; even the constellations keep changing. It's getting harder to read them."

I just stare at her, but Will says, as if to reassure me, "This is how prophets talk. They're all mad as hatters."

Merrow is much shorter than Trow and me but she manages to make herself seem much taller. "Excuse me," she says, offended.

"Iceland," Will muses. "That makes some sense."

"Why?" I ask.

"Because it's closed to travelers."

"Not quite," Ben says. "We can get in but we can't get out."

"Like the room at the Boston Public Library," I recall.

"Exactly."

"Which is why your mother would have liked the place to hide a fay. No one would have guessed," says Will.

"You can get out at Thingvellir," the Erlking says suddenly.

Ben looks at him.

The Erlking shrugs. "We goblins have always known the traveler loopholes."

"Yes," Ben says. "I bet you have." He looks back at Merrow. "Iceland, you can understand, isn't a place I'm keen to go. In fact, it sounds like a trap to me."

"All of a sudden you're worried about traps?" I say, because I can't help it.

Ben frowns.

Merrow says, "This whole thing is messy right now. There are prophecies upon prophecies. They fold in on each other and contradict each other, and one says what the next doesn't say, while the next says what the next after that *can't* say. You see? The patterns in the salt don't match the pepper, the patterns in the honey don't match the bees, the patterns in the sneezes don't match the coughs. And don't even get me started on the stars. Plus the air is thick here; the salt wasn't falling properly, and the sugar was clumping. Is it always like this in Boston?"

"That's the Seelies getting closer, throwing off the chemistry of the sky," says Will nonchalantly.

Kelsey and I exchange panicked looks.

"So what does it all mean?" I ask. I hope I don't sound desperate and panicked, because I want to be coolly in control the way Merrow seems to be, but I feel like I can't help it. Everything is a mess and my father is missing and a battle is coming and the air is growing too thick to breathe and the clock keeps ticking and Merrow's just sitting here talking about salt and pepper.

"I think that none of it is settled. None of it is prophesied. And all of it is prophesied. It is all existing at once. The time is spiraling. It's because we're in the middle of it. You can't prophesy what you're actually living. All I know is that the next word I can read is Iceland. Actually." She blinks at Ben. "*You* have to get it."

I look between her and Ben. "How do you know?"

"Can't you tell from the dust motes?" she asks. "I wish I had my tarot cards. I could do this so much more easily."

"Well," remarks Ben. "This seems like a genuinely terrible idea, so I'm sure we're going to do it, right?" He glances at Will.

"What else can we do?"

"If you're going to Iceland, you're going to need to talk to the Hidden Folk," says the Erlking. "I know the Hidden Folk there."

"You can take us to them?" Will asks.

"They keep to themselves, as you know. But they'll speak to

the Erlking of the goblins of Goblinopolis."

"Why?" persists Will.

"Trade treaties, of course. They have a terrible weakness for goblin silver. It *is* the best," the Erlking allows.

"You have trade treaties with the Hidden Folk?" Ben clarifies. He sounds disbelieving.

"The world is getting smaller, Benedict," remarks the Erlking. "Even *this* world."

I honestly don't know which world he means by that.

"So you can get us to the Hidden Folk?" Merrow asks.

"I can," the Erlking confirms.

"Awesome. Then we should leave immediately," Merrow announces. "Probably the three of us and you." She points to Ben. "And him." She points to the Erlking.

I bristle, because Merrow seems a little bossy, and I'm offended that she's just drifted in here at the end and made it seem like this is all so easy to do.

"And me," says Will.

"I'm going too," adds Safford.

Ben looks at him. "Safford," he begins.

"I'm the expendable one of this group, aren't I? Don't you need an expendable one?" He asks it dryly, but the truth is that he has something of a point, which is terrible.

"I didn't want you to be this involved," Ben says. "You weren't supposed to be this involved."

"I really never had a choice, Benedict," says Safford. "I have never had a choice, not since the Seelies named my parents and flooded our world and cursed me to Mag Mell simply for *sport*. Actually, that's not true: I *had* a choice, and I've made it. So. I'm coming."

"I'm coming too," says Kelsey immediately.

I look at her. "Kelsey," I begin.

"I'm coming, Selkie," she tells me, giving me a look. "We've come this far in saving the world. I'm not going to stop now."

I look at my aunts, and then I look at Merrow and Trow. Merrow beams at me. Clearly she thinks we are already fast friends. Trow looks a bit bemused.

"Excellent," says Will as if there is nothing more to discuss. "We'll leave immediately."

Ben says he feels well enough to jump all of us to Iceland. Except that he can't jump the Erlking due to the fact that he can't work when the Erlking is touching him. The Erlking says not to worry about him—he has other ways to get to Iceland—and then he leaves the house.

"He's going to meet us there, right?" Kelsey says to me as we watch him go.

"Definitely," I say, feigning a confidence I don't feel.

Kelsey can tell. "Do you trust him?"

I look at Ben, who is listening to something Will is saying to him, his nose wrinkled in displeasure. "I don't trust anyone," I say.

"Yeah," echoes Kelsey as she rests her eyes on Safford. Poor Safford, who seems so sweet and straightforward and may have the world's most terrible fashion sense, but other than that just seems *lovely*.

"I don't know that Safford's like that," I tell her, feeling bad that I've colored her crush with the whole disaster that happened with Ben.

"Never trust a faerie, right?" says Kelsey, sounding half-grim and half-wistful.

"It's so great to meet you," Merrow gushes, coming up to me. "I feel better now that we've got three of us. We'll go to Iceland, find the fourth, and rewrite the story."

"Rewrite the story," I echo.

"It's what my mom told me we have to do. We have to rewrite the story to…fix a lot of things." Merrow is speaking bouncily and sunnily, but there's a shadow lurking in her eyes. I feel bad. Something tells me she has just as much inner turmoil going on as I do; she's just hiding it better.

"You guys should have some sort of secret fay handshake," Kelsey says, and I wonder if she feels a bit left out.

Trow smiles at Kelsey. "So you're not a fay?"

"Not a fay," Kelsey agrees.

"How'd you get roped into this?"

"I'm just the world's greatest best friend," Kelsey explains.

"She speaks the truth," I contribute and turn to Merrow. "So you know…everything?"

Merrow snorts. "I wish. No. Not even close."

"How much do you know?"

"She knows just enough to be dangerous," says Trow.

Merrow ignores him. "I know there are four of us. I knew you were here because the stars told me. I know we have to go to Iceland, although I can't tell if that's because the other fay is there. It doesn't feel right, but I don't know what else it could be. And I know we're supposed to rewrite the story." Merrow pauses then says slowly, "My mother is…Whatever they did to her, it's…"

I think of Trevor and Milla, the little children I saw named right in front of me, for no reason other than because the Seelies *could*. I can't help but shudder. I don't know what I would have done if that had happened to my aunts or my father, right there with me watching. If Merrow had to see that…"I'm sorry," I say, aching for her. "It's…horrible." It is hardly an accurate word but it's the best I can do.

"Did they attack your family too?"

I look at my aunts, who are standing in the corner, looking terrified and heartbroken. "Excuse me," I say to Merrow and go over to them.

"There's nothing we can do," Aunt True says, her voice laden with tears. "We can't keep you here. We can't stop you. And they have Etherington…"

"I'm going to get him back," I vow. "That's why we're going to Iceland. We're going to find the other fay, take on the Seelies, and get Dad back. I promise."

"Oh, Selkie." Aunt Virtue looks at me, and her eyes are wet.

She looks as if she is trying to catalogue everything about me, as if this might be the last time she ever sees me, and I can't bear the thought of that.

"I'll be back before you know it," I say desperately. "We'll be so fast."

"Please be careful," Aunt Virtue says. "Please don't be *heroic*."

"I'm never heroic," I say, confused.

Aunt True and Aunt Virtue both make noises that could be close to laughter.

"I'm *not*," I insist. "It's just that sometimes…I have to do stuff. But I'm not—"

"Just be careful," Aunt Virtue repeats. "We'd come with you, except that we're two more people to worry about, and Boston's defenses need all the help we can give them, and—"

"We're going to keep everything here safe for you," Aunt True tells me with the air of a promise.

"Good. When I get Dad, we're going to bring him home." I've made this decision already. We can figure out some way to accomplish this. Maybe we can even make him better. Maybe Will knows some kind of spell. Maybe Ben can help.

I hug my aunts, refusing to hug them for longer than I would normally hug them, because I want this to be just like any other parting.

And then I turn to the knot of people in the center of the room. The people I'm supposed to save the world with.

Ben says, "Ready?" and I nod.

CHAPTER 17

We are outside, in darkness. It is cold, and we are surrounded by a wet, drizzly fog that presses against us. I am near enough to Ben to feel him flinch and hear the curse that he mutters under his breath at the damp.

"Where are we?" Merrow asks cheerfully.

"*Iceland*," Ben half snaps at her. "Isn't that where you told us we had to go?"

"It's awfully dark," says Merrow, undeterred. "How do we know it's Iceland?"

"It's Iceland," says the Erlking suddenly from somewhere in the darkness. "And it took you long enough. It's 11:48 now."

"How did you get here so quickly?" Kelsey asks in surprise as the Erlking strides up to us, slightly darker than the night.

"Who says I got here quickly?" the Erlking replies mildly. "It's possible I took the long way around and just happened to meet up with you."

Kelsey stares at him. "No," she says. "That's not possible."

The Erlking ignores her and says to Ben, "It was obvious of you, wasn't it? Coming to this part of Iceland?"

"Isn't it the right part?" Ben asks. He is suppressing shivers now, and I can tell the wetness all around is seeping into his bones. I have a vivid recollection of the way he was in Tir na nOg. "Aren't we near the Hidden Folk? Certainly this place is covered in magic."

"You're quite close," the Erlking agrees. "I just thought landing so close to where you wanted to be is *obvious*."

"Or sensible," says Kelsey.

The Erlking shrugs. Then he takes a few confident steps away from us and disappears. I blink in confusion then realize that there is a rock ahead of us with a gap in it: the entrance to a cave. *Shelter*, I think, and I am relieved.

The Erlking's head reappears, poking out of the cave. "Come along."

We follow him obediently. Will sends one of his lighted orbs up to the ceiling of the cave, where it floats, illuminating the size of the cavern. It's really more of a passageway than a cavern, a narrow hallway hewn into the rock. There isn't much to see, but I don't know what we're looking for. I glance at Ben who looks drawn and exhausted, droplets of water shining in his dark hair.

"Take your coats off," Will tells him. "They're getting you damper."

Ben obeys, slipping out of his trench coat and pulling the windbreaker he's wearing underneath it over his head, leaving his hair in unruly and wet disarray. The blue-and-white striped long-sleeved polo shirt he's wearing over a bright tangerine shirt seems mostly dry.

"What's the matter with him?" Merrow asks, sounding curious.

"He doesn't like water," I answer.

"He doesn't like water," repeats Trow, as if trying to make that make sense.

"Here," the Erlking says and carefully hands across the cape he's taken off.

Ben looks both surprised and jubilant. He wipes his face and towels off his hair with the inside layer of the cape, which seems to have remained dry, and then hands it gratefully back to the Erlking, careful that they don't touch each other. "Thanks."

"Don't mention it." The Erlking twirls the cape dramatically around himself and fastens it back around his neck. "This way."

We set off following the Erlking, although I'm not sure where it is we're going. The Erlking moves slowly, cautiously, and I sense that he needs it to be quiet. None of us says a word.

We've only gone a few dozen feet when the Erlking, in a movement so quick that I don't even see him execute it, pulls out his sword and points it toward the wall. I'm confused, wondering if he's suddenly lost his mind, and then I become aware that he has pinned a *person* there, up against the wall of the cave. A person who is a stranger to our group. A person I didn't notice until just that moment.

"Where did he come from?" Kelsey whispers beside me, clearly as shocked as I am.

The person is a young man. His face is sculptured and striking, beautiful bow lips and lovely, high cheekbones, but the effect is somehow not attractive. His eyes dart around at us from underneath a mop of thick brown hair falling over onto his forehead. He is dressed in trousers and a filthy blue shirt, tucked half in and half out, and his shoes are on the wrong feet.

And he says, "There's no way that you can see me."

The Erlking smiles a wicked, terrifying smile and edges the point of his sword closer to the man's Adam's apple. "Reconsider," he suggests smoothly.

The cornered man gulps and tries to look cross-eyed at the sword cornering him. And then he frowns. "Hang on just a pig's whisper," he says and looks up at the Erlking in amazement. "Is that goblin silver?"

The Erlking smiles again, a bit more nicely this time but still silkily. Then he lowers the sword and bows gracefully, his cape swirling about him dramatically. "I am the Erlking of Goblinopolis," he announces.

The man blinks in astonishment. "Are you really? Well, isn't this amazing!" He launches himself at the Erlking, and I flinch, expecting it to be an attack, but he simply shakes his hand enthusiastically. "It's wonderful to meet you. *Marvelous* to meet you," he exclaims.

The Erlking looks as if this is to be expected. "Thank you, thank you," he says, although he might as well be saying *Of course, of course.*

"What brings you to the humble land of Ingolfur Arnarson?" the man asks.

"A quest," answers the Erlking. "A most important quest." He steps aside, gesturing to Merrow. "These are the fays of the seasons—"

"The fays of the seasons!" the man interrupts, sounding astonished. "Well, why didn't you *say* so? You will need to see Their Majesties."

We follow our guide. He is chattering a mile a minute to the Erlking, and I can't really follow the conversation. It doesn't seem as if the Erlking can either; he just keeps *hmm*-ing every so often to keep up his end of it. The walls and floor of the hallway are covered in red carpet so plush we sink into it and leave footprints as if it is snow. Golden sconces line the walls, candles burning merrily. Over our heads, from the ceiling of the cave, chandeliers drip delicate crystal and blaze away. It seems to be an entire palace existing in a cave.

Eventually, the hallway opens into a large room. The floor is stone, like the floor of the cave itself, but it has been polished until it gleams like a mirror, reflecting the chandeliers high above it. Looking into it has a dizzying effect, the doubling of the world at one's feet. I can't look away from it, staring into my own startled eyes. It isn't like looking at a reflection, not entirely. It's like looking into a puddle, like there's a me on the other side of it also looking into a puddle, and I lean closer to it, inexorably...

And tumble in, through cold marble that gives way with a splash, and then I find myself struggling my way out of a weed-choked pond in a forest, and nobody else is anywhere in sight.

CHAPTER 18

O h!" exclaims a voice, and I jump a mile, because I
could have just sworn that I was all alone. "Oh! Oh!
Oh! A *visitor*! Oh, a *friend*! A *soul*! *Mate*!"

I try to locate the voice, peering through the undergrowth,
and then the owner of it bounds into view. He is a skinny, old,
bald man, with a long face and a long nose. He has a straggly half
goatee that seems to be the only hair on his body, and he is filthy,
dressed in rags, apparently from living by this pool of water.

He is an ugly little creature, and he looks utterly *delighted*
to see me.

"Hello, hello, hello!" he enthuses and bounces up to me.
"Welcome, welcome, welcome! Are you thirsty? Would
you like some food? Please stay and have some food! Please
stay *forever*!"

"Uh," I say very intelligently. "I have to get back..." Even
though I have no idea how I even got *here* in the first place.
I look down into the pool of water and try to determine if I
should swim down to the bottom. Would I emerge out of the
marble floor? I can't see the bottom of the pond at all—the
water is filthy—but it's the only idea I have.

I hold my breath and dive down toward the bottom. It's deeper than I estimate, and I don't even find it the first time I try. I do find it the second time I try, but it seems to be nothing but mud and…other things I decide not to think too hard about. I dive down again and again and again, but I always just end up surfacing in the forest, with the skinny, old, bald man watching me with interest.

Finally, I give up. However I get back to where I was, it's not through this pond. I'm hoping that the rest are looking for me by now.

"Are you going to stay?" the man asks me eagerly as I straggle my way out of the pond. "Please stay at least for a meal! It is so *lonely* here. *Please* stay!"

"I was just in Iceland," I tell him. He just looks at me politely. "With…" Damn it, what was the name they'd said. "Arnarson?" I guess, hoping it's right.

The little man just says, "*Please* stay here for a meal."

He is so insistent. Maybe he's trying to tell me something. "Okay," I decide slowly. "I'll stay just to have something to eat. Then I have to be on my way."

The creature screeches with delight and goes gamboling away from me. "A guest, a guest, a *guest*!" he chants. "This way, guest! It's this way!" He gestures to me, into the undergrowth.

I hesitate then decide I might as well follow him. He *seems* harmless, and I don't know what else to do. I don't have time for any of this, but I have no clue how to fix it.

The undergrowth gives way to a cozy clearing, in the center of which there is a fire, over which a rabbit is roasting.

"Look!" exclaims the creature. "I caught a rabbit! We can share it!"

"Excellent," I manage. I've never had rabbit to eat before, and I'm not sure I want to start now.

"Sit down, sit down!" He practically shoves me down onto a patch of moss and thrusts a dirty glass of water at me.

I take it. "Where'd you get the glass?" I ask. It is a stupid question, but it is literally the first thing that occurs to me.

The creature laughs with delight. "It was a gift! Another visitor left it for me!"

"Do you get a lot of visitors?" I ask and take a tentative sip of the water. It seems to be drinkable.

The creature's face falls. He sits on the moss opposite me and looks like the saddest thing in existence. My heart aches for him.

"Hardly any," he says wistfully, looking out into the distance. "Hardly any."

"I'm sorry," I tell him sincerely. "It must be lonely."

"So lonely," he says. "I am the loneliest thing in the *world*."

"I'm sorry," I say again. He looks *so* miserable. I almost feel bad asking my next question. "Where are we?"

"This is the Urisk's clearing. *I* am the Urisk," he adds after a second, as if afraid I won't understand that. "I am the only Urisk that there is!"

"Yes, but what's this forest?"

The Urisk looks at me quizzically, as if he doesn't understand the question. Then he flops melodramatically onto the moss. "You're going to leave, aren't you?" he wails. "Everyone always *leaves*."

"I need to get back," I try to comfort him. I almost want to tell him to come with me, I feel so terrible for the poor little thing.

The Urisk sits up, sniffling, and pokes at the roasting rabbit. "It's okay. Don't trouble yourself. I will be fine. Lonely, but fine. Just oh so lonely. Have some rabbit." He tears some off for me unceremoniously and drops it in my lap. "*So* lonely," he mutters and munches at his rabbit.

There is a scrap of cloth on the ground, faded red in color, long and thin, ripped from something. I pick it up absently and tuck it into my pocket. "I have to get going," I tell him. "I'm sorry, but I have to try to figure out where I am. Are there any towns near here? Any people?"

"No," declares the Urisk mournfully. "There is no one around here. There is only me. Only me. And it is so very, *very* lonely."

"I'm sorry," I venture again uncertainly. "You could come with me, I suppose?"

The Urisk shakes his head. "I will stay here. Alone. It is my destiny. Alone, alone, alone. Always alone. No one ever stays." He stares at the moss as his slender fingers pick at it, apparently taking no notice of me.

I stand up, wondering what to do. "Well," I tell him.

"Thank you for the food and the water." I receive no response. "Good-bye."

"Good-bye, good-bye," says the Urisk without looking at me. "Good-bye."

I push out of the clearing and take a moment by the pond to collect myself. What a strange, sad little creature. I feel terrible for him, melancholy weighing me down.

I dive into the pond once more, just to make sure, but its bottom stays stubbornly mud. I give up and get out and start walking, not knowing what else to do.

I walk for not very long, maybe half an hour, before reaching another pond. For a second, I stare down at it, wondering if I've walked in a circle.

Then a voice I recognize cries, "Oh! Oh! Oh! Oh! A *visitor*! Oh, a *friend*! A *soul*! *Mate*!"

The Urisk comes rushing into view, eager to greet me again, bounding up to me.

"A *visitor*!" he exclaims. "A *guest*! How lucky to have you! How fortunate! Won't you stay for some food?"

I look at him quizzically. "But...we just ate."

He laughs as if I am delightful and hilarious.

I continue to stare at him. "You ate the rabbit, remember?"

"Do you catch rabbits? How very useful!"

"No, *you* caught the rabbit," I remind him.

"*I* caught the rabbit?" This gives him pause. "But I haven't caught a rabbit in *forever*."

"But you did, you just did, we just—" I cut myself off,

realizing something. This little creature is dressed in blue rags. The Urisk's had definitely been red. It's the color of the scrap of fabric I took with me. So unless the Urisk had changed his ragged clothing…which I suppose is a possibility…"Wasn't that you, Urisk?"

"I am the Urisk, but we have not eaten together."

"But we must have. You said there's no one anywhere around here, that you're all alone and lonely. You said you're the only Urisk in existence."

"Well," he says. "That's true. I am. And there *is* no one anywhere around here. I am all alone and lonely. Won't you stay *forever*?"

I continue to stare at him. "So we didn't just eat together?"

He looks offended now. "I would remember. I never get visitors. I would remember a visitor in my clearing."

"But…then that means there's two of you."

"What?"

"There are two Urisks. There's another Urisk just through the trees, not a long walk at all. I just ate with him."

The Urisk gapes at me for a moment. And then he bursts into loud, shuddering sobs, burying his face in his hands as he cries messily.

I don't know what to do. "But this is good news," I point out, bewildered. "The two of you can be friends. You don't need to be alone anymore."

"Oh, you are *cruel*," sobs the Urisk. "You are *cruel*, you are *cruel*, you are *mean*! Telling me that there are other Urisks in the forest, when I know I am all alone, all alone, all alone."

"But you're not—" I start to protest.

"Leave!" he shrieks at me, lifting his tear-splotched face from his hands. "Leave! Haven't you done enough? *Leave!*"

"I…" I stammer.

He rushes at me as if to attack me, and I stumble away from him, not really scared but extremely confused. Then he collapses to the ground in a heap and cries as if his heart is breaking. I stand and stare at him, unsure what to do.

"He's not far away," I venture quietly. "Only about half an hour—"

"*Leave!*" shouts the Urisk and throws something at me in anger.

I dodge it, but when I look at what it was, I realize it's a key. An old-fashioned scrolled skeleton key. The Urisk is still sobbing behind me.

"Do you need this—" I start to ask him.

"Why don't you *go*?" he shrieks at me violently.

I decided that maybe I am making things worse. I tuck the key into my pocket and follow it with a long, thin scrap of fabric I find on the ground. Blue this time. And I continue walking.

"Oh! Oh! Oh! Oh! A *visitor*! Oh, a *friend*! A *soul*! *Mate!*"

Another Urisk bounds out of the woods by the new pond I've reached, identical to the other Urisks, only this time dressed in yellow rags.

I sigh, resigned. "I don't suppose you would believe me if I told you there were two other Urisks living not far from here?"

His face scrunches in confusion. "But *I* am the only Urisk! I am all alone in this enormous forest! It is the loneliest life in existence!"

I sigh and decide it's not even worth the effort. I walk past him.

"Won't you stay?" he calls after me. "I almost never get guests."

"Two other Urisks," I call over my shoulder to him. "Not far from here. I swear."

"You *lie!*" he accuses furiously. "Why would you tell such a terrible *lie?*"

The sound of his sobs carries over the air to me, and I pick up a yellow scrap of fabric, and then I stop and look at the pond I'm standing next to. *Maybe I should be checking every pond*, I think. *Maybe one of them will get me out of here.*

I walk over to the pond, the Urisk still sobbing, and I look into it.

And there's me, looking back from the palace, the chandelier beyond my head.

I lean closer. And tip.

CHAPTER 19

I sit up with a gasp. And there I am, back in the large room with Kelsey and Merrow and Trow and Ben and Safford and Will and the Erlking. I am perfectly dry, as if I hadn't just spent a little while thrashing around filthy ponds. And everyone gives me a look, as if I'm being dramatic for no reason, as if they didn't even notice that I had gone anywhere at all.

Maybe I hadn't.

But there is a key in my pocket and three scraps of fabric when I check.

Kelsey hisses at me, "Are you okay?"

I nod dazedly, because it's too much to explain right now. I put my hands down on either side of me, bracing against a sensation of falling, even though I am perfectly still. Our guide has disappeared, but instead there is another man blinking down at us, accompanied by a woman. They have the same striking features as our guide, but they are more attractive, their cheeks rosy and their eyes bright with evident amusement. Did they send me to the bizarre forest with the Urisks? Maybe the Hidden Folk are as crazy as the faeries.

Both the man and the woman have masses of dark hair.

The man's hair curls playfully down to his shoulders, like a French king in the age of Versailles, but the woman's is gathered into a heavy bun at the back of her neck. Each of them is wearing a heavy gold crown, the sort of ornate, bejeweled affairs you see in illustrations in faerie tales, and this makes sense, since they are dressed in velvet and ermine.

"Three fays, a human, a goblin, a traveler, and a wizard walk into the court of the Hidden Folk," proclaims the man who is evidently the king. He sounds delighted, like he's telling his favorite joke. Maybe the Urisks are just an elaborate joke. A girl walks into a forest…

"And him," responds his queen, pointing to Safford.

"And him," agrees the king. "Three fays, a human, a goblin, a traveler, a wizard, and *him* walk into the court of the Hidden Folk."

They have been staring at all of us, studying us closely, and we are too astonished to say anything.

Then the king abruptly turns to Ben. "Speak to us, traveler," he commands. "Tell us the words of your prophecy, and beware, for you are in the court of the Hidden Folk, those who assist at will and at whim."

Ben hesitates. I don't know what he thought the Hidden Folk would be like, but I can see that this isn't it.

So I'm the one who speaks. "We're the fays of the seasons," I tell the king. "We're prophesied to save the Otherworld. But we need to find the other fay to do it, and we think he or she might be here."

"The fays of the seasons," answers the king musingly. "And a traveler."

"The box, my love," the queen tells him gently.

"Oh! Yes! The box! Ingolfur Arnarson left the box specifically for Benedict Le Fay. Would that be you, traveler?"

Ben, startled, nods.

And the king beams. "Oh, excellent. What has taken all of you so long?"

There are thrones at the other end of the room, and the king and queen lead us over to them. They don't offer any seats to us as they settle themselves.

"Erlking of Goblinopolis," the king says to him.

"Your Majesty," the Erlking responds politely with a small bow.

"The crowns are quite lovely. My wife adores them. Thank you."

The queen beams at the Erlking and blows him a kiss flirtatiously. I wonder if the Erlking has his special seduction power set on high. And I'm annoyed, because the clock is ticking. We don't have time for *flirting*.

"Good," the Erlking replies. "I am pleased."

I want to lean over and ask him what time it is, just to remind him that we're on a schedule, but before I can, the king says, "As for the rest of you, none of you have gained proper entrance to the court of the Hidden Folk. We grant you this hospitality at will and at whim."

"Thank you, Your Majesty," Will says respectfully.

"You, sir," the king says to him sharply. "Through the looking glass, you do not exist."

"So I have been told," Will responds.

I notice Ben look at Will with his eyes narrowed, and I wonder what the phrase means.

"Faerie Le Fay," announces the king. He has a goblet in his hand now, gold and heavily bejeweled, like everything else in this place. I have no idea where it came from. "You have come for the box."

"Well," says Ben. "I thought we were coming for a fay."

"We have no fay here. Only the box. Do you know how long the box has been sealed? Waiting for the touch of Benedict Le Fay?"

"I do not," Ben confesses.

"Neither do we." The king sips from his goblet and considers. "But it's been a long time."

"Or no time at all," contributes Will.

"Spoken like a wizard." The king smiles at him.

"Where is the box?" I say, tired of this pointless conversation.

"In the museum, of course," answers the king.

I can't wait to have conversations that don't constantly make me feel like an idiot. "What museum?"

"'What museum?' she asks," scoffs the king. "'*What museum.*' What a mopple you *have* made of things, if you have to ask me what museum. Don't you know where you are? You're in Iceland. What other museum would it be in, but the Museum of Iceland?"

Ben contributes, "But...I have never heard of the Otherworld having museums."

"Don't be daft, faerie," snaps the king. "We had to keep the box safe, didn't we? How would we ever have accomplished that in the Otherworld? Seelies listening at every corner and rattling every box, for that matter. And naming travelers with a quickness. How, I ask you, could such a thing be safe in the Otherworld, as a box meant for a traveler?"

"It's a *human* museum," Ben realizes.

"Of course it's a human museum. Have you ever heard of any other type? Dear me, *what* a mopple. Are you sure you're Benedict Le Fay? I had the notion he was going to be clever, was Benedict Le Fay. Perhaps you'd better verify your identity. Perhaps a middle name or two."

"Ingolfur Arnarson left the box for me, with middle names as collateral?" Ben drawls.

"And what if he did?"

"Your Majesty," Ben responds calmly. "I am the best traveler in the Otherworld."

"So I have heard. If that is the case, Benedict Le Fay, by all means, collect your box, sir." The king makes an expansive motion with his hand.

I wake with a gasp, lying on cold, dewy grass growing in a scraggly manner amid waves of rolling black rock.

Ben stands up beside me and brushes himself off, nose crinkled with distaste.

"I just had the strangest dream," Kelsey gasps.

"I think we all did," I reply grimly and sit up.

"We're in the middle of nowhere," says Trow. He has already stood up and is surveying the ocean of black rock stretching around us for as far as can be seen. He turns and helps Merrow up and says, "What do you propose we do now?"

"Well, obviously we have to go to the Museum of Iceland, like the king said," Merrow replies.

"And where is that?" I ask. I know I shouldn't sound sour—Merrow's just trying to help—but I hate how confidently know-it-all she seems to be. *I* want to be confidently know-it-all like that, and instead I never know what I'm going to do from moment to moment.

"Come along," Ben says. "I'll get us there."

Merrow looks at him. "You know where it is? A second ago, you'd never even heard of the place."

"I'm the best traveler in the Otherworld," Ben tells her, and we all join hands.

The Erlking says, "I'll meet you there."

And then we are standing in front of an unassuming and modern building that is helpfully labeled the National Museum of Iceland. The Erlking is lounging against the wall by the door, and I wonder once again how he seems to manage to get everywhere before we do.

"What time is it?" I ask him.

"11:52," he tells me. "And I think we should really stop checking. There is nothing we can do about it."

Ben walks through the front door of the museum, which slides open accommodatingly, and we follow him and stand in the lobby, which is a high atrium with windows. Ben turns in a circle in the middle of it, looking up.

"So we're going to steal an artifact from a museum?" says Kelsey.

"Looks that way," responds Trow.

"Then shouldn't we wait until it closes?" she suggests.

"Why?" Ben counters absently.

"I don't know." Kelsey looks at Merrow. "Does the prophecy say we're going to be successful stealing this?"

Merrow frowns briefly, saying, "That's not how prophecies work. I wish it were. I didn't even know we had to get something here."

Ben sets off up the escalator in front of us, walking with swift purpose. No one stops us or asks for any tickets or anything. We follow Ben through the galleries. He is moving quickly, wending through them without hesitation, until he abruptly stops. It is as if he knew all along where the thing was.

"Here we are," he says. He is looking down at a small wooden box, only about the size of a brick, trapped under glass and clasped with an old iron lock. There is nothing overly remarkable about this box, other than the fact that it looks to be old.

Curious, I lean over Ben, reading the description of the box.

"It says here that only a knowledgeable man named Benedikt could open this box," I note and look at it. "Have you opened it before?"

He doesn't look away from the box. His eyes are an extremely pale blue, like a sun-bleached sky. He shakes his head.

"Then why does it say that?"

"Because Ingolfur Arnarson left it for me. It's a message for me."

"A message in a caption by a museum exhibit?"

"Can you think of a better place to put a message to someone?"

"Maybe in a letter," answers Kelsey pragmatically, reading the caption over my shoulder. "It says here that the man named Benedikt was a man of many skills. Is that true?"

"Inconclusive," I say.

That gets Ben to look away from the box, his nose crinkled in annoyance. I smile sweetly at him.

"Well," says Merrow. "I guess you should go ahead and open it. Maybe the whereabouts of the other fay are inside."

Ben lifts up the glass that had been protecting the wooden box. I'm pretty sure you're not supposed to be able to lift up that glass, but he does it effortlessly, and nothing happens in response, no alarms or anything like that.

He touches the box, hands grasping either side of it.

And then he frowns.

"We have to go," Will says.

"Something's wrong," Ben replies, not taking his eyes off the box. "There's something wrong with the box."

"We'll figure it out later. Take it and let's get out of here." Will's voice is low and urgent, and I look at him in surprise.

"What's wrong?" I say.

"It's not opening." Ben turns the box over, still frowning at it, clearly trying to make it function properly.

"I'm telling you," Will says, "we'll deal with it later. Right now—"

Will cuts himself off. I look up and all around, and see nothing out of place, but I can't help feeling panic. And it's contagious. I can feel everyone else draw closer to each other too.

"What?" Kelsey says, sounding a bit frantic. "What is it?"

"Run." Ben grabs my hand, tucking the box against his body. And he takes off at a sprint, dragging me behind him just as I finally hear it: the chiming of bells.

CHAPTER 20

P anic makes us sloppy. Merrow half slides down the staircase we are descending, which almost starts a chain reaction of all of us sliding. Ben's hand is firm in mine and he doesn't let go, keeping me upright and moving. He is running like he has a goal in mind, although I don't know what the goal could be.

The chiming grows louder. The ground starts vibrating beneath our feet. For a brief, wild moment, I wonder why we're even running. If the Seelies are this close, then they'll catch us easily; they're so very fast. I look over my shoulder, but they don't seem to be behind us. They seem, rather, to be all around us, a terrifyingly invisible presence that is going to swoop over us at any moment.

We've reached the ground floor, the lobby with its wall of windows. Ben's pace does not slow. He rockets toward the glass in front of us. I register our pale reflections superimposed over the gray world outside, quickly getting larger and larger as we get closer and closer, and I am sure the look on my face is alarm. Just as I am about to ask him what he could possibly be doing, he smashes head-on into the glass.

It splinters all around him, almost in slow motion, slivers cracking and then falling, drifting down like petals from a flower. I duck instinctively, trying to shelter my head from the onslaught of glass, but there is…nothing.

I lift my head and realize that we are in a tunnel, underground, much like the one we walked through to get to the court of the Hidden Folk. The bells have stopped chiming, and Ben stops running, drawing to a halt. We all stop around him, gulping down breaths.

"What was *that*?" Kelsey asks.

"The front door," Ben responds. He still has the box tucked against his side and is looking up and down the tunnel intently.

"Oh," says Kelsey. "Of course."

"What *was* that?" Merrow demands.

"Seelies," Will answers grimly. "That's what we're saving the world from."

"Where are we?" I ask Ben.

"I don't know." Ben sounds slightly panicked. He drops my hand and takes a few steps in one direction then the other. "I don't know," he repeats, and his panic is more than slight now.

"How can you not know?" the Erlking snaps at Ben. "You're a—"

"I know," Ben cuts him off angrily. "Shh. Let me listen." He stares intently to his left and then his right. "It's an enchantment," he announces finally, shaking his head. "They're blocking me. The Hidden Folk or the Seelies or somebody. I don't know where we are."

"What should we do?" ventures Merrow.

"You're the one who told us to come here, and this is a *trap*," Ben shouts at her. "This was always a trap! You led us here and I can't get us out!"

"Hey," Trow says, his voice hard. "That is not necessary—"

"We needed to get whatever that is!" Merrow shouts back, gesturing at it.

"It's a *box*," Ben says. "It's *nothing*. I can't even *open* it! It's *broken*! And now we're trapped here. Is that what you wanted all along?"

"Of course it wasn't what I—"

"This isn't helping." I stand in between the two of them. "Please. We'll figure this out." I look at Ben. "We've been in worse spots, you and I."

"What does the precious *prophecy* say?" Ben snarls at Merrow before taking a step away from her in impatience.

"We have to get to Thingvellir," Will interjects calmly. "That's the way to get out of Iceland, remember?" He tosses something up into the air. A tarnished brass arrow. It floats over our heads. "Thingvellir," he calls up to it, enunciating carefully.

After a second, the arrow swings around, pointing to our right down the hallway.

Ben looks at Will in relieved astonishment. "I didn't know you could do that," he says.

Will looks at him. "You've always thought you were the only one with tricks up your sleeves."

"I could kiss you right now," the Erlking says.

"Maybe later," Will replies. "Let's go." He walks resolutely down the tunnel in the direction the arrow indicated to us, and we all follow him.

I think of the chiming bells that sounded right on top of us in the museum. The tunnels are eerily silent by comparison. "What time is it?" I ask. "Is it twelve o'clock?"

"Don't worry about the time," the Erlking responds shortly, and then, after a second, he says almost apologetically, "but it's not quite twelve o'clock. We haven't quite lost."

"Yet," I can't help but mutter darkly.

"Can I ask a question?" Trow requests with the air of not really caring what the answer is.

"No," says Ben.

Trow ignores him. "They'll know we have to get to this place to get out of here, right? So shouldn't we have a plan?"

"How is it you're a fay?" Ben mutters. "How are all these fays so obsessed with *planning*?"

"They're all only half faerie, Benedict," Will tells him. "That's kind of the point. And we don't have a choice," Will says to Trow. "There's only one way out. And we have to get out."

"So this *was* a trap," Trow says.

"We needed whatever was here. The box," Merrow insists but with only a shadow of her former bravado, and her face is very pale. I feel a bit bad for her. "We had to come and get it."

"Don't worry about it," Will says breezily. "I am not a faerie, and I knew what we were getting into, so I have a plan."

Ben looks at him in evident surprise. I'm surprised too. This is the first I'm hearing of a plan more detailed than "go to Iceland."

"What's the plan?" I ask.

"We have to get to Thingvellir."

"That's not a plan," I point out, annoyed. "That's just a destination."

"What's that noise?" asks Kelsey suddenly.

I've been distracted by everything that had been going on, but I hear it now that Kelsey points it out. It's a dull, thundering roar, like a great rush of air somewhere in the distance. Ben draws to a halt, and we all follow his lead, listening.

"Is it…what is it?" asks Safford.

"It's a waterfall," the Erlking says. "You've taken us to Gullfoss."

"I don't think so," Will responds slowly. He resumes walking, taking the lead.

Ben, clearly dreading the prospect of a waterfall up ahead, drops behind him.

We walk forward more cautiously now. The air around us is pounding, reverberating with the force of whatever's ahead. The tunnel begins to lighten, murky daylight filtering in from an opening before us. We are all silent as we walk through and emerge before a sheet of water.

It's not a waterfall. Or at least not the kind of waterfall that exists on Earth. In front of us is craggy, rocky land, uneven and scrabbly, which drops off into an abrupt cliff. And just beyond the cliff, a ribbon of water hovers in the air, a waterfall tumbling down from another world into this one. It stretches along the cliff in front of us, as far as we can see to the left and the right, dense and thick and silver. It looks as if we have reached the end of the world, like there is nothing to do but turn around and go back.

The noise of the gushing water is so loud that it is impossible to have a conversation without shouting. Ben is hanging back, still in the shelter of the tunnel, looking grimly at the water in front of us, and I stand next to him and stare at it as well. Everyone else is standing out by the edge of the cliff, clearly trying to come up with the next step we should take.

I dimly hear Ben say something next to me.

I turn to look at him. "What?" I shout.

"We're trapped!" he shouts back to me.

I shake my head, mostly because I want to come up with something that will deny what looks to me like the inevitable conclusion that we're trapped. Will had a *plan*. Didn't he say that he had a plan? But Will is just staring at the waterfall like the rest of us.

And then we hear the bells begin to chime, somehow louder than the water in front of us. Everyone out by the cliff looks to their left, and I look that way as well, edging closer to Ben without even realizing I'm doing it, until my hand curls into his.

Confusion has erupted out by the edge of the cliff. Everyone is making a mad dash back to the safety of the tunnel, but Seelies have begun swooping into existence off to our left. They shine brightly in the gloom of the landscape, looking cold and triumphant, and my stomach sinks in horror. I am not sure what they will do, but I know it will not be pleasant.

Trow is the first to gain the safety of the cave where Ben and I are standing, tugging Merrow in right after him. Kelsey stumbles just in front of Safford, tumbling to the ground. I utter a little cry, but Safford helps her up. The Erlking guards their escape, sword out as they run for the caves. I watch the Seelies gather, somehow growing taller and brighter, swooping toward them, and I feel Ben's hand tighten on mine, tugging me back before I even realize I was trying to go to them.

And then the Seelies collide midair with something invisible and fall to the ground. Will dashes by the Erlking, glancing behind himself at the contained Seelies. *There*, I think. *That must have been Will's plan.* I have every confidence Will can block the Seelies and keep us safe.

I turn away from the Seelies, viciously banging on the invisible wall, their faces contorted with murderous fury. Kelsey is limping, supported by Safford as they make their way to the cave, straggling behind Will, the Erlking bringing up the rear. I rush over to them even as Will sweeps his hand impatiently, a gesture that apparently has the effect of muffling the sound of the water so that we can hear.

"Are you okay?" I ask Kelsey anxiously.

"My ankle," she says, wincing as Safford helps her to the ground. "I think I twisted it."

I look at her ankle, clearly already beginning to swell.

"How long will it hold them?" I hear the Erlking ask from behind me.

"Not long enough," Will responds. "We have to put the plan in motion."

The Erlking says, "I'm still not sure that I—"

"It's nonnegotiable," Will snaps at him.

Something in me pricks in alarm, and I manage to turn from fussing over Kelsey to look at Will. I want to ask him exactly what this plan entails, but just then, Ben throws the box violently to the ground, startling all of us.

"What the devil are you doing?" Will asks him in alarm.

"I'm trying to break it open," he responds, frowning at it when it remains intact. "We need to get into this box. How else are we going to get out of this?"

"Stop it," Will snaps. "Are you mad? You need whatever's in that box *intact*, not smashed to smithereens."

"Do you have an *idea*, Will?" Ben shouts at him. "Because I would love to hear it. Your ingenious plan is only going to hold them for so long, and in the meantime, I need to get us out of here, and I can't jump us from here, and one of us can't *run*." He sweeps an arm out toward Kelsey.

Kelsey looks from Ben to me. "I'm sorry," she says, her voice small.

"Don't be ridiculous," I say to her. "Do *not* apologize. It's my fault you're here in the first place, and I have a key." I say it in a rush as I suddenly remember. How had I not remembered before this?

"What?" Ben says blankly.

I rush from Kelsey to the box, fish the key out of my pocket, stick it into the lock…and nothing happens. I can't turn it. I rattle it around in frustration. How can it not work? Everything I pick up always ends up *working*. How can the prophecy be failing me *now*?

"I think Trow can help with the running at least," says Merrow as I continue fiddling with the lock. "With the ankle. He's…a caretaker."

I have no idea what she means by that, and I'm still too distracted by the key conundrum to care. Ben has dropped to his knees next to me, trying to help but really just interfering. Before anything else can happen, Will says, "I can take you off the map."

I don't know what that means, but it gives Ben pause. He regards Will for a moment, and then he shakes his head. "No, you can't."

"Yes, I can."

"You can't take all of us off the map when there are Seelies just outside. Stop talking nonsense. It would kill you," Ben bites out and bats my hand away to try jerking at the key again.

"Benedict Le Fay," Will says, but he hasn't named him, hasn't said it with intent, because Ben doesn't even glance up at him, wiggling the lock back and forth in an attempt to loosen it instead.

"What?" he responds absently.

"I'm sorry," Will says.

"For what? This isn't *your* fault. Well, not entirely at least."

"For this," Will says, and then he turns and runs.

There is a moment of stunned reaction time, and then Ben leaps to his feet.

"Wait," Ben calls. "Will! Don't—"

The Erlking lunges at Ben suddenly, grabbing his arm. Kelsey gives a shriek of surprise. I am frozen, uncertain what I should be doing, if I should aid the Erlking or attack him. I can feel my hesitancy mirrored in Safford and Merrow and Trow, all of us staring, unsure.

"What is happening?" I demand, thinking of what Ben just said, of how Will couldn't do what he was going to do, how it would kill him. "What is he going to do?"

Ben is squirming in an attempt to throw the Erlking's hand off of him. "Let go of me," he pleads. "Let go of me."

"I can't." The Erlking doesn't sound unkind. He sounds, in fact, gentle, despite the fact that I can see his grip on Ben is iron. "I promised him I wouldn't let you follow him."

"Why would you make that promise?" Ben demands of him, sounding horrified, and then he switches to fury. "If you don't let me go this instant, Erlking of Goblinopolis, I'll—"

There is a noise like a thunderclap, and all of us jump. Then there is a furious, blinding flash of light. My eyes close involuntarily against the force of it, and when it fades away, the tunnel is completely silent except for Ben's heaving breaths.

I open my eyes. Ben is staring toward the opening of the tunnel. The Erlking has let go of him, but he's not moving. The silence is total. The sheet of water has disappeared. There are no Seelie bells chiming.

"What happened?" Merrow whispers. It seems like anything more than a whisper would be rude.

The Erlking answers in a low voice. "He took us off the map."

"What does that mean?" Kelsey asks. Her voice is also quiet.

Ben turns toward the Erlking abruptly. He is coiled with fury. "He asked you to stop me."

"Benedict—" the Erlking begins, hands raised in placation.

"He was *planning* this!" Ben is shouting, and his voice echoes off the cavern around us.

"He said he had a plan," the Erlking begins in answer.

"That? *That?* He called *that* a plan?" Ben demands. "He never said *that* was his plan!"

"You wouldn't have let him do it," the Erlking says.

"Of course I wouldn't have let him do it! What are we going to do now?"

The Erlking reaches underneath his cloak and produces a scroll of paper sealed in old-fashioned wax that he hands across to Ben.

Ben takes the scroll but he doesn't look at it. He stares at the Erlking for a very long moment, and then he turns and marches out of the tunnel.

I have an inkling of what's happening, but I don't want to be right. I want to be very, very wrong. "What's going on?" I ask the Erlking angrily. "Where's Will?"

The Erlking hesitates and then says, "Do you know how a wizard harnesses a great deal of magic, all in one place, all in one time?"

"No," I retort. And then, just like that, I realize that that's not true. I *do* know what a wizard has to do to do that. I watched Gussie do it when we were escaping Tir na nOg.

"He does it," the Erlking continues slowly, even though I now know exactly what's coming, "by sacrificing himself."

CHAPTER 21

Ben is sitting on the edge of the cliff. Next to him the scroll of paper, its wax seal broken, flutters slightly in the breeze. Ben stares across the chasm to the land on the other side, and he does not give any indication of knowing that I'm there.

I don't want to sit on the edge of the cliff, so I sit a little bit behind him and try to think of what to say. I look at the scroll of paper. I can just make out the first word on it, written in an old-fashioned, curly-cue handwriting. The word is *Benedict*, followed by a dash. It's a letter, I think.

"Do you know how I got involved in all of this?" Ben asks abruptly.

It saves me the effort of coming up with something to say to him. "How?" I respond and watch him as he speaks, never taking his eyes off the horizon he's looking at.

"It involved water," he says, his tone flat and dry. "It was the only way he could get me to stay still long enough to listen to him. So I listened to him. How he got me to *trust* him is another matter entirely. And I really should have known better. All this time, I've been trying to teach you not to be so trusting, and I'm the one all along who should have been taking the lessons."

Silence falls, and I try to come up with something to fill it. "Ben—"

"Did you know about this?" he demands, turning swiftly to look at me.

I shake my head and swallow and say, "Is he really dead?" I need someone to say it, bluntly, so I can process it.

His eyes are the darkest gray I've ever seen them and as unreadable as they usually are. "That's a very human term for it. But yes, a roughly accurate one."

I think of the first time I met Will, at the Salem Which Museum, and I think of how he had become, somehow, the ally I trust the most. Ben I'm in love with, and that can't be helped, but Will made me feel safe, like no matter how volatile Ben and our relationship might be, I would have Will, and this whole prophecy would turn out okay, because there was Will. Will who knew more than me, who was a link to my aunts and the past of Boston, who knew more than any of us, it seemed, about what Boston had been designed to do. The absence of him is a cold hollow of dread inside of me, and I realize it must be thousands of times worse for Ben. Ben, I think, might not realize it, but Will was his friend.

"I'm sorry," I say, blinking my tears away to focus on Ben.

"For what? You didn't know this was going to happen."

"No, I'm sorry you lost him."

He looks away, back out to the horizon. "So am I," he sighs. "I don't really want to be in charge of this whole thing."

I pause. "I'm sorry you lost him because you liked him."

Ben doesn't respond for a moment. He squints at the horizon and wrinkles his nose. "That," he proclaims eventually, "is another very human thing to say."

And, I think, another roughly accurate one. I stand slowly and take a cautious step on the rocky, uneven ground, until I am standing next to him on the cliff. He looks up at me, watching as I take a deep breath and sit next to him, my legs dangling over the side into space. The height is dizzying, and I try not to think of it.

"I don't know what do next," Ben says. "I'm hoping you do."

I take a deep breath. "We should get back to Boston. And we should fight. I'll ask random people on the street for their birthdays again. That seemed to work last time."

Ben shakes his head and huffs out an amused sound that isn't quite a chuckle. He looks around and says, "Well, we're at Thingvellir. The only place in Iceland where I can jump us. And Will's brought us here and bought us the time, so we'd better use it. Let's get going."

He takes a deep breath then stands easily, offering me his hand to help me up. I brush the dust off of me and turn toward the cave, but Ben doesn't move away from the edge of the cliff, and I turn back curiously.

He stands where he is, looking out into the immeasurable distance, and he cups his hands around his mouth and shouts out into the countryside, his voice bouncing off rock and seemingly the sky itself, reverberating all around us. "I give you William Blaxton," he shouts, "known as Blackstone, wizard and founder of the realm known as Parsymeon and eventually as Boston. Here shall the force of his magic be felt forevermore. So be it." He sweeps his hands down sharply with the last proclamation, and a sudden gale sends me staggering a few steps in his direction. Leaves and twigs and even small pebbles swirl around us, and across from us, with a loud dramatic crack, a crevice appears in the cliff, from which water bubbles in a steady, trickling waterfall. The gale dies down, and we watch the flow of the water over the cliff opposite us.

Ben nods, and he looks at me and smiles. He seems much better. His eyes are a clear, pale blue. "That was old magic," he tells me. "Old *wizard* magic. Not my style at all. I've never even tried that before. Will, I think, would be very pleased with the result."

Because Ben looks so happy with it, I agree with him. "I think he would be too."

And I think, *Benedict Le Fay will betray you. And then he will die.* Nowhere did anyone ever mention the loss we've actually suffered. I wonder if it's true, what everyone has been telling me, that my mother was lying. And even if she wasn't, Will just sacrificed himself instead, to save Ben. It doesn't seem to me outside the realm of possibility.

We walk to the cave, Ben's steps firm and purposeful.

When we enter, everyone stops talking and looks at us expectantly.

"We're at Thingvellir," Ben announces. "We can go."

"Back to Boston?" says Safford.

"Yes. We're going to drive the Seelies out of Parsymeon once and for all, and out of the Otherworld as well. I hear that it's almost twelve o'clock."

CHAPTER 22

A moment of silence follows Ben's announcement.

Kelsey is the one who breaks it, saying, "I'm going to need a bit of help." She gestures to her ankle.

Ben frowns at it.

"Can you fix it?" I ask him.

He shakes his head. "Not my kind of magic, unfortunately."

"Right," says Merrow. "But it is Trow's."

Ben looks at him in surprise. "Are you a caretaker?"

Trow looks uncertain. "That's what they say, but I…Look, I'm not *magic*."

"You're a fay," Ben says. "You must be magic."

"Right, but…I don't know. What they seem to tell me is magic is just something that kind of…*happens*. I don't feel like I'm *doing magic*."

I think of my naming magic, and how I never really had to know what to do—I just *did* it. "It just comes to you," I say at the same time as Merrow says the exact same thing. We look at each other for a moment of pleased solidarity.

Merrow turns to Trow. "At least try," she says.

"Um," says Kelsey nervously. "Don't you think that *I* should have a say? I mean, no offense, but you don't know what you're doing. What happens if you do it wrong?"

"I have no idea," says Trow.

"Comforting," says Kelsey after a beat.

"Look," sighs Ben, "I don't mean to be practical here, because it's not really my forte, but Will's sacrifice is only going to help for so long, and then we'll be back on the map and the Seelies will find us in a pig's whisper. If you're going to do it, do it now."

Kelsey licks her lips. Her breaths are labored and her face is white with pain. "Do it," she commands. "Before I change my mind."

"Just kind of let it happen," Merrow tells Trow and squeezes his hand comfortingly. "Like you did when I burned my hand in Roger Williams's kitchen."

No, seriously, I think. What are our *lives*?

Trow kind of *looks* very hard at Kelsey.

Kelsey gasps, and for a moment I'm worried that Trow has actually made everything much worse, but then Kelsey says in surprise, "Oh," and she doesn't sound like she's in any pain at all. Her ankle, in fact, looks back to normal. She moves it around experimentally.

Then she looks at Trow in shock. "That was *amazing*."

I am looking at him in shock too. "That was fantastic!" His talent seems a lot better than my naming nonsense at the moment.

"Yes, yes, it's caretaker magic," grumbles Ben. "It's pretty standard in the Otherworld."

"Not unique and showy," says the Erlking, deadpan, "the way a traveler is."

Ben glowers and says, "We'll meet you back in Boston? We're going to need your army."

"It has been at your disposal." The Erlking bows low with a dramatic sweep of his cape. "I'll meet you in Boston. I take it you won't be obscuring yourself?"

"I do not intend on keeping a low profile," Ben says. "Hold hands, everyone. Stay together. Next stop Boston."

The next thing I know, we're all crowded in a dark, cold, damp cement room.

"Where are we?" Kelsey asks.

"Where did I say we were going?" responds Ben. "It's Boston."

"It's not Beacon Hill," I point out. In fact, I have no idea where we are.

"I wasn't aiming for Beacon Hill," Ben replies darkly. He is regarding a chained door in front of us. *Warning*, reads a sign on the door. *Alarm will sound.*

"That's a fire exit door," Kelsey tells him.

"I know."

"An alarm's going to go off."

"Let it," he says, sounding satisfied at the prospect. "I want every bell in Boston ringing." Ben flings out his arm, an appropriately dramatic gesture, and the door flies open in front of us.

Bells begin to clang, loud and insistent, but they are

high-pitched enough that they don't have any effect on me. We are standing at the top of a staircase, and Ben descends it. I follow close behind him, and when we reach the bottom, I realize that we're at the end of the Red Line platform in Park Street, where the fire exit staircase is located. Chaos is reigning. People are hastily trying to get off the platform, assuming there's some kind of emergency.

Ben leads us through the melee of the station until we get aboveground.

"Was that really necessary?" I ask him.

"I told you I wasn't keeping a low profile," he replies, not pausing as he strides through the Common toward my house. "We're here. I want them to come and get us."

"Is that a good idea?" I ask. "To taunt them?"

"Yes, actually," Safford replies from behind us. "They're not terribly rational beings, and they'll be even less so incensed like this."

"And it's almost twelve o'clock anyway," Ben says and gestures to the clock on the bell tower of Park Street Church. Ominously, it reads 11:59.

The half-light seems a bit brighter than it had been before. The lavender windowpanes at my house are picking up the brightening rays. And the air seems thinner, much easier to breathe.

Kelsey says, "It's almost like the sun is trying to come out. Are we fighting back?"

"No, they're just getting closer," Ben says grimly. "This is enchanted air. Can't you feel it? They'll strangle us slowly, the way they do in Tir na nOg."

I remember how I didn't even know I wasn't breathing right in Tir na nOg until the moment we cleared the prison walls and Ben told me to take a deep breath. He's right that the air in Boston feels startlingly similar to that right now.

My aunts must have sensed our return, because they open the door for us as soon as we cross Beacon Street, and they fall upon me in tight hugs.

"Did you find the other fay?"

"No." Ben looks disdainfully at the box, which Safford has been carting around. "We got *that*."

Aunt True has been looking around and says suddenly, "But where's Will?"

There is a moment of silence. I remember it then, that my aunt and Will had a history from long ago. I look at her and say gently, "Aunt True..." I don't know what to say next.

Aunt True, her eyes wide with horror, shrinks away from me, stumbling. "No," she whispers. "No. It can't be."

"He did it to take us off the map," Ben says solemnly. "It was—"

"Noble," Aunt Virtue finishes, putting an arm around Aunt True to comfort her. "He saved our Selkie for us. You see? As he always promised us he would. He kept his promise in the end."

"How can there…how can there be a Boston without Will? He was here before us. I thought he would be here after us." Aunt True looks stricken.

"Something tells me it won't be the last thing to change about Boston before this is all over," says Ben grimly, going to look out the window.

Not helping, I think at him furiously and join Aunt Virtue in hugging Aunt True, who is weeping softly.

"First Etherington," she is saying, "and now Will…"

"Dad's not dead," I insist. I feel everyone look at me, but it's Ben I look back at in challenge. "He's not!"

"Have you heard any news?" Ben asks after a moment of silence.

"Just the clock ticking," Aunt Virtue answers, still comforting Aunt True with one arm around her shoulders while with the other arm, she gestures at the grandfather clock on the landing. I glance at it. 11:59, just like the Park Street Church clock. "The bells have already begun chiming. We have heard reports. Every non-Seelie enchantment in this world is dying."

"What are we going to do next?" Aunt True sniffles.

Ben looks at Merrow. "What does the prophecy say?"

"It doesn't say anything," Merrow says, sounding miserable. "It said to go to Iceland. I thought that would help."

We all look at the box, still stubbornly closed.

"Maybe we got the wrong thing," says Safford.

"Maybe we need all four of us to open it," I say. "And we've only got three."

There's a moment of silence.

"I guess I'll go outside and start asking people for their birthdays," I decide.

And then there's a knock on the door.

We look at it, and then I swallow and move forward and peer through the window on the side of the door. As if the Seelies, if they showed up, were going to *knock*. The Erlking. I open the door for him.

He steps in and says, "Benedict," and then pauses.

Ben looks at him questioningly.

"Can you…" The Erlking pauses again. Whatever he's about to say, it's paining him to say it. "Can you hide names?"

"No," Ben replies, a bit sourly. "My mother could, but I don't know how."

"Ah," says the Erlking and nods.

"I could obscure them," Ben offers. "Maybe. For a bit."

There is a moment of stilted silence. I look between the two of them. "That would be helpful. If you could. If we could dilute the power of the Seelies' words, just for a little while. Otherwise it's going to be a slaughter."

"I can do it," says Ben. "Although I need to know the names to cast the enchantment. And it would only be temporary. It would be like wrapping the name up in a bow. They'd need to rip through the ribbon before they could do the naming, but they'd do it."

"Any time you can give us at all," the Erlking insists. He pauses and then says, "It's Kainen."

I'm surprised. I look at Ben, who also looks surprised, but he nods and says, "Right. Done. What about the rest of your army?"

"Could you come?"

Ben looks at all of us.

"Go," I tell him. "All I'm going to do is ask people on the street."

We have one minute left, but luckily the length of a minute depends on the time you're keeping, so I am able to stand outside with Kelsey and Merrow and Trow and Safford and canvass up and down the street, asking people's birthdays. My aunts stay in the house, "fortifying," although I don't especially know what that means. I wonder if they are offering to help out the gnomes they've been fighting with my whole life, if perhaps having a greater enemy in common will help finally forge an alliance.

I hope they're having success "fortifying," because we get nowhere.

Kelsey and I end up pausing together. I look out over Boston Common and think how this is so weird: it could be any other day, except it's *not*.

"How's your ankle?" I ask.

"Good as new, actually. That was some amazing magic."

"I wish I had magic that useful," I say. I wonder if he'll be able to heal some of our casualties in the battle. What sort of casualties will they be? Will there be blood? Will there be weapons?

"You've got pretty useful magic. Well, it seems that way to me anyway." Kelsey pauses. "Wait, what's your magic again?"

She is saying it to tease me. I pretend to laugh for her sake and say, "Stop it. I can name people."

"Well, that's apparently terrifying if you're an Otherworld creature, right?"

"Apparently. I don't know what good it's going to do me though. I don't know any of the Seelie names. I don't know what I'm going to do." I pause. "I guess I can heal a bit by giving people my name, but I don't know how much good that will do. Have you gotten in touch with your mother?"

Kelsey shakes her head. "Not picking up. I left her another message."

I think of my father and wonder. "Do you think she's okay?"

"None of us are okay, right? What happens if the Seelies win here?"

"I have no idea," I admit.

"Will it be the end of the world? Or just the end of Boston? Or will Boston even notice that all of its supernatural inhabitants are suddenly going to disappear? I mean, are you going to disappear? I would have noticed if you disappeared."

"Not if they make you forget I ever existed," I point out and try to sound frank and matter-of-fact about all of this.

"Hi," Merrow says, pausing by us. "No luck?"

Kelsey and I shake our heads.

Then I say, because this person has dropped into our lives out of nowhere and we're somehow connected and we might all be dead in a few minutes or hours or days, depending on the time you're keeping, and I don't know anything about her, "Do you live here?"

She shakes her head. "Rhode Island. Me and Trow."

"Oh, right," I realize. "Roger Williams makes sense then. When did you find out you were a fay?"

"Yesterday. Or decades ago. It's weird. It's like I can't tell."

"I know exactly how you feel."

Merrow looks at me and gives me a hesitant smile. "What's your magic?" she asks.

"Naming."

"Be happy it's not telling the future. I feel like none of it is ever anything good. I'd like to have a vision of something good, you know? Like me in my wedding dress or something. But no. I get to have a vision of some random thing in Iceland. And then, after that, nothing."

"Nothing?" I ask.

Merrow looks at me.

"Does that mean we lose?" asks Kelsey after a moment.

Merrow doesn't answer.

CHAPTER 23

B en looks tired when he comes back from casting enchantments over the army and meets us on the street. We've scattered again, back to asking for birthdays.

I just shake my head at him. He walks up the front steps, pokes his head in the front door, then comes out and sits on the stoop.

"Still 11:59," he says in answer to my querying glance.

"Will it just stay like that forever?" I ask, frustrated.

Ben sighs and leans back on his elbows. "They're toying with us. They love to toy."

I look down the street, waiting for a pedestrian that Merrow, Trow, Kelsey, and Safford haven't cornered yet. "How did the army thing go?" I ask awkwardly.

"Fine," he says, which I think is a silly answer considering our topic of conversation, but then I guess my question was a silly question to start with.

It's getting brighter out. I could almost use sunglasses. I wonder if anyone is commenting on the weird weather. Then again, Boston is prone to weird weather.

I look back at Ben. His eyes are closed. "We need the other fay, don't we? To even have a chance."

Ben doesn't answer. He takes a deep breath.

"You're tired," I say.

"A lot of energy expended just now. And the air is thin. I'll be fine. Just getting my bearings."

I look at him and think of how I've helped to recharge him before, so I go and sit next to him and slide my hand into his. He opens his eyes in surprise, and there is a moment when we look directly at each other. I am waiting for him to ask me a question, and I don't know what the question is going to be or how I'm going to answer it. But then he just closes his eyes again.

"You can say my name if you want," I say.

He shakes his head. "Not just yet. We'll save it for something bigger. I don't want to dilute it. I wish Will were here, just so I could have you name him." Ben opens his eyes and looks at me. "I'm sorry, you know," he says. His eyes are dark and heavy and sad. "For leaving you on the Common that day. I'm just…sorry. You've always taken me by such surprise, and I've always behaved so poorly in response."

I hold my breath, lick my lips, and say, "Ben." Then I don't know what else to say.

"I really am so sorry, Selkie," he says. "For everything."

"Don't talk like it's over," I tell him, because I realize suddenly what he's doing. "Don't tell me good-bye."

"I don't know what else to do," he says, his voice urgent. He sits up and lifts his free hand. He pushes my hair behind my ear and leaves his hand on my cheek in a caress, and I am furious that he would do this *now*.

"We have to beat them. We have to win."

Ben shakes his head a little bit and closes his eyes.

"Ben. Listen to me." I lean over him a bit more, getting myself closer to him, as if with proximity I can convince him of what I'm saying, even though his eyes aren't even open. "How can we fight? We don't know their names, so we can't name them, so tell me what else we can do."

"I don't know," Ben groans. "We don't know the right words."

"What does that mean?" I demand.

"There's power. In words. If we could find the right ones, the right combination…That's why the Seelies don't write things down—they don't want to capture the power in the words. If we could find the right words, the right story to tell, then maybe…But the fourth fay must be the key, because otherwise I've no idea what…" Ben opens his eyes, realizes for the first time exactly how close to him I am.

"The right story to tell," I echo him. "We need to rewrite the story."

"I guess," he says, "that would be one way of putting it."

"It's what Merrow said her mother said to do. Rewrite the story. It's what you're saying to do too. Find the right story."

"Words have power. You know that. But the right story involved four fays, and I don't know what you're going to do without them."

And then Park Street Church starts chiming the hour, the grandfather clock in the house echoing it.

One, two, three, go the chimes, and Merrow, Trow, Safford, and Kelsey all leave off talking to the pedestrians and instinctively hurry back toward where Ben and I are sitting on the steps of the house.

Four, five, six, go the chimes, and Ben draws his hand out of mine and stands warily. I follow suit.

Seven, eight, nine, go the chimes, and we are all looking around us, waiting for something to happen.

Ten, eleven, twelve.

CHAPTER 24

There is a sharp, resounding crack, and Seelies tumble headlong from the sky over the Common. On the sidewalk, people have stopped to look. The cars on Beacon Street have slowed to a crawl, as their drivers are clearly gaping at the supernatural hole that has opened up over their heads.

"They need to keep moving," Ben says. "Why don't they keep moving?"

"Because do you *see* that?" says Trow, pointing at the hole in the sky.

"That's exactly why they should keep moving. *Humans.*" Ben takes a step forward, as if to prosaically direct the traffic away from the Seelies, just as a howling noise starts up.

"What's that?" Kelsey asks.

"Wind," answers Ben, as if there can be nothing worse than that.

It's frequently windy in Boston, so I don't know what to make of that.

Ben shouts at everyone around us, "Run! Run for your lives!"

The people on the sidewalk look at him in curious puzzlement.

And then the wind slams into us. It's so strong that, for a moment, I think an actual enormous hand has reached out and slapped me backward, up against the front door, holding me in place. But it's just the wind, so forceful that I can barely breathe.

It ends just as suddenly as it started, and I flop unceremoniously to the top step of the stoop without the wind there to hold me up. There is a moment of complete silence, because none of us had been able to get up enough breath to scream or utter any noise at all. And then noise rushes in—the people on the street screaming and shouting, children wailing.

I stagger to my feet and take stock of everyone else. Breathless but basically okay. My head is buzzing a little bit from where I knocked it hard against the wall, but I can push through that.

"Everyone okay?" asks Trow, looking around at us, and I have this thought about him being a natural caretaker.

Ben has recovered. "Go!" he is shouting at the panicked people in the street. "Get out! Move!" And then he turns back to us and says hastily, "Get in the house. It's safest there. Don't move." And then he leaps lightly down into the street, toward the Seelies assembling on the Common.

Like hell I'm going in the house while he runs out into battle. Traffic has thronged around a car accident, and people are abandoning their cars. I don't see the Seelies anymore, which is terrifying to me. Weren't they just tumbling out of the sky? I can't even hear any bells chiming. Did they just blow a wind and leave? It seems unlikely, but I don't know what else to think.

"Go, go, go!" Ben is shouting at people as he darts among the cars, opening doors and pulling people out of them.

Everyone looks shocked, like they don't know what to make of him, and I don't blame them. But I understand what he's trying to do. Wherever the Seelies are, they haven't gone forever. They're going to come back. All they've done so far is blow a little wind, but I am sure they can do much worse.

So I run out into the street, following his lead, urging people along, off the street. "Where are we sending them to?" I shout to Ben.

"What are you doing out here?" he snaps at me, and then he is off, trying to turn some cars around that have joined the melee.

"Ben said the house was safest," Kelsey says by my side. "Can we put a bunch of them in the house with us—"

There is a flash of white light so bright that it blinds us. The screams which had been dying down are renewed, except that now no one can see, so people are stumbling around, knocking me this way and that. And when the light dies down, the howling starts again, from far away.

Wind, I think and dive for the nearest car, ducking down behind it. But then the street underneath me starts shaking. I look down at it in shock. The people around me actually fall quiet. We are all looking down at the pavement underneath us as it starts to crack and buckle.

I look up at Ben, who is staring off down Beacon Street, toward the Public Garden. I follow his gaze, and what I see doesn't make any sense. I blink, trying to figure it out, but it looks like…a wave. A wave of…concrete, rising up and then over the buildings and trees, cars gathering in front of it like foam would in water. That can't be possible. But it seems as if all of Boston is turning into an ocean of movement right in front of us.

"Get off the street!" Ben shouts, and then he reaches for me. I see him do it, almost as if in slow motion. I see him lean to grab me, and then the street underneath me jumps, flinging me off like I'm nothing but a rag doll.

There is a moment as I'm flying through the air when everything seems silent and still. And then I land with a thud, with a crack in my ear that I imagine is my own skull. I try to pick myself up, but I put weight on my arm when I do it and it gives way with blinding pain. *Broken*, I think. It seems that way.

I try sitting up again, more carefully this time, and wait for a nauseous moment of dizzying pain to pass. I'm on the Common. From the street, there is still screaming and shouting, although there is less, and I think about what that might mean, of the people who must already have died. The concrete and cars are still going this way and that, tossed in a tempest, and I can see people's bodies flying through the air, the way mine did. A woman in jeans and Uggs and a black pea coat lands not far from me with an unpleasant crunch. Blood spreads out underneath her onto the dead grass, and she doesn't move again. There is a little girl crying nearby, hands pressed around her thigh, blood pouring through her fingers.

I should get to her, I think. Although what am I going to do? How am I going to help? I feel powerless, and I wonder where Ben is. Or Trow. Trow has healing powers, right? He could heal my broken arm, and then maybe he could also do something for these poor people.

And then I think of the rags in my pocket, taken from the Urisks. *Tourniquets*, I think, and get up and struggle over to the little girl. Someone else has stopped to help, which is good, because I still have a broken arm to deal with and can't tie.

"She needs a tourniquet," I gasp and thrust the fabric at the man.

He looks panicked but also like he understands, taking the proffered fabric and getting to work.

"What's your name?" I ask the little girl.

"Hannah," she manages.

"*Hannah*," I say gently, infusing it with all of the warm intent that I can.

And Hannah stops sobbing, her face lightening. She actually almost smiles. "That feels better," she tells the man still tying the tourniquet, who looks up at her, surprised.

I stand, pleased that I was able to make it better for her, and look around, getting my bearings, trying to find someone else who I might still be able to help.

As I am thinking it, just like that, a Seelie appears in front of me. And smiles. "Selkie," this Seelie says, and the pain is like a vice around my brain. I find myself falling back to the ground, writhing with pain, and those moans of agony I hear, those are mine.

When the world stops swirling Technicolor with pain, I pant for breath, lying on my back, staring up at the Seelie over me. He smiles, one of those anti-smiles that they're so expert in, and I brace myself, wondering if he knows enough of my name to name me, if this is the end, what it will feel like—

A man suddenly throws himself onto the Seelie, knocking him to the ground, and once he has him pinned, he pulls out a sword and slices it clean through the Seelie's neck, severing his head. I cry out in surprise, because I can't help it, but then the Seelie's head reattaches and he smiles his anti-smile again.

The goblin—I can only assume it is a goblin—starts just hacking away at the Seelie, not that it seems to matter, because the Seelie just keeps fixing itself. But at least he's distracted. This is my opportunity, I know, as they grapple with each other, but in my haste, I jostle my arm enough that pain blossoms through me anew.

When I get to my feet, I can see that the Common is dotted over with skirmishes, Seelies clashing with goblins. The goblins are all flashing swords that glint in the bright, artificial Seelie sunlight as they heave them around, stabbing through Seelies who all seem completely unaffected by it.

I don't know what to do. The world seems to be swimming

around me, but I can't tell if it's from pain or because I feel like I can't really breathe or if it really is pitching and heaving to and fro. I try to struggle back to my house, but I feel like I am never going to get there. I wonder where everyone else is, if they're okay, if the house is even still standing. The street in front of me is still a frothy tempest of concrete and cars.

And I feel like I have barely taken two steps when my mother says, with false sweetness, "Selkie."

I wince at the pinch of the pain, not as severe as when the other Seelie used my name. My mother, I think, is just toying with me, the way Ben said: the Seelies like to toy.

"I don't think we finished our discussion," she says pleasantly as she falls into step behind me.

I limp another step forward, feeling like every bone in my body is a protesting bruise, and then I whirl on her. "Where is my father?" I demand between my teeth.

She anti-smiles at me. "Wouldn't you like to know?"

"Yes," I retort. "I would."

She leans down, puts her face very close to mine, and whispers smoothly, "Would you? Would you like to see your father?"

I answer before I can think. "Yes," I say furiously.

A sharp pain runs through me, and I convulse with it. I have the strangest sensation, as if my blood is spilling out of my fingers and onto the floor, although my hands look perfectly normal. There is just *pain*, spreading through my center, spreading through the *world*.

I look from my hands to my mother, who is watching me with detached satisfaction. "What are you doing?" I gasp out. "What are you doing to me?"

"Selkie!"

I hear Ben shout my name, and I even turn in his direction. He is dashing toward me, Kelsey behind him, but they seem far away.

"Selkie!" Kelsey screams, launching herself toward me. "Grab my hand!"

Why does she want me to grab her hand? I wonder. *Where does she think I'm going? Why doesn't she just lean over and get me, I'm right there—*

—And then I'm not.

I am in a huge, light room overlooking a vast ocean.

With my mother.

CHAPTER 25

The room is gorgeous, hewn out of a bright white stone, and, except for me and my mother, completely empty. Archways run across the opposite end of it, open to the air, and warm, delicious breezes drift through. My mother anti-smiles at me and then walks confidently away, over to the archways, and then she turns to the left.

"Where are we?" I shout at her. "Where is everyone? Where's *Dad*?"

"Come along, Selkie," her voice drifts back to me. I wince in reaction and then hurry up to follow her.

We walk beside the archways. The view beyond them is an expanse of deep blue sea stretching out to meet a paler blue sky. It's gorgeous, frankly. The castle appears to be perched on a cliff right at the edge of the water.

"Here you are." My mother opens a door that appears in front of us onto a large, airy bathroom, tiled over completely in colorful mosaics in shades of rose and gold and turquoise. There is a huge tub that seems to have been made out of a seashell, and a matching seashell sink and sea-shell toilet. And there is a bright blue Seelie dress hanging by the window opening in the wall, edged with tiny, jingling bells.

"It matches your eyes," my mother tells me.

"Where is my father?" I ask, voice steely.

"All in good time."

"No," I insist. "Not in good time. Now. I don't have time for this."

"Oh, you delightful little creature." She looks down at me from her full height and tsks. "You have nothing *but* time. All the time in the Otherworld and the Thisworld. Because of the time you're keeping. You think you need to get back home to fight your little battle." And then she laughs. "Don't worry. No matter how much time you spend here, we will still be able to bring you back to Boston in time to see it fall, to see it topple back into the sea it was stolen from in the first place." And then she closes the door behind me.

I stare after her. Because I'm pretty sure that where I am is Avalon. *A fay on Avalon*, Ben's mother had said. The warring prophecy. I am helping the wrong prophecy win. I have to get away from here.

Somehow.

I tear out of the bathroom with no clear idea where I'm going, which is as faerie of me as I've ever been, to have not even a shadow of a plan.

My mother is standing at one of the archways, talking to someone else. She turns toward me immediately.

"Ah. Selkie," she says, and I bite my tongue with the hiss of pain that comes with it. "You didn't change."

I have nothing to say to that. I look around, trying to find some way out, but I have no idea where I could run where I wouldn't be caught immediately.

"No matter," says my mother. "I did not expect you to be satisfactory, even now. Come here, my dear."

I do so, because now I recognize the faerie at her side.

"You know our darling Benedict's mother, don't you?"

Ben's mother smiles at me. "It's so nice to see you again, Selkie."

"Likewise," I lie and smile sweetly. *I'm half Seelie*, I think. *I can play this game too.*

"It seems you've injured your arm," says Ben's mother, and just like that, it stops hurting me.

I look down at it, move it experimentally. It's as good as new.

I refuse to thank her for that. I look at my mother instead. "Where's Dad? What have you done to him?"

She blinks at me and puts a dramatic hand to her throat, as if taken aback at my accusation. "Why, I've done nothing at all to him! He is going to join us for dinner."

"Now that you mention it," remarks Ben's mother, "isn't it time for dinner?"

"Depending on the time, indeed." My mother waves her hand, and it sounds as if she's ringing a tiny dinner bell.

A table appears by one of the archways, laid out with a bright white tablecloth and gleaming china, silver, and crystal.

I take my seat slowly. My muscles are literally jumping to get away instead, but I need to play this game until I can figure out a way to get out, to save the right prophecy. My mother walks away to the right, into a hallway that swallows her into darkness. I wonder if this is my chance to make a break for it, but Ben's mother looks hard at me and I think not.

The room pulses with the energy of named faeries—I can feel it in my bones. They whisper around me, crying out for help. I think of all of these voices begging me for help, and I don't know what to do, what I *can* do. I am failing right now at saving my own *father*, never mind the rest of the faeries who are counting on me.

Ben's mother sits next to me and studies me. "I must say, I am *very* surprised to see you looking so…well."

I think of the cursed coat that should have killed me. "You shouldn't be. He's stronger than you. You know it, and he knows it. If I were you, I'd be worried."

Ben's mother doesn't look worried. She just lifts her eyebrows. "Bold words from a young fay trapped on the Isle of Avalon."

"I've been trapped before. Haven't you heard? I escaped from Tir na nOg."

"You did that with Benedict. Benedict can't get to you here."

"What makes you so sure?"

"Because we're on an island, Selkie."

She does not say my name with intent. She doesn't have to. She has said the one, simple fact that finally begins to make me worried. We're on an island. I look out at the ocean, at the expanse of limitless water, and nerves knot in my stomach.

But I didn't have to swim to get here. Maybe Ben won't have to swim to get here. Or maybe someone else will get here to me. Merrow was good with prophecies. Maybe she'll see something that will tell her where I am, and they will come and save me, the way they all came and saved me before.

Except that they are in the middle of fighting a losing battle that I've abandoned them in.

A tiny voice inside me says, *Why would they even want to save you now?*

"Here she is!" exclaims my mother gaily.

I immediately leap out of my seat, turning to face her. My father is standing with her, looking lost and confused, which is just how my father so frequently looks. It is my *father*, and I run to him, flinging myself onto him, and I realize that I am crying as I bury my face in his shoulder. He smells like my father. He feels like my father. He is *alive*. I cry with relief.

He lifts his arms and closes me into a hug. "There, there," he soothes me and lays his cheek on my head. "There, there."

"It's me," I weep against him. "It's Selkie."

"I know who it is." He sounds offended.

I laugh at his offense. He sounds like normal. This is such an unexpectedly wonderful thing to have happen, and my crying shifts suddenly, away from relief, back toward despair. I want to have a happy ending. I want us to go back to Boston.

I want Ben to be back on the Common. I want to lie in the sunlight and drink lemonade. I want it so much I ache for it.

I am never going to get it, I think.

"There, there," my father says again. "It will be okay, Selkie. It's all true. Didn't I tell you? It's all true."

I try to catch my breath, to stop my tears. Now, alone with my father depending on me to get us out of this, is not the time for me to fall to pieces. "What's all true?" I ask and lift my head to look at him.

"*Everything*," he says.

"Yes," I agree, because it makes sense to me. "Yes. It is."

"Now." My mother claps behind us. "Touching reunion concluded, it is time for us to eat."

I walk with my father over to the table and we sit down together. The food is Seelie food, fluffy mashed potatoes that taste like fresh strawberries and heaps of turkey that taste like milk. I pick at it, pushing it around on my plate, and debate how to escape. Water doesn't bother me. Could *I* swim away? Could I make it with my father? I can't *leave* him here.

"Don't you want to know the story?" my mother asks eventually.

"The story of what?"

"The story of *you*."

"I know my story."

"No, you don't. You know part of your story. You know bits and pieces of your story. But the whole thing. Your story

270

is the most important thing. Stories *are* the most important things, you know. The stories we tell. The words we use. Selkie Stewart. The fay of the autumnal equinox. So much *prophecy* around you. Your name shows up in the very oldest of the books about Boston. Did you never wonder about that?"

I think back to before I ever knew any of this. Flipping through an ancient book Will had given me from the Salem Which Museum.

My mother doesn't wait for a response. "For so long, Selkie Stewart. For so long, we have been waiting. You included, although you don't remember it. Will was very good, very clever. You leaked through to some records, but in many—in most—you never existed. Impossible to find. Hidden from view. Protected by the very strongest enchantments he could find. Present company excluded." My mother indicates Ben's mother.

Ben's mother inclines her head and sips her wine. "Of course."

"But we have been planning this. I know what you're thinking: how very shocking, for the Seelies to *plan*. I must admit, it was very difficult to get the other Seelies to go along with it, and they do keep forgetting and losing their way every so often. But Ben's mother is so very good at it. Planning comes naturally to her."

I look at Ben's mother, who anti-smiles at me.

"And so," continues my mother, "we have been planning. How to get to *you*. You all have your weak points, each of you fays, because you are none of you fully faerie, and therefore you are none of you entirely strong. Because all of you *love*. It is the great vulnerability, you know. All of this *affection*. So it could have been any of you, any of you fays that we went after, but in the end, it was you who had to be the fay chosen to come here to Avalon to seal the reign of the Seelies forever. At first, we thought that the great weakness would be through Benedict. Your feelings for Benedict are so adorable, so quaint. But that turned out not entirely as prophesied." My mother sends a dark look to Ben's mother.

Ben's mother says lightly, "On your end, as well. Don't forget, she escaped your prison before she escaped mine."

My mother ignores her. "Benedict turned out not to be the key. It was your father. Your love for your father would drive you here, and it would keep you here, willingly. And thus, we would have you, your power, your strength, here in Avalon, keeping us safe forever."

But this is all unnecessary, I think. They would be safe forever because we don't know where the other fay is. Because Ben's mother hid the other fay from us. Wasn't that part of their original plan?

But I don't say that, because I don't want to say anything.

"So, in the end," my mother continues, "we won. Here you are, alone on Avalon." My mother's eyes turn hard upon me. She is not smiling now. She is the most terrifying I have ever seen her. "Centuries ago, William Blaxton founded Parsymeon as a refuge for those who refuse to submit to the will of the Courts. Today, Parsymeon falls. Today, we ensure the harmonious ruling of the Courts forever."

My mother and Ben's mother clink their wineglasses together. It is a sound like a chiming jingle bell. I sit in dread.

"What is it?" my mother snaps, surprising me, and I realize she is talking to a small creature who has come bounding up to us.

"It's an Urisk!" I exclaim, unable to help myself.

"I am the only Urisk," he tells me mournfully. "There are no other Urisks in existence."

"Yes, yes," my mother interrupts impatiently. "What have you come in for?"

The Urisk hesitates, bouncing on the soles of his feet, and then he leans up and whispers in my mother's ear.

Her entire expression changes. She lights up. "*Really?*" she drawls. "Well, that is excellent news." She smiles at the Urisk, and then she says lightly, "Urisk."

The Urisk gives a little cry and disintegrates on the spot into dandelion fluff that drifts away through the room.

And the awful thing is that I see it, and it's horrifying, but I also feel the burst of power that comes from it, warm, like sinking into a hot bath. There is a piece of me I can feel that would bask in that, that understands why the Seelies do such things, because if I reached out and let myself grab it, it would feel heavenly.

My mother and Ben's mother both breathe deep and smile, satisfied, drinking in the little burst of power.

"Why did you do that?" I manage to choke out.

My mother looks at me, her hard eyes glittering. "Why not?" Then she gets to her feet. "Shall we go for a stroll?"

CHAPTER 26

We leave the castle, because I don't know what else to do, and anyway I want to get out of that room with its leftover naming power making me feel itchy. We walk down steps roughly carved into the cliff until we come to an expanse of beautiful white sand beach. The waves curl and lick over the sand, coaxing it into ripples under the weight of the water. The beach stretches around us in either direction, as far as I can see, uninterrupted except for a bundle of something a few hundred feet away from us, noteworthy as the only blemish on the postcard nature of the scene. I know I should be focused on it, but I can't; I am mostly focused on the fact that I have ruined everything. *Me*. After spending all of this time trying to set the prophecy into motion, I have been the one to destroy it.

My mother strides confidently over the sand to the bundle, followed by Ben's mother. I struggle to keep up with them, keeping my hand firmly in my father's. Now that I've found him, now that I have effectively given up everything else for him, I'm not going to let anything take him away from me.

The bundle takes on a shape. It's a person, I can see that now. A person sprawled on his or her side, the waves still sliding at their legs. A man, I realize, as we get closer. A man with a tumble of dark, thick curls…I draw to a slow halt, my feet dragging in the sand, as I stare at the form in the sand. His face is turned away, but I would know him anywhere, of course I would.

Anxious with fear, I drop my father's hand and dash over the sand, past Ben's mother and my mother, dropping to my knees in the sand beside Ben and pushing him over onto his back. He is very still, his pale skin tinged with blue, his eyelashes stark against his cheekbones.

"Ben," I say desperately, my mind a panicked maelstrom of *Benedict Le Fay will betray you. And then he will die.*

He doesn't respond.

His jacket is sodden, sticking to his skin with wetness. I tug clumsily at the zipper, finally forcing it down, and struggle to pull it off of him. He is heavy and limp and reacts not at all to the poking and prodding and shoving I am doing.

"Ben," I say again. "Benedict." I look in dismay at the soaked shirts he's still wearing and curl my hand into his. "Come on, Ben." I lean my forehead down onto his shoulder. "Come on," I whisper.

Ben does not move. He does not breathe.

"Ben," I beg, and I tell myself that the sound I make is not a sob.

"Look at that," I hear my mother drawl behind me. "True devotion. That's what that is."

"I don't understand," I say, and I lift my head and shout at her. "What happened to him? What did you do to him?"

"*I* didn't do anything to him. He swam to you, my dear."

This doesn't make any sense. "What do you mean? He knows how to swim?"

"No," she answers. "Obviously not."

"Then why did he do it?" I know the answer even before I ask the question: he did it for me.

My mother must reach the same conclusion—that I already know the answer—because she doesn't bother to reply to me. She walks over and drops a blanket unceremoniously next to me. I look at it, blinking through my tears, wondering where it came from. "Dry him off."

"But—"

"Get him dry, Selkie. He'll be fine. And then I can name him. It's no fun naming a half-dead faerie. You get barely any charge out of it at all." She walks away through the sand to the castle.

I look at Ben's mother, who gazes inscrutably at Ben's body on the sand, and then turns and follows my mother. I look at my father for a moment, and then I swipe at my tears and concentrate on getting Ben dry.

After a bit of struggle, I eventually get Ben out of his soaked shirts. My father sits in the sand near me, watching and biting his thumbnail nervously. I can tell that he is concerned for me, but that he doesn't understand why or what I am doing.

I consider taking off Ben's jeans. I had ideas about the first time I would take off Ben's jeans. These ideas did not go like this. I fret about it, and then I decide that I have to save him and I have to get him dry to do it, and the jeans aren't helping.

So I take off his jeans.

Not as easy as it sounds, since the jeans are wet and difficult to work with. Ben remains unresponsive, but I manage to get them over his bare feet and toss them aside. I steadfastly do not gape at the sight of Ben in his underwear, because now is not the time for such things. Although I look enough to know that he's wearing underwear, which is a relief. I wasn't sure if faeries believed in such things, and I can barely take the intimacy of seeing Ben's bare feet, never mind Ben completely naked.

I spread the blanket over him and rub at him briskly.

When I've gotten Ben as dry as I think I can get him, I flip the blanket over so that the driest side is touching him, and I lie down next to him and curl my hand into his. And I wait.

She said he wasn't dead. I have to trust that he's not dead. But he stays still and cold next to me, while the sun dips into the ocean stretched beside us and the stars come out overhead. Dusk glows around us, and I stare at the rhythm of the waves as they push and pull at the shore, half-mesmerized by it. I think about the battle in Boston, and whether they've already lost it, and whether everyone has been named.

Ben takes a sudden, deep, shuddering breath beside me and then rolls over away from me, choking and sputtering. I sit up in alarm, watching, uncertain what I can do to help, and eventually he catches his breath and rolls back toward me. He looks exhausted and unwell, half in twilight shadow, and I can't even tell what color his eyes are as they gaze up at me.

"Selkie Stewart," he says thickly, as if his tongue is swollen.

"Did that help?" I ask anxiously. "Use my middle name. I'll give you both of them."

He shakes his head against the sand. "It helped." His voice does sound clearer. "I'm naked," he remarks.

I probably blush. "Not quite."

"Were you taking advantage of me? Because I wanted to be conscious for that."

"Shut up," I tell him. "My father's here."

"Your father?" He shifts his head a bit, looking beyond me to where my father sits in the sand. "Good. Your father. I'm glad you found him. Is he okay?"

"Yes. He seems to be."

He looks back at me. "Tell me how you are."

"I've ruined everything," I blurt out to him. "I'm a fay on Avalon, and that will fulfill the warring prophecy, the one that your mother mentioned, about how the Seelie Court power will be cemented forever—"

"That's why I'm here: to help you stop that."

I shake my head. "It's too late."

"Why do you think that? When I left, we were still in the middle of the battle."

"But we've been here for hours," I tell him. "It's nighttime now. The battle must be over and—"

"You're keeping the wrong time," Ben interrupts me calmly. "You can still save the battle."

"How?"

"Leave." Ben says it like it's so simple.

I blink at him, annoyed now. "*How?*"

"You can leave anytime you like. You're a Seelie. Seelies can come and go from Avalon as they please."

"What about Dad? And you?"

"How do you think they're going to get you to fulfill their prophecy and stay?"

I pause, thinking things over, thinking of how I was lured here in the first place, thinking of my fatal flaw of *loving too much*. I look out at the ocean. I think of all the lives I ruined because I wanted to save just one. I wonder how selfish I can be. I look at Ben. "How do I leave?"

"I have no idea. That's Seelie knowledge."

That's no help at all. I shake my head and tangle my fingers into my hair. "Your mother's here," I tell him.

"I figured. She's been playing the long game, my mother. Your mother too."

"What are we going to do?"

"I have no idea. I don't really have a plan. Then again, I usually don't. I thought it was a faerie trait, but this entire situation is making me reconsider."

"My mother said that Parsymeon would fall today."

"Well, she would, wouldn't she?" Ben's gaze has shifted beyond me again, and I look over my shoulder. Beyond my father, a figure is approaching. An Urisk.

He hops up to us and peers down at Ben. "Can you walk?" he asks, a little rudely.

"Why?" retorts Ben.

"If you can walk, your presence is requested."

"I bet it is," mutters Ben and sits up with what I can see is obvious effort. He even winces a bit.

"We don't have to go," I tell him.

"Yes, we do."

"We could…make a run for it."

"I can't run anywhere right now. And, anyway, there's nowhere to go. This is an island, and the Seelies control every inch of it. *You* can go."

"But I don't know how to yet." I look back at the ocean and wonder if I really should just start swimming. I wonder if the reason I haven't tried it is because I really can't bear to leave Ben and my father behind.

Ben stands up slowly, weaving a bit on his feet, keeping the blanket wrapped around him. "We'll go then. I want to see how this ends, finally."

"Ben…" My protest is halfhearted. I know, in a way, that he's right. All of this time on the beach, this stolen time with him, is just delaying the inevitable.

He walks over to my father and pauses, looking down at him. "Etherington," he says in greeting, with a graveness belied a bit by his state of undress.

"Benedict," my father says in response, his head tipped back to look up at him. "You promised to keep her safe," he accuses.

"I know," Ben replies. He glances at me. "I'm trying." And

then he starts limping toward the castle, holding the blanket close to him.

I pick myself up off the sand, gather my father, and we follow.

CHAPTER 27

Ben's progress up the staircase in the cliff is slow and agonizing, but eventually we reach the castle's promenade along the ocean. My mother and his mother stand at the opposite end, watching our approach. No one says a word except for the named faeries murmuring constantly, their pleas for leniency intermingling with the crash of the waves far below the window.

"It was very foolish of you to come," my mother finally says to Ben as we draw to a halt a few paces away from them. "We had everything we needed with her father. You are extraneous."

"Do I normally do intelligent things?" Ben inquires cheerfully.

"You're in a very good mood for a faerie about to be named," she replies coldly, and then she says meaningfully, "Or *are you*?" My mother looks at me, anti-smile firmly in place.

I don't know what's coming next, but I know I'm not going to like it. My hand in my father's, I can't help but shrink away from her a bit. Cowardly, I know, and it leaves Ben two steps in front of us, alone. But I know Ben can defend himself, at least better than my father can.

"You see, Selkie, this is your choice. Your final choice, here at the end, which I give to you out of sentimentality. We are going to kill the other three fays today. The prophecy is broken. You will stay here, on Avalon. Because so long as you stay here, you may keep one of them. But you may not keep both."

At first, I don't understand. "Keep one of what?" I ask, and I know my confusion is evident.

Ben is not confused. Ben looks at me immediately. In the glow of the candles of the candelabra lining the promenade, his eyes are as clear as the starlight outside. "Choose him," he tells me.

This doesn't help my confusion. "What are you talking about?"

"Etherington Stewart," says my mother, and my father cries out in pain, leaning more heavily on me in obvious agony.

"Stop it!" I shout at my mother desperately.

"Or Benedict Le Fay," she continues.

Ben staggers, catching himself on the nearest archway to keep himself upright. I stand supporting my father and stare at Ben in horror as he gasps for breath.

Even my mother seems surprised. "My, you're very weak," she remarks to him.

"I just went for a *swim*," he reminds her through clenched teeth.

"You'll just require the merest of nudges," my mother says and looks at me. "So it's your choice. I'm going to name one of them, now. You tell me which one."

"Let her name me," Ben insists from over by the archway. "Save your father."

I look from him to my mother. "What does it matter what I say? You're just going to name them both anyway."

My mother laughs like I am the funniest creature she has ever met. "My, Selkie." My skin crawls. "You *have* learned, haven't you? Finally. Never trust a faerie. You don't have to believe me. But I tell you the truth. It is your reward for staying here, with us, forever."

"What if I refuse? What if I just leave?" I ask with bravado I don't feel. But Ben said I could leave this island anytime I want.

"You can leave. But you will leave with neither of them. I will name them both right now. This way, you can be assured of the continued existence of one of these creatures you so foolishly love. Tell me which one."

I cannot think. I keep trying to form thoughts—to *think*—but I can't. Is she really asking me to...? I can't even comprehend it. My father leans on my shoulder, gasping for breath, and I think how all he's ever done wrong was to give me life, to want a child enough to ask for one, to sacrifice everything for me. I've loved him, always—he's my *father*—and I would do anything to protect him. I look at Ben, leaning on the archway, his ridiculous blanket askew and his sand-scattered hair creased into salty cowlicks all over his head. Ben, who I have loved for nearly as long. And we may have had our issues, he and I, but I am in love with him. I think I will never *not* be in love with Ben, with everything about him, even the strange, odd otherness that I think I will never be able to fully capture, and I cannot imagine ever hurting him, never mind *ending* him. I want to make him laugh at me, I want to cuddle him and kiss him, I want his smiles and his whispers in my ear. I want to make him happy, and I want it for the rest of our lives, for whatever length of time that might be.

And I shouldn't even be thinking these things at all, because I should be *leaving*. I should be saving everyone else that I condemned when I foolishly chose to come here.

I hear a noise like a squeak escape me, and I lift a hand and press it to my mouth, willing myself not to burst into tears, because I know this is what my mother wants. I feel like I am breaking inside, like the shards of me will fall onto the floor if I open my mouth.

Ben's eyes are steady on mine. "Tell her to name me, Selkie." His voice is so even, so calm.

And surely he should know that I should just *be leaving*. Isn't that why he came back to get me? I shake my head helplessly. "I can't…I can't…" I feel on the verge of hysteria, like I can do nothing more than hiccup my breaths. Here, at the end, I think I am finally going to lose it.

"Listen to me," Ben continues. "He's your father. You'd never forgive yourself."

Something occurs to me suddenly. I look at my mother, composure building inside of me as I reach the realization.

"But you can't name him," I point out. "You don't know his whole name."

My mother smiles her chilling smile at me, and it sends ice drifting through me.

"Benedict Le Fay will betray you," she says, "and then he will die. Isn't that the prophecy? He betrayed you, didn't he? He betrayed you, and he led you to the Unseelie Court, and there was put upon you...a curse." My mother moves forward, toward me, and I cannot move away from her. I have forgotten how to do anything except feel the cold panic consuming me. She reaches out a hand and lays it against my cheek, in what would be a caress from any other mother. I flinch. "You should be dead," she coos to me. "Do you know why you're not?"

I don't. I have no idea. Ben did something, that's all I know. Something that frightened Will. Something he wouldn't tell me.

My mother keeps her eyes on me. "Why don't you tell her, Benedict?"

Ben doesn't tell me. Ben, with a gasp, slides to the floor. I take my eyes off of my mother's to stare at him in horror.

"Ah," she says. "He's not really in a state to tell you. I'll tell you for him. He used the power of his hidden name to save you, Selkie. He can't keep it hidden anymore."

My eyes flicker between my mother and Ben. His head is tipped against the stone of the bottom of the archway behind him. It's true. I know that it's true.

"So," says my mother. "Choose."

I stare at Ben, who is not looking back at me. I feel the weight of my father beside me. My mind whirls with the impossibility of the choice.

Then Ben, with an effort that is tangible even from several paces away from him, which I am, lifts his head and looks at me. "This is what I am trying to tell you," he says distinctly, forming the words carefully. "Benedict Le Fay will betray you. And then he will die." He gives me a meaningful look.

I'm actually *angry* with him. What use is *that*? Repeating the prophecy back at me? He thinks that's helpful? He—the *prophecy*. It dawns on me suddenly, the way it must have dawned on Ben. It's *our* prophecy, his death. It's not my mother's prophecy, not the prophecy of the fay staying on Avalon. It's the prophecy where the four fays are victorious. If I let my mother name Ben, then maybe I can get our prophecy back on track. Maybe we can *win*, without sacrificing my father.

But at the price of Ben.

I stare at Ben, processing this. He seems to realize I've understood, because he nods almost imperceptibly and leans his head back against the wall behind him, closing his eyes. *This isn't better*, I think at him furiously. I had never wanted that part of the prophecy to come true. I had wanted to *change* that part of the prophecy. And now I find that, all along, I was going to be the one who fulfilled it.

But I recognize that I am powerless. If my mother is going

to force me to make this choice, I want to make the one that will end up destroying her. And I know that Ben would want that too. And this way I can save my father, which I cannot do if I just walk away from Avalon myself. Otherwise, I will end up killing both of them.

I gather myself, the power of the fury within me, and look at my mother. "Name Ben," I say firmly. "Do it."

My mother considers me for a moment. "I genuinely did not know which you would choose. Interesting."

Ben's mother speaks suddenly from where she is staring at the heap of him against the stone wall. "Have you ever read the prophecy?" she asks, and I don't know who she's talking to.

My mother is the one who answers her. "What? What do you mean?"

"The prophecy is both clear and vague. There is always a Le Fay in the prophecy. But the prophecy does not say *which* Le Fay. Did you know that, Benedict?"

Ben has lifted his head again and is regarding his mother curiously. "I did," he admits after a moment.

"So Will told you, did he? He chose *you*. He wanted *you*. I volunteered, you know. I was willing to do it. But Will wanted you. You, he said, would be so very strong. The strongest of the Le Fays. He was right. And I don't think you even understand why."

Ben looks extremely confused. "I…" he says.

"What are you doing? What are you talking about?" snaps my mother.

Ben's mother raises a hand, and my mother freezes in place, unable to move. Her lips move soundlessly, ranting and raving, I can see the fury in what she's saying.

Ben's mother looks at her scornfully. "So arrogant, all this time. You've always thought you could control the Le Fay power to your own ends. And that has never been true. Never trust a faerie."

His mother turns back to Ben, who is absolutely gaping at her. "It is our joint enchantment, Benedict, your hidden name. You never realized that, did you? I sealed it for you, years ago, with the power that Will told me you would have, the power which carries the strongest of enchantments. We Le Fays have always been susceptible to it." Her voice is trembling with emotion. I dart my gaze between Ben and his mother, unsure what is going on. Ben looks incredulous, astonished. "My *darling* boy," she says, her voice actually breaking on it. "The prophecy is that a Le Fay is to die here today."

Ben's mother tosses something across to him, something he catches reflexively. He stares down at it for a moment of complete and utter silence. Then he gapes over at his mother, who smiles at him—not an anti-smile, but a sweet, adoring smile.

Then my mother shrieks, "*What is that? What have you done?*"

Ben's mother looks back at her. "Ah, starting to shake it off, I see." She turns back to Ben. "Well, waste no time. You were slow enough with the curse that it was a much closer call than it ought to have been. Try to avoid the same mistake twice, my dear."

Ben springs into action with an energy that I can tell startles all of us. He skids into my father and me. "Hold your father's hand," he gasps at me. "Don't let go of it."

"Ben, what—"

"Kiss me," he says.

"*What?*"

"Do you trust me?"

"Yes," I answer without hesitation. Because it's true. I can't help it. I do. And it takes that moment, that split-second decision in a castle in Avalon, after all of the other agonizing decisions I've had to make today, to make it so abruptly, blindingly *true* to me.

"Good. Hold your father's hand, and kiss me."

I do. I let Benedict Le Fay kiss me into oblivion.

CHAPTER 28

When I say I let him kiss me into oblivion, that is not just a figure of speech. I kiss him, and the world seems to explode around us, lightning bright. His hands close into my hair, clench into fists, and he kisses me like I am the only thing left in the universe. For a second there, I think that maybe I am.

We are still kissing when we collide, hard, with something that knocks us apart. My hand still clinging to my father's, I look up into a sky of roiling gray clouds. There is a moment of silence so complete all around me that I think it's possible I went deaf. Then the sound rushes up and captures me, a cacophony of shouting and pounding and clanging and more shouting.

I sit up. We are in the middle of the Common, with the battle raging all around us. The light is uncertain, diamond bright and then pitch-black. It is dizzying and disorienting.

The Erlking comes running past, sword drawn, then stops and backtracks, frowning at us. "How many times do I have to get you troublesome fays off the field of battle?"

An arrow lands beside me before I can answer, a bit too close for comfort, quivering with the force of its landing.

Someone grabs my hand. Ben, with the blanket shrugged off one shoulder. "The battle's going to turn," he says to the Erlking. "Night's going to fall. Have your army ready."

"How do you know that?" the Erlking asks and slides his eyes up and down Ben. "And what are you wearing? Or… not wearing?"

"Would you turn off your seductive superpower?" Ben responds impatiently. "We don't have time for this. Let's go," he says to me.

I take Ben's hand, letting him pull me up, and I pull my father up beside me.

"Did we get the prophecy back on track?" I ask as he pulls me up the Common in a mad dash.

"Yes, and I know who the fourth fay is."

"What?" I want to ask more questions, but we reach Beacon Street, which is a rutted mess of towering crags of pavement and deep valleys at the bottom of which sit destroyed cars. And sometimes people. I look away, swallowing back nausea.

Ben says under his breath, "Oh, I haven't got time for *this*," and just like that, we are on my front step.

I stare at him in astonishment. "You were just a mess," I point out, because he had just been a crumpled heap on Avalon. "And how do you know who the fourth fay is?"

"Because my mother gave it to me. She gave me *all* of it."

He pats his pocket, where he's put whatever it was his mother threw to him. Then he touches the front door of my house, which opens for him.

Everyone piles into the doorway to the living room, staring at us.

And then all hell breaks loose. Kelsey flings herself onto me, while Merrow and Trow and Safford all start exclaiming.

"What *happened*?" Kelsey demands.

"It's a long story," I manage.

"And you." She turns to Ben and shoves him.

Ben hadn't been paying attention to her, so she catches him entirely by surprise, staggering him. "Ow," he says and rubs at his shoulder.

"You can't just run off and not tell any of us what you're doing," Kelsey snaps. "You scared us. Both of you."

Ben looks confused, and I can tell the idea he would be worried about never even crossed his mind. "I…oh," he says and crinkles his nose as if this is too much to deal with.

"And what are you wearing?" she demands after a second.

"It doesn't matter. None of this matters. Where's the box?"

Merrow is looking at us curiously. "It's here in the living room." She turns to me. "You came back from Avalon."

"That was the wrong prophecy," I tell her. "That's not the prophecy I want to succeed. We have to win."

"But we need the fourth fay, don't we?" asks Aunt Virtue, sounding confused.

I hug both of my aunts on my way into the living room.

"Ben knows who it is," I say and then turn to Ben, who has dragged the box out into the center of the room. "What do we have to do to get him? Or her, I guess?"

"We have to do this. *Kelpie*."

Kelsey utters a little cry, wheeling backward. My eyes widen in surprise, and I start to demand what Ben's done to her, and then it hits me.

I turn to him in shock. "Wait. *What?*"

"Fourth fay." Ben points to her. "Hidden. Hidden so deep that her *name* was hidden. A special talent my mother's perfected. But what did she tell you, my mother? She gave us the clue all along. You have a habit of collecting the most important things you need. And you collected *Kelsey*."

"You're insane," Kelsey tells him. "I'm not a *fay*. Selkie, tell him. I haven't been able to do *anything* this whole time."

"Kelpie," he says again, and Kelsey cries out in pain again.

"What are you *doing*?"

"I'm naming you."

"Yeah, stop it." I frown at him.

"Selkie, I wouldn't be able to name her if she wasn't a fay. She's a fay. And now the four of you need to open this box and see what's inside it."

"But I don't have a secret power like—"

"You do," I realize suddenly. "Your secret power is *being here*." I kept saying that we should step onto the street and ask the birthdays of random people. I should have started with Kelsey. Because it sweeps over me suddenly, and I should have seen it so much sooner: *I don't know when her birthday is.* "Kelsey," I say. "When is your birthday?"

"It's March 21," she answers readily, and then her mouth drops open.

"Exactly," I say smugly. Then I take the key out of my pocket, go over to the box, and insert it in the lock.

"All of you, help me." Trow, Merrow, Kelsey, and I all grab the key. It turns easily, as if it hadn't given us all sorts of trouble in Iceland. And we'd had the four fays all along. If only we'd known, if only we'd *realized*, if only we'd said the right words then, Will would never have had to—

I don't let myself finish the thought. We have no time to get caught up in what-ifs right now. We haven't had time in a while.

Time to find out what this all-important thing we sacrificed Will to get actually is.

We open the box.

And pull out four old books, the leather binding them cracking with age. Each of them has a symbol stamped on it in flaking gold: a snowflake, a sun, a leaf, and a flower.

I hand them out, corresponding to our season, and then I flip mine open. Nothing. Completely blank.

"Because we have to *rewrite the story*," Merrow says.

I think of my mother on Avalon. *Your story is the most important thing.* My story, I think. *The stories we tell. The words we use.*

"We have to tell our stories," I hear myself say. "Words

have power. They're the most powerful things—it's why Seelies don't allow histories to be written down. We need to use our words to tell our stories." And I suddenly realize that everyone has been telling me this all along. I didn't need any special powers. What I needed was just to be *me*. That was what I needed.

And then the windows blow in, the lavender windowpanes exploding all over us.

There is an entire Seelie army outside my house, and for a moment, we all look at each other, and then chaos happens.

"Get them out, get them out, get them *out*!" Safford shouts, and for a moment, I think he is talking about the Seelies, but then I realize he's talking about *us*. The fays.

"Upstairs!" Ben shouts at me as one of the Seelies must name him, because he doubles over in pain.

"We can hold them off!" Safford gives me a shove. "Get up the stairs and *write your stories*."

I try to protest, and then Safford, right in front of me, fades into dust.

I scream. I can't help it.

Someone names me, one of the Seelies, because I feel the pain, but it feels like it is far away, because I am covered in the dust that was Safford, who ferried me across Mag Mell when this whole journey was still so new. Safford, who tagged along because he was expendable, and because he wanted, so badly, for us to defeat the Seelies.

Ben shoves at me, and I turn and run up the stairs, pulling

Kelsey in my wake, Merrow and Trow on our heels. We pile into my bedroom, and I slam the door shut and lock it.

"Are you really locking the door?" Trow exclaims, as down below us I hear what is unmistakably my aunts screaming. "You think that's going to stop them?"

I don't let myself think about the war going on downstairs. Ben has all of his mother's power apparently, and he'll hold them off as long as he can, and we need to write our stories. We need to fix this.

"Write," Merrow commands Trow. "We need to rewrite the story. Just like my mom said, remember?"

"Write our stories," I say. "The story we *want*. We can fix this. We need to find the words."

I find pens on my desk, throw some to everyone else, and I sit on my bed. For the first time since this whole thing started, I know exactly what to do. Because now that I have to write my story, I know exactly where it begins.

One day my father walked into his Back Bay apartment to find a blond woman asleep on his couch.

CHAPTER 29

When spring comes to Boston, the populace always seems dazed. They wander out to the greening spaces, as if they can't quite figure out what happened. Where did the snow go? Where did the sun come from? What is this strange sweetness in the air?

The seasons shift and tumble, and we never question it. We wake up one day and the world is different, the day is longer or the night is shorter, and we move forward, until the time when the day is shorter or the night is longer. It is its own kind of magic, the march of time in this fashion.

I notice it now because, for me, spring really does come out of nowhere, even more than it usually does. One minute I am writing down my story in my bedroom while underneath me a war rages, and the next minute the clock on the landing is chiming one o'clock and I am waking from a doze. My aunts are hunting for gnomes in the conservatory and pretend not to know what I'm talking about when I ask what happened. I know they are pretending, and I know they think this is what they should do, that maybe everything will go back to normal if they don't acknowledge everything that happened.

This is the special talent of my ogre aunts, I think: the ability to only recognize the reality they want. And frustrating as it is, I am so relieved to have them back that I can't help but love them for it.

And in this world I have wakened into, it is spring.

I stand with the door open, looking out at the traffic on Beacon Street. The street is paved smooth. In fact, it is smoother than I have ever seen it, clear of potholes. There are tourists taking photos of the lavender windowpanes in my house, and there are besuited businesspeople hurrying past. I think that one of them, a particularly attractive one, pauses and salutes at me, a funny little half wave, half bow. I blink at him.

"Selkie," a voice calls to me from the staircase, and I turn away from the doorway.

"Dad," I say in shock, because there he is, looking *wonderful*, descending the staircase toward me. "You're here!"

"Of course I'm here," he tells me. "Where else would I be?" He hugs me, and he whispers in my ear, "Well done."

"But what happened?" I ask, bewildered.

He draws back a bit and cups his hand onto my cheek. "We won," he answers simply. "Thank you. Now." He drops his hand. "Your aunts are going to pretend nothing ever happened. We can let them do that. In the meantime, Arawn and I are going for a drink."

"Who?" I turn as my father walks past me, pausing by the open doorway to pull a bowler hat off the coat stand by the door. That bowler hat has always been on that coat stand. I have never seen anyone wear it before. I never even thought about the fact that it must have been my father's. Just the sight of him in it makes me want to cry.

"Your faerie godfather," my father says, as if this makes total sense. "I'll be back later."

"My…what?" But my father winks at me and, whistling, steps out onto the doorstep and then down the street.

"Aunt True?" I call. "Aunt Virtue?"

"Yes, dear?" Aunt Virtue calls back.

"I'm going to the Common," I tell them and step out and close the door behind me.

Ben is not on the Common. I stand in the middle of the swirling crowds in and around Park Street and feel lost and bereft. *We won*, I think. I got my father back, and the Otherworld is presumably much better off. I wrote the story I wanted. But my story had Ben. And I can't find Ben.

I turn away from Park Street, walking up and over to a patch of sunny grass, where I sit.

And as if on cue, Kelsey and Merrow and Trow are there. I'm not sure where they came from.

They don't seem to know where they came from either.

Kelsey says dazedly, "What *happened*?"

"I have no idea," I answer.

"But you were the one who told us to do this!" she points out.

"But I didn't know what I was talking about. I was just making things up as I went along."

"We rewrote the story," Merrow says. "I've been reading prophecy after prophecy and…we won. We made the world we wanted. Everything is the way it always was. Only everything is *better*. We saved *everyone*."

"We won," I say and look out over Boston Common. I want to know how to find the rest of the Otherworld creatures. Where are the Erlking and his goblin army? If I snuck my way into a subway tunnel, would I be able to find him? Or are we cut off now? Is that part of my life over? Is the rest of my life just going to be…normal? Was that the story I wrote for myself? I feel like I didn't get that far.

And where is Ben? When I saved the world, did I send him back into the Otherworld? Will he just stay there now that his job is over, now that he doesn't need to protect me anymore?

"So the Seelies are gone?" I say.

"Seems so. I don't know. You were the only one of us who ever actually got to go over to the Otherworld."

"Kelsey did too," I tell her. "And it's not really something to be jealous of. Trust me."

"Agreed," says Kelsey, nodding emphatically.

"I don't know." Merrow shrugs. "Maybe now it will be. Now that we've fixed everything. Maybe we can ask your traveler boyfriend if he'll take us."

"I'm not going to run *tours*," says Ben good-naturedly from behind us, and I whirl around.

He smiles at me. His eyes are green like the new grass all around us and blue like the bright sky above us. I want to fling myself into his arms, but I am aware of the audience and I am also aware that I don't know where we stand. Not quite.

"We are third, fourth, and fifth wheels," Merrow remarks.

"I'm always the third wheel when it comes to all of you," says Kelsey.

"I'm sure you won't be single long," Merrow tells her. "I mean, us faeries are pretty irresistible. Right, Trow?"

"Being a faerie myself, I wholeheartedly endorse that," replies Trow.

"Know a good ice cream place?" Merrow asks.

"Do I ever," says Kelsey, and they all pick themselves up from the grass.

I sit, awkward, trying to decide if I'm supposed to go with them.

"You're supposed to stay here," Kelsey says. "But later, you and I are going to have a long discussion about my being *supernatural*."

"I don't know anything about that," I say. "I don't know anything about being supernatural."

"You're doing a pretty good job with it," Kelsey replies.

"I'm not." And then I say honestly, "I'm just trying to be me."

Kelsey smiles at me, and then she moves off with Merrow and Trow, and they are laughing about something. I think how maybe saving the world together is kind of a huge bonding experience.

I watch them go, and then I look at Ben. Ben walks over to

me and stands with his hands in his pockets, looking down at me.

He is so dazzlingly beautiful, I think. It's been a while since I thought that, in the middle of all the running for our lives we've been doing. In the middle of how angry I've been with him, how betrayed I've felt by him. It almost hurts to look at him, he's so gorgeous. I squint up at the cloudless sky then look back at him. "You're the only person on Boston Common wearing a raincoat today."

He doesn't smile. "Glockenspiel," he says.

"What?" I ask, wondering if he's started speaking another language.

"It's Glockenspiel," he repeats.

He's not making any sense. "What is?"

He sighs and sits beside me on the grass. Next to me, closer to me, I can see he looks tired, smudges of exhaustion under his eyes.

"Are you okay?" I ask in concern.

"In my time, everything happened two minutes ago."

"In my time too."

"Not really. It just seems that way to you." He lies down on his back on the grass and looks up at the sky. "It's been a very long day, Selkie."

I think of his mother, and I say again, "Are you okay?"

"Yeah," he sighs. "Just tired."

"So we won?"

"We won," he confirms.

"And what happened? How are things in the Otherworld?"

"Wonderful, actually. Safford sends his gratitude."

"So that worked," I realize. "Writing him back in. What about Will?"

"Ah," says Ben and almost smirks. "You should ask your Aunt True about that one."

I wince. "Stop it," I tell him.

He looks at me, abruptly serious. "Speaking of the Otherworld. I could, if you wanted, spend, you know, a lot more time *here*."

I swallow thickly, my pulse racing wildly. "More time than you spend now?"

"I could spend forever here."

My heart feels too full for me to talk. "Forever's a long time," I tell him.

"It's the blink of an eye," he counters.

"I don't want to just stay in Boston. I want to see everything. I want to see it all without being afraid for our lives the whole time."

"I will take you anywhere you would like to go. Say the word."

I don't know how to respond to that. I take a deep breath. It's exactly what I wanted Ben to say, and yet at the same time, it's all too much.

"So she loved you," I say abruptly. "Your mother. She was protecting you all along, helping you, in a convoluted, faerie way. Right?"

"She was protecting all of us. By making it look as if she wasn't. But she found the way to get the prophecy to be fulfilled in exactly the way she wanted it to be fulfilled, and she saved all of us in the end."

"She also caused a lot of problems," I say, thinking of the cursed coat.

"She was a faerie," Ben says and looks at me. "We always cause more problems than we intend to."

"Why didn't she just *help* us at the Unseelie Court? It would have saved us so much trouble."

Ben says after a moment, "I wasn't...I wasn't trying to manipulate you."

"When?" I ask, confused. I have no idea how that answers my question.

"When I asked you to kiss me to escape from Avalon. It's what my mother was talking about. Giving enchantment the ultimate strength: love. It has never been the weakness the Seelies have always presumed it to be. It has always been the source of the Le Fay strength. That's why she didn't help us at the Unseelie Court. Because you still could have been manipulated away to Avalon through love of your father. Everything still could have fallen apart. But if she sealed the whole thing with *love*, if she took the power of that love and turned it against the Seelies, against *their* prophecy and toward *ours*, then she would seal the prophecy forever. That was why I had you kiss me. I could get us out of there, but I needed you to *love* me to do it."

I look down at him on the grass and I say it out loud. "I always love you."

"I know you do." He sits up. "And you trust me. You said you did."

And I shouldn't. And yet. "I do. I trust you."

"And I trust you. That's why I'm telling you. Glockenspiel."

"I don't know what you mean when you say that, Ben," I tell him. "Is it some kind of faerie vow?"

"No. It's my hidden name."

My breath stalls in my chest. He says it so simply, as if it's nothing at all. "It's your what?" I whisper when I can form words again.

"My hidden name." He smiles at me, looking delighted with himself.

"Why would you tell me that?" I ask, astonished.

"Because I trust you." He leans forward and brushes a kiss over my lips. "Also because someday you might need to know my whole name to save me. I do foolish things sometimes, you know."

I feel like this is the equivalent of a marriage proposal, this knowledge he has given me. I tremble with the power of it, with how matter-of-factly he is placing himself in my hands. I clench my hands into the front of his raincoat. "Ben…" I say shakily.

"Shh. I gave you my whole name. You should say it. Say it the way you love me."

"Benedict," I whisper and brush a kiss over his left eyelid

as it flutters beneath my touch. "Will o' the Wisp." I brush a kiss over his right eyelid. "Celador." I kiss the bridge of his nose. "Glockenspiel." I kiss the tip of his nose. "Le Fay," I finish. I linger close to him, our noses brushing together. "It's a beautiful name."

"Only when you say it. I give you the power of my hidden name, Selkie Stewart. And I seal it with love."

Benedict Will o' the Wisp Celador Glockenspiel Le Fay kisses me into oblivion. Metaphorically speaking, this time. Because he's the best kisser in the Otherworld.

Faerie tales end with *happily ever after*. But that's just where our tale of faeries is beginning.

ACKNOWLEDGMENTS

As usual, many thanks to the small army of people that make a book possible:

My agent, Andrea Somberg, whose cheerleading has been invaluable and who also understands that breakfast is the best meal of the day.

My editor, Aubrey Poole, who made this book so much better and did it with aplomb and flair and infinite patience, and made this all so much incredible fun.

The rest of the team at Sourcebooks, including Katy Lynch and Derry Wilkens, who perform publicist wizardry on a regular basis, Jillian Bergsma, Cat Clyne, Kay Mitchell, Valerie Pierce, Katherine Prosswimmer, Becca Sage, Jennifer Sterkowitz, Brittany Vibbert, and Christina Wilson.

My friends, for continued wisdom, talking-off-ledge-ness, and hilarity, including Sonja L. Cohen, who stayed up late helping with copyediting and provided design services; Claudia Gray, who basically knows everything in the world in the best way possible; and Larry Stritof, for ongoing tech support.

Tumblr and Twitter and all who reside there, for saving my sanity and being madly inspirational.

And as always, my family: Mom, Dad, Meg, Cait, Ma, Bobby, Jeff, Jordan, and baby Isabella, for being people I love to come home for.

ABOUT THE AUTHOR

Skylar Dorset grew up in Rhode Island, graduated from Boston College and Harvard Law School, and has lived in New Orleans, Mississippi, and Washington, DC. But she actually spends most of her time living with the characters in her head. She hopes that doesn't make her sound too crazy. Visit www.skylardorset.com.